Try Not to Die

By Your Own Hand

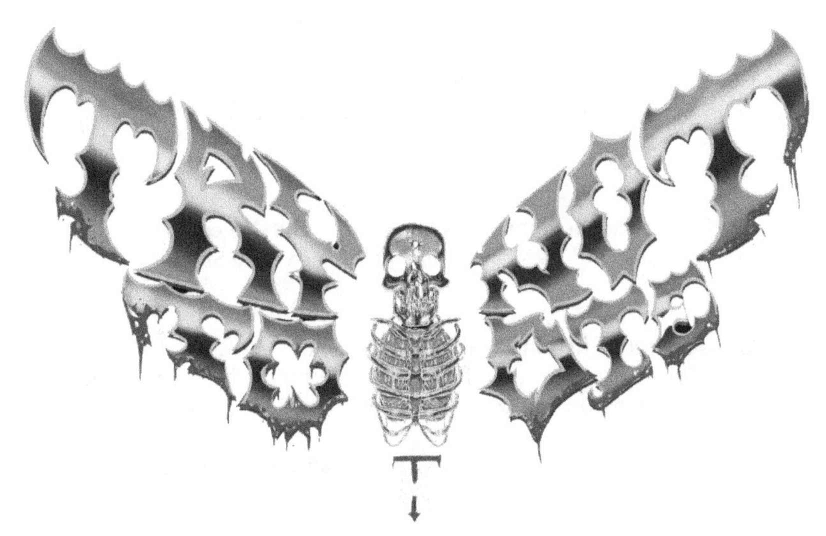

RENÉE S. DECAMILLIS

Published by Vincere Press
65 Pine Ave., Ste 806
Long Beach, CA 90802

Printed in the United States of America
First Edition

ISBN: 9781961740464
Library of Congress Control Number: 2025917108

Cover by Jun Ares

Please Read:
An Important Note from the Publisher

Before you start this story, I want to make sure you understand what you are about to encounter. This book is unlike all the other *Try Not to Die* books where I want readers to make the wrong choice and suffer a brutal death. Death scenes are my favorite parts of the books to write, and it typically makes me sad to think someone might not read them. But in this book, Renee and I want you to make every correct choice. We both understand how difficult it can be to know what the correct decision is when all hope is lost, and that many times we might even crave the wrong choice, not caring how extreme the consequences can be. This book is more about the story and less about decision-making. Please make the smart choice. Help keep Dahlia alive.

I also want to share how difficult it was deciding if we should create this type of book. I didn't decide to pull the trigger until after a talk with my good friend, jiu jitsu coach, and the co-author of the upcoming *Try Not to Die: In the Tournament of Mortem,* Wes Levine. Over the prior year, Wes and I had several talks about how much we'd been affected by losing loved ones to suicide. When I told him what I was considering doing with *By Your Own Hand* along with my motivations for doing so, he assured me it was a worthy goal and that I should do it, especially as I promised that all profit would be donated. He agreed that he and I could co-author half of the book from a male's perspective while Renee wrote the other half from a female's. When I approached Renee, she agreed, very aware it was going to be an incredibly heart-wrenching and painful process.

Well, Renee did what she promised, but life got in the way for Wes and me. We had to postpone *Tournament of Mortem* and he was forced to drop out of this project. That left it up to me. After a week of mulling it over and talking with my therapist, I realized I was not in a safe place to take on such an emotional book. I can't tell you the number of times I've had a gun in my mouth or stood in front of the bathroom mirror with a razor blade to my wrist. Speeding over 100 mph, I've wished I could crash my motorcycle into a wall or fly off a cliff. I absolutely hated myself most of my life and wanted to end it. I'm not sure when the urge lessened and finally disappeared, but it isn't until now at 53 that I can finally look in the mirror and be proud of myself and the contributions I've made to my family, friends, and possibly you, the reader.

Renee was incredibly understanding when I told her we had to change things up and I had to bow out. I felt like a coward, but I knew I needed to respect my limits and not take on things that would cause more pain than healing.

And that's how I hope you go about this story that includes some very sad and disturbing events, including sexual assault. If this isn't the type of book you feel is right for you, please send me a message and I'll send you a different *TNTD*. If you're interested in the story but aren't sure you want to risk making the wrong decisions and ending Dahlia's life, please read the survivor version which takes out all the decisions and deaths. And if you do read the interactive version, I hope you make all the right choices. If you do encounter a death, please forgive Dahlia and give her another chance, something I wish I could give to my friend, John Powers. We lost him nearly 30 years ago, but I still think of him often.

All of us who worked on this *Try Not to Die* wish you the best wherever you may be in your journey through life. If there is one thing I hope you take from the book; please understand that reaching out to others for help and support is one of the strongest acts you can ever do. Much love.

May you always try not to die and make the absolute most of your life.

Mark Tullius

Trigger Warning

As mentioned in my note, this book contains numerous intense and potentially disturbing themes. While the following list covers many of the most prominent triggers, please be aware that it may not capture everything. Please read with caution.

Content Warning Includes:

- Sexual Assault
- Physical, Emotional, and Psychological Abuse
- Self-Harm and Suicide
- Alcohol/Cannabis Abuse and Addiction
- Forced Captivity and Kidnapping
- Mental Illness

Please proceed with care and know that your well-being is important.

If you would like to skip the death scenes, please read the Survivor Version on page 132.

In Memory of

Joseph "Joey" William Petruk

2/24/1979 – 12/12/2023

Gone too soon, but never forgotten.

♫♪♫

Dedicated to Jesse

Always & Forever

Try Not to Die: By Your Own Hand
Interactive Version

Our band's last song wails and thunders across the fog-filled venue. The crowd jumps and thrashes against one another. I step up to the mic, spotlight hot against my skin, and belt out the second verse.

> Sinking lower, they're dragging you down
> Parallel plane, disappear in the dark.
> Chains confine you, constricting movement,
> Stealing your breath, silencing all your words.
> Now stagnation threatens to bloom
> As the flames lick at every inch of your skin.
> Are you content to crawl with vermin, the bottom feeders,
> Are you happy where you're at?

Just as we're about launch into the chorus, I peer out over the audience, trying to see if Beth showed up. She looks like a no-show, but there's a tall, burly hooded figure standing in the back corner, sweatshirt zipped up to their neck.

Alone.

Not moving.

Just staring.

Did we attract an A&R rep to our gig? We have been playing a ton of shows lately. Maybe word got out we've been attracting some big crowds. I *hope* it's a recruiter of some sort.

That must be why the person came alone. That must be why their hands are empty, no drink. That must be why they don't join in with the jumping and moshing.

Mike tears into his guitar solo. I step back from the mic, glance over at Ronnie on bass. Curiosity paints his face as he looks from the hood in the corner to me. I try to stay focused on playing guitar, but memories flash through my mind.

Aiden backhands me, shoves me into the dug-out hideaway-escape-hatch under his trailer and locks the trap door above my head.

Cuffed to the bedpost, tears stream down my temples as Aiden, with a knife held to my throat, straddles me while professing his undying love and tearing off my shirt. Above the bed, his graffiti art of me as an angel surrounded by roses and skulls stares back at me in violet, black, and crimson with drips like blood. Pointy, knife-like lettering arches over the top of it: *Angel Baby*. I try to pretend I'm somewhere else, somewhere peaceful.

With a few whips of my long hair, I headbang the horrors out of my thoughts. Turning back-to to the audience, I watch for the cue from our drummer, Kyle. Right after our synchronized stop, I spin back toward the mic and belt out the final chorus. Shivers run through me as I sing.

The hooded figure remains still, staring.

A sinking sensation hits me.

I can't help but feel like I'm the one he's staring at.

Our set ends. The audience goes nuts. Mike's best bud, Wally, jumps on stage to help break down our gear so we can clear the stage for the last band to set up.

We head to the bar.

The three drinks I had before our set make me trip as I walk up the steps leading to the pool table and bar area. I grab the railing, steady myself. Out of the corner of my eye I see the hood slowly swivel, following my every move. Stay with your people. Don't go anywhere alone. I bend down to adjust my pantleg, making sure my throwing knife's in place and at the ready. For some reason, the hope of an A&R scout checking out our band has shifted and twisted into nothing I want to consider.

At the top of the stairs I see Jen, lead singer from the opening band, Blood Rain. "Hell yeah! Here comes the growler."

We high-five.

"I still can't believe that big voice comes out of such a little lady." Gordon, Jen's lead guitarist, spiked bracelet around his wrist, throws me the metal horns.

I glance around, look over each shoulder, then turn back toward them. "What? Where's this 'lady' you're talking about?"

They laugh.

I smirk and walk over to the guys at the bar.

Harry, the bartender, already has my margarita waiting for me. I plop my ass in the stool between Mike and Ronnie and take a refreshing sip. With the cool glass against my lips and the tangy libation filling my mouth, I glance over to the corner of the mosh floor.

The hood's now watching the bar, face masked in shadow, reddish-auburn hair hanging down to their burly chest.

That final detail evaded my perception while on stage.

Now I don't need to see their face to know who it is.

My muscles tense. I take another sip, wash it away.

"So, another packed show," Harry says. "You guys really know how to tear people away from their computers and out of their houses. What do you cats say? Can I book you every third Friday of the month?"

The guys each bump their elbows into my arms, looking at me with excited expressions. Kyle, standing behind us, leans in and reaches his arm across the bar.

"Fuckin'-A-right we will!" Kyle fist bumps Harry, then throws looks to the guys and me. "What? Come on, I knew you'd all say yes."

We laugh, nod our heads, and say, "Yeah," in unison. We bump shoulders and sip our drinks, excited for regularly scheduled gigs.

Damn. It's only taken me all through my twenties and early thirties to finally get into a band dedicated enough to score recurring gigs at Geno's, Portland's legendary dive bar and rock club. Hell, recurring gigs period is freaking awesome. Man, why's it been so hard to keep a gigging band together? It's not like I'm gunning for fame. I just want to write tunes and perform. Now I've got it. This is freaking awesome!

After Harry walks off to go write us into the bar's gig schedule, I ask my bandmates, "Hey, did you guys notice that person all alone in the corner, hiding under their hood?"

Ronnie nods, is about to say something when Kyle says, "No. Where? What guy?"

Ronnie's eyes follow mine as I turn toward the dark corner in the back of the mosh floor. The corner is empty.

I jump off my stool and frantically search the crowd all around the bar and near the pool tables behind us, wondering if the guy followed me. I can't find him anywhere.

The fucker disappeared.

♫ ∎ ♪

At the 24-hour diner after the show, we sit at the corner booth next to the large front windows so we can see Mike's tricked-out hearse parked out front with most of our gear loaded in the back. It's pretty sweet he doesn't mind hauling my gig amp back to our practice space for me after our shows. Saves me a lot of time and hassle. But my guitar always stays with me.

Ronnie scooches over close to my side. Leaning toward my ear, he whispers, "So, the guy in the hood, I noticed he never took his eyes off you. Freaked you the fuck out, I could tell. Is this someone I need to take care of for you?"

With a shrug, I turn away, look out the window.

I don't want to think about it. Not. At. All. And I don't want to think about what will happen to Ronnie if he tries to take care of this problem for me. Nothing good, I know that, especially considering the psychotic who hid under that hood.

I wish Beth had been at the show. She'd have pointed that lunatic right out before I even stepped off the stage, her recognition pulling him out of the shadows, not allowing him to hide. She despises him *almost* as much as I do. Knows how much he ruined high school for me. Plus, he never liked me hanging out with her; we had too much fun together going to parties. If Jordan were still coming to my shows, he'd've pulled me off stage and ushered me right out of there. Jordan knows the nightmares I've dealt with because of that psycho.

"I'm not sure," is all I say as I open the menu.

Ronnie needs to stay out of this, or he'll end up in the hospital, or worse. Plus, I'd like to enjoy my buzz after the great show we just had. Recurring gigs at Geno's!

Turning his head, Ronnie throws me a squinty side-eye. "Hmm, why don't I believe you?"

I refuse to look at him. Lies—not my forte. The truth always clings to me like a second skin.

"Let's just enjoy some food, talk about it tomorrow. I don't wanna ruin this night." I glance up from my menu, look around our booth: Mike, Kyle, Wally, Ronnie. Dropping the menu, I pound the table with my fist. "Monthly gigs at Geno's, man! If that ain't sweet-ass fucking news I don't know what is. Now, let's order some grindage."

"Hell yeah!" They shout in unison.

Everyone in the diner, all ten customers and four employees, throws us dirty looks. We ignore them and pass high-fives and fist bumps around the table.

But the hood from the gig dominates my thoughts. Man, my head is swimming right now. I wish the diner sold booze.

After we order and our food arrives, Mike and Kyle keep the gig conversations going strong. Thank god. It allows me a breather from Ronnie's questions and my thoughts of the corner creeper.

"Now, if we can score monthly gigs down at the beach this summer, we'll be gold." Kyle stuffs a forkful of French toast into his mouth.

"Don't forget Lewiston. That city loves metal bands. And that shit ain't seasonally dependent. Recurring gigs up there, man, *that's* what we need." The scraping of Mike's steak knife against his plate as he carves his meat makes me cringe. That nails-on-chalkboard feeling, but deeper, darker. And the bloody red inside that rare steak makes this vegetarian want to gag.

"Shit. Don't dis the beach, man. That place is packed, and not just with locals. We can hit the fucking tourists too, dude."

As Kyle and Mike go back and forth, I sense Ronnie watching my every move. I try to ignore it. Pretend I don't notice.

My stomach flip-flops. Shoulders ache. My knee bounces so fast the booth shakes. After smothering my home fries with more ketchup, the bottle slips from my sweaty hand, hits the table hard, and topples over. The guys jump. Red pours out of the top of the bottle like blood oozing from an open wound.

Ronnie pulls a wad of napkins out of the dispenser and wipes up the spill as I stand the bottle back up and clean off the top.

"How many drinks did you have tonight, Growler?" Mike winks at me as he slices another chunk off his thin slab of steak.

"Not enough, that's for sure." I stuff a forkful of ketchup-smothered home fries into my mouth. Then I notice Ronnie wearing a strange expression as his eyes dart back and forth between Mike and me. Not sure what that's about, but I don't have long to ponder.

Wally points out the front window. "Guys…Some fuckers are stealing your gear!"

We bolt out of our booth, knocking silverware, napkins, and jelly packets onto the floor. The table wobbles, spilling our coffees all over the place, and sending the ketchup bottle splatting to the ground.

We rush toward the door.

"Hey, you haven't paid your bill!" A server waves a slip of paper in the air as we fly past.

"We'll be right back," I yell over my shoulder.

Platform boots make it difficult to run, but I sprint down the sidewalk with my bandmates. Nothing holds me back. The thieves are right there, not too far ahead. It's like I could almost reach out and grab them.

The distance grows between us. Maybe if we didn't drink so much at the show, we'd be able to catch up to these scumbags.

They toss our shit into the back seat of a car, jump in, and peel out.

Shit. Why didn't we just jump in one of our vehicles, dammit? It's too late to turn back now—the highway's so close I can practically spit on it.

The four of us—Wally stayed back with the car, and to hopefully call 911 and pay our bill—chase after the car that just took off with most of our band equipment. *And*—I know that car. A dark blue

Buick. The license plate and the old Chippendales sticker and the "*Trucker's Wife*" window decal.

My thieving former sister. Sara's her given name, but she *earned* the name Satan.

She lost her name when she physically attacked me for standing up for *my* mother and then took my niece, Zoe, away from me—my mini-me. But I couldn't let her keep stealing from Mom and not call her out on it.

Not only do I know that car and the person driving, but we also saw that hooded figure—the corner creeper—jump into the passenger's seat after tossing Mike's Marshall amp head into the backseat. His hood fell off while running, long, red straggly hair clear as a slap in the face.

What the hell is she doing chumming around with my abusive ex from high school?

Who freaking knows? He's probably buying his coke from her and her husband now.

I run as fast as my boots and the electric shocks of nerve pain shooting up my legs allow me. But none of us can outrun a cokehead behind the wheel of a car filled with hot goods ripped off from the little sister whose life reminds that driver how much of a lowlife she is.

I really wish we were driving instead of running right now.

Just as the thieves run a red light, a huge Peterbilt pulls in front of their car, slowing them down as both vehicles merge onto the highway's onramp. Ronnie, with his long legs and spastic energy, jumps onto the trunk.

I pause, reach down to slip out my throwing knife. But I hesitate.

What if I hit Ronnie instead of a tire?

But I gotta do *something*. What other options do I have? I can't run fast enough. And they have my band's gear!

Oh, shit. Nausea gurgles in my gut as I wobble in my platforms. Dizziness hits hard. My fingers fumble trying to unsnap the sheath.

What the hell am I thinking? This isn't a damn movie! No matter how good I think I can throw, I'll never hit that freaking tire. I'll probably stab Ronnie instead.

I straighten up, rub my stomach, try regaining my balance. Doesn't work.

Bending forward, I hurl undigested home fries and ketchup and a whole metal show's worth of alcohol onto the sidewalk.

Maybe I shouldn't've had that fourth margherita.

I wipe my mouth on my forearm and stand back upright.

Satan swerves back and forth, making the Buick shimmy. Ronnie slides side-to-side a couple times before one arm loses its grip, dangles.

"Fuuuuuuuck!" I start running again.

Ronnie slips off the back of the trunk.

His legs hit the pavement, but he grabs onto the bumper. As the car drags him further up the on-ramp, his feet scrabble for purchase as though he could run along with the car. The Peterbilt swerves onto the highway. Satan punches the gas and follows suit, and Ronnie loses his grip. He hits the pavement hard and rolls off the side of the on-ramp into the ditch.

All we're left watching are the red taillights of the Buick as the thieves speed off down the highway through the foggy full moon night.

And I'm left in awe at…well…everything. Ronnie really put in some extra effort. Maybe I've finally found *the one*.

Or maybe he just really wants that gear back.

♫ ▮ ♪

At work the next day, my supervisor's face twists with shock when I tell him about filing police reports at the Portland PD until four in the morning.

"After the night you had, I would've understood if you called out. Remember, I'm not just your boss. We're friends, Dahl. And we don't have any burials today." Jack rests his liver-spotted hand on my shoulder. "Wanna go home? Get some rest?"

I shake my head. "Nah. I'd much rather be here. Work is a welcome distraction from last night's bullshit. But thanks." I straighten up a bit, rigid, scoot to the edge of my seat. "Dude, we just scored recurring gigs at Geno's after our set, then that thieving psycho stole half our gear. You'd think I'd be used to this sort of thing by now since that's how my oh-so-great life tends to roll—take a step forward only to get kicked backwards three more steps." I shake my head, sink back into the desk chair.

Jack's eyes widen. "Recurring gigs at Geno's? Dahl, that's kickass! Are you sure you don't want to go home, try to find your gear somehow? Maybe check with some local pawn shops?" He pauses, runs his hand down his long beard. "Or you *could* always borrow my amp. That will at least cover you until you hopefully get yours back."

I consider this a moment.

"Thanks for the offer, but your digital Line 6 has a completely different sound than my tubed Mesa, and it works so differently. It'll mess me all up. Pawn shops though? That's a great idea! Thanks! But nah, I really shouldn't leave work. I can't afford to lose the hours. Plus, Ronnie's tending to his road rash, and seein' that bloody mess gives me the ick-shivers."

A new look sprouts on Jack's face. Not just shock, but confusion. So, I'll bite my tongue about Ronnie's newfound jealousy rearing its ugly head when we got back to my place this morning. I don't even want to think about it, let alone tell someone who I already know doesn't like him. I haven't even had time to think about it. Everything happened so fast. And my exhaustion makes my thoughts all rattled.

"Ronnie's at your place right now? Without you there? Did he stay the night?" He steps back and leans against the office counter beside me.

I look up at him, serious as all hell. "Yesterday, he just showed up at my place with all his shit packed up in his car, ready to move in. Made me literally speechless. He has his own house, so it makes no sense. Though his house does need a shit-ton of work." Groggy, I shake my head, try knocking the confusion against my skull to make it make sense without me needing to think too hard right now. "But still…I was shocked mute. And with our gig last night, I just haven't had time to address it yet. Plus, I have no idea what the fuck to say."

"You tell him no—*that's* what you say. Shit, Dahl. What the hell is Jordan gonna think when he finds out?"

Dammit. Leave it to Jack to sound like a dad. Maybe I should've waited to tell him that too, at least until I figure all this shit out myself. "If only it were that easy." I stuff a handful of almonds and raisins into my mouth and turn away.

"Um, yeah, I'm pretty sure it is." An irritated huff comes out of him.

"Yeah, but Jack, he was so sweet about it, saying how he just wants to wake up next to me every day, and knowing I live where I live to help Mom, he saw this as the only way."

Jack rolls his eyes.

"Yeah, I know. It's way too soon. But I don't know how to break it to him. You didn't see the excitement on his face."

Silence. Uncomfortable, like neither of us knows what to say.

"Oh, yeah, forgot to tell you the rest of my good news." The sarcasm filling my voice causes Jack to cock his head and stand at attention. "The divorce papers were delivered to me yesterday too."

"What? Divorce papers? I could've sworn you two would end up back together, that this was all just a hiccup. Man…" Jack shakes his head and rubs his sweaty forehead with the back of his dirt-caked hand. "You two are made for each other."

"Huh…Yeah, that's what I thought too, once upon a time, but all fairy tales—real fairy tales—end in tragedy." I turn away. "Huh…Tragedy…Story of my fucking life."

As I pick at my raisins, knowing I should eat more but not really feeling it, I think back to my last argument with Jordan. Heat rushes to my cheeks.

When I had left the last marriage counseling session with Jordan, I could barely breath. The things he'd said…

"I've never wanted kids."

I asked, "Then why did you act all excited and start planning to have a baby with me? You even went as far as picking out names with me and deciding we'd start trying after my graduation? We even joked about how we'll probably embarrass our kid when he's a teenager. We've talked about teaching him how to play music, how we want to play music together as a family, buying a camper van and going on family vacations. Why did you make all these plans with me when you knew none of it was going to happen?"

"It made you happy. I've always loved your smile—it's intoxicating."

"Do I look happy *now*?" I'd been crying through most of the session, and my face felt flushed, my eyes stung.

"Well, not now, but you were then."

"So, how long did you think you could keep me happy telling me fantasy stories? Making false promises? Did you think I'd never find out?"

"I guess I never thought about that."

"You never *thought about it*?" Rage bubbled up inside of me, and I yelled, "A five-year fucking lie and you never thought about it?" I didn't mean to raise my voice, but something came over me as he sat there staring at me, unblinking, like a deer caught in the headlights.

He shrugged, and silence fell over the small, white and sea green room. The counselor had remained quiet.

How could Jordan sit there and not shed a tear? How could he suddenly seem so cold and nonchalant? It was a side of him I'd never seen before.

After a few moments of my sniffling, sobbing, and stuttered breathing, the counselor said, "Dahlia, tell Jordan how that makes you feel."

It took me a moment to control my breath enough to form words. I grabbed a tissue, wiped my nose, and said, "I thought we were going to grow old together, play music together with our kid, hold hands until our dying breaths. You're my home. Every picture of my future…you're in it. But now…" My sobbing kicked back into overdrive, and I just shook my head and wiped my nose, unable to finish my sentence.

He yelled, "I'll be a terrible father! Is that what you want?" He paused, lowered his voice, and shrugged. "I guess I'm just selfish. I like my time."

I told him how I felt, and he yelled at me?

The weight of his words pressed down on me, suffocated me. I couldn't speak. Only cried.

The session ended when the counselor said, "I think the only option for you two is divorce. I don't see either of you coming out of this."

That was it in a nutshell. Jordan said nothing, though I saw him nod slightly. My sobs increased so much I thought I might hyperventilate.

When we got out to the parking lot, he grasped my hand gently before I walked off to my vehicle and said, "I'm sorry, Dahl. I didn't mean to hurt you like this. I didn't mean to make you hate me."

The look in his eyes felt like pity. It hurt so much, I couldn't hold eye contact. Sobs overcame me. I turned away, got in my Jimmy, and left.

It felt like he'd pulled my whole life right out from under me.

I've been free falling ever since, into an abyss of loneliness and uncertainty, with no place to call home, no one to cry to, every battle I now have to fight alone.

And I've been fuming ever since that last encounter. I did *not* need him to feel sorry for me. He took the pain he caused me and turned it on himself, trying to make me feel bad for his hurt feelings over me hating him for this. Really? "*Selfish*" was certainly the right word to describe him. Add "self-absorbed" to that too.

"Maybe you should try talkin' to him again?" Jack cocks an eyebrow.

"Yeah, well, maybe he shouldn't've lied to me for the past five years and gone through all the motions of wanting to start a family after my grad school graduation in three months. He completely fucked me over. Not only did he leave me high and dry financially, but my biological clock is *tic-tic-ticking* its final countdown." Tears welling in my eyes, I remain turned away. I hate looking weak. "And based on our argument at our last counseling session, all these months apart haven't changed his mind. Guess he'd rather be without me than take on another adult responsibility." A *ping, ping* sounds near my feet as a few almonds hit the floor from the baggy I'm crushing inside my clenched fist. "He's nothing but a selfish little man-boy, too scared to grow the hell up. Just kick back in his recliner, pound another beer, watch TV, go to the bar or a concert whenever he pleases. Fucker!"

Tension squeezes every muscle in my body as a lump forms in my throat. Eyes sting. I can't handle this conversation right now. It hurts too much.

Anger is much easier to deal with.

"Sorry. That really sucks. I just don't get him." Papers crinkle as Jack shuffles around through the upcoming burial records, obviously feeling uncomfortable and trying not to look at sad and pathetic little me.

Releasing the death grip on my lunch, I shake the baggy of almonds and raisins and consider reaching in for another handful, but my stomach has other plans. I lurch, cover my mouth. With eyes wide and holding back what I know is coming, I hold up a finger to Jack as I jump from the office chair and run to the bathroom.

Bent over the toilet and hurling everything out of my stomach, I hear Jack knock on the door. "I'll be out back having a smoke. Feel better. Meet me outside when you're done."

After swirling my gut chunks down the drain, I wash my hands and splash cold water on my face. The mirror hangs above the sink, taunting me, trying to lure my eyes to my reflection. I refuse to look. Not wanting to see the mess I've turned into, I turn away, grab a paper towel, and head back out into the office.

I grab my work gloves and head toward the front door. My old, black GMC Jimmy sits parked out front in the gravel patch between the road and the office. Just as I step down the front steps, a dark blue car speeds past. Something flies out of the driver's side window.

A loud, metallic *bang* and a shattering *crash* sound as the back window of my truck implodes. It stops me in my tracks. Shards of glass fly and scatter everywhere.

"What the fuck?" I run down the side of the road, chasing after the car. "You motherfucker, I know who you are, you crazy cunt!"

An arm pops out the driver's open window, middle finger held high, as the car—a dark blue Buick—speeds around the corner out of sight.

By the time I stop running and turn to head back to the office, I see Jack, cigarette in hand, running out from behind the office.

"What the hell was that?" Red paints Jack's angry face as he stubs out his cigarette on the bottom of his steel-toe boot.

Fuming and ready to rage, I shake my head. "Just another visit from oh-so-loving Satan."

"What the hell is your sister's problem?"

"My existence, apparently." I grith my teeth. "And *never* call her my sister again. It's Satan."

He nods, smirks. "Well, now she's fucking with my workplace. This shit needs to stop."

The window of my truck now lies in pieces across the ground. It's mixed with what look like ceramic shards.

"What in the world did she throw? A rock?" Jack leans in close to inspect the shattered window. Broken glass peppers the inside of the truck.

Bent over, I search the ground. "I'm not sure, but I don't think it was a rock." I kick around some pebbles, looking for any sign. "Motherfucker! I don't have money to fix this…and I sure as shit don't have time for her fucking bullshit."

Something shimmers differently from the bulk of the mess near the rear tire. I slip on a work glove, reach down, and grasp a shard of what looks like ceramic. Red and white and green paint. The words *Ho, ho* and the tip of a candy cane image decorate the surface.

"Found it!" I stand upright and turn toward Jack.

He pulls his arm out of the back of the truck with something held in his gloved hand.

The red ceramic handle of a coffee mug.

We hold our finds out on our palms, hands side-by-side as we inspect.

Jack looks into my sunglass-covered eyes. "A Christmas mug?"

A loud, sardonic laugh shoots out from deep down in my core.

"What's so funny?" With quotation marks etched into the skin between his eyes, Jack looks confused, and a bit concerned. Or am I reading that wrong?

"Her idiocy, *that's* what's so funny." My hand curls into a fist around the sharp shard of ceramic. "Don't you remember what she wrote in the comments of my Facebook post a couple weeks ago? Calling me a hypocrite for celebrating Christmas with our family and a Satanist for my Wiccan beliefs? Come on, Jack, don't you see the connection? And last night, my band's stolen gear and her car speeding away? Shit." I turn away, lean against the Gator loaded with landscaping tools parked beside my truck.

With the toe of his work boot, Jack's kicking around debris at the side of the road, searching for more evidence.

I shoot my free hand out. "Stop! Don't mess with the crime scene."

His foot freezes. Eyes wide, he looks back to me and nods. "Shit. Yeah, my bad." He tosses the mug handle back into the truck and pulls his cell out of the leg pocket of his cargo pants.

"I'm so exhausted and there's all this shit going on, I forgot to tell you who else was at the show last night. Her partner in crime."

"What are you talking about?"

"Aiden."

Jack's eyes widen.

"What? *Aiden* came to your show?" He steps closer to me. "And he *helped* her steal your band's gear? What the fuck is going on?"

Words don't come to mind. I just shake my head and shrug my shoulders, feeling frustrated and angry and cornered and ready to explode…or just un-exist. *Poof.* Gone. No more stress. No more crazy. Death, a welcome escape.

I shake my head, try tamping down the darkness like tamping down a freshly filled grave.

Man, I really could use a toke and a drink right now. Maybe I *should* leave early, go home and call Beth, party at her place like the old days, blow off some steam with a buddy and forget my shitty life.

Jack holds up his cell and heads toward the office. "Let's go call the cops. I'm your witness. I saw her too."

Unsure how I'm supposed to keep my shit together, I look up at Jack, no idea what to say.

He winks. "Yes. Sure as shit…I saw that bitch. I saw her throw that mug too. That crazy cunt isn't getting away with this."

I dread the idea of calling the cops again. Spending the morning before work at the Portland police station sucked, and I'm exhausted! I didn't get any sleep. Can you have a hangover if you never slept?

And the number of times I've had to call the cops on the same person—a sibling, no less—is getting old, time-consuming, and extremely tiresome and embarrassing. It doesn't help that the cops look at me, the little woman that I am, and think I'm bringing them my petty family drama, which is so far from the truth I could spit nails. And all the times I had to deal with cops in my teens because of bullies at school and because of Aiden, whom they never busted for all the abuse and stalking and terrorizing he dished out on me and my family. When your calls to the police station become so frequent they've memorized your phone number, address, and your name, it doesn't reflect well on you as a person no matter what the issue is that you're calling them about. They simply get tired of dealing with you, and they brush your problems aside as quickly as they can. My history of dealing with the PD in this town has left a bitter taste in my mouth. Plus, I'm not too keen on dealing with authority figures with my "Fuck you *and* your rules" attitude. I despise their smug, power-hungry stares.

But I sure would love to finally get Satan busted. With Jack backing my story, maybe they'll believe me this time.

I don't know. Going to Beth's sounds a lot more enticing.

Call the cops to get Satan busted. Turn to page 23.

Call Beth, go party, and forget my shitty life. Turn to page 17.

Thank goodness Beth answered when I called earlier. "Come have some drinks with me and forget that bullshit." The exact words I wanted to hear. Yeah, Jack sent me home early from work to go home and get some rest when I refused to deal with the cops again. Thankfully, Ronnie went to his parents' place to do his laundry. But I'm wound too tight to sleep. I need to escape.

"You Can't Bring Me Down" cranks through the open windows of the house when I pull into her driveway.

It doesn't matter that it's the middle of the work week and not even 5:00 yet. Tunes are always cranked to eleven and guests are always present whenever I show up at Party Central.

I wonder if Suicidal Tendencies is playing just for my arrival. Sure feels like it. But no one knows what I've been thinking. No one but Jack takes the time to ask.

Thanks, my so-called friends.

What is that term Mom uses? *Fair-weather friends?* I guess that sort of applies here, in a sense. Beth always wants me to have fun and party with her. So, yeah, I guess it does.

And my party pal knows I love this band. We've cranked these kickass cats since high school.

The bright sunlight blinds me as I reach out to knock on the door. Before my knuckles connect with the wood, I hear Beth's boisterous voice yell, "Put that damn thing away, you paranoid freak! It's just Dahl." Loud laughter follows.

"Hey, hey, hey, chica! Long time no hang!" Beth's face, hair disheveled and cheeks flushed, appears in the open daylight-basement window of her game room and home bar.

"How the hell did you know I was already here?"

"I could smell your patchouli through the open window." Beth laughs. I'd laugh too, if I could drag up the energy from my blackhole-soul. Beth's always told me how much she loves my patchouli, can always smell my presence before she knows I'm nearby. "You ready to party or what?"

Or what.

Whatever. Doesn't matter. I'm here. I'm not alone. And I'm on my way to Forget All Bullshit Zone.

"Yeah, yeah! Now open this damn door and let me in!"

"Woo-hoo!" Someone hollers as footfalls thud up the front hall stairs toward the front door.

Beth smushes her face against the window screen. "Tony's on his way…"

"Nope." Tony, the drummer Beth dumped last year, yanks open the front door. The knob slips from his grasp, slams into the wall. "Already here, and now…" he spins back around, "already gone!" His last word comes out loud, long and drawn out as his feet twist and he stumbles down the stairs. He rolls like a bowling ball down every step and lands, laughing and *apparently* unharmed, on the carpeted cellar floor.

"Holy shit, man!" I step inside and close the door behind me. "You alright?"

Brian, the bassist for Sea of Corpses, steps through the game room doorway on the left, fifth of Jack in one hand and a small black lockbox in the other. "Good thing he's fuckin' wasted, or he might be a whole lotta *not* alright."

Damn! A drummer and a bassist. Maybe I just found my new band.

Or Beth's a closet groupie. Or she never told me about her side-project.

Maybe both. Let's see where this shindig takes us.

Beth pops her head around the side of the open barroom door. "Yeah, he's not *at all* alright. Never was. Never will be." Her voice booms over the music. Loud laughter rushes out of her just before she raises the red Solo cup to her lips and takes a long chug. Dark liquid dribbles down her chin.

Back on his feet, Tony reaches out, hands me the fifth of Jack. "Want a swig?" Eyes barely open, a goofy grin plasters across his sweaty face. "I like to share."

Beth and Brian burst into hysterics. "Yeah, he *sure* does," they say in unison, then laugh some more.

I grab the railing and make my way to the bottom of the stairs. I grab the bottle and take a throat-tearing swig.

"Oh, *so* yummy," I lie. The only *yummy* is the effect. "Just what the doctor ordered. It's been a bitch of a month." I wipe my lips. "Scratch that. It's been a bitch of a fucking life."

I've fought my way away from this type of party lifestyle most of my life, but my darkest and loneliest mind pulls me back again and again.

"I hear that, sista! Fuck this life! Let's get fucky and forget it all," Tony shouts, though we're all standing close by. With his long straggly black hair sticking all over his sweaty face, he swipes the hair from his eyes, looks over at Beth. "You know what time it is?" He winks.

Her face lights up. "Ooooh, yes, I do." She grabs the black box from Brian then disappears into the game room. We all follow.

I gab with Brian and Tony about our respective bands, tunes, gigs, and whatnot as Beth wanders behind the bar and then disappears through a side door. Brian grabs a tray and a bag of ganga, then plops on the couch and rolls a couple blunts. A few minutes pass, then Beth strolls back in as soon as Brian lights the first joint.

She went searching for her Ecstasy to turn my melancholy into love, but they've been drinking since 10:00 A.M. She can't find it.

The black lockbox box has also disappeared, tucked behind the bar.

"Whatever you got to make the world go away, I'll take it." My words come out strained as I pass the blunt to Tony. "Fuck it all! That's my new motto." I try to smile, but I hurt so much my face won't comply.

The three of them yell, "Fuck it all!"

We all pass around fist bumps along with the blunt.

Beth leaves the room.

She comes back with a tray covered with Jell-O shots.

I dive in the deep end.

Suck down the blackhole sun.

Six in a row.

Warm and cozy. Rush to joy. Floating euphoria. Not a care in the world.

Nothing can bring me down.

The feather flows and floats with the wind as though it can fly, alone.

But even the feather eventually falls.

Unsure how much time has passed since I first arrived, I sit in the corner of the game room in an electric blue beanbag chair between the bar and the Ping Pong table—I *think* that's where I am—hugging my legs to my chest, unable to lift my head off my knees.

Darkness.

Lids try to open.

A sliver of a star.

Is that the sunrise I didn't want to see?

I look away from the light.

A black metal box behind the bar.

A shiny clasp mocking my mood.

I grab the box.

I flip the latch.

I open the secret.

A shiny revolver sits nestled inside.

When did Beth start packing?

Who cares.

I pop the cylinder open.

Full.

Pop it closed.

Cock the hammer.

Barrel to my temple, I pull the trigger.

Crimson rain splatters.
Red rivers rush.
Screams ricochet.
Gone but here.
Floating.
No.
Flying.
This feather will never fall again.

At the cemetery, Beth sits beside Dahlia's freshly filled grave, shoulders bouncing, tears flowing, hands covering her face. The laminated letter sits atop the headstone.

Dear Dahlia,

I can't believe what happened. I can't believe you're really gone. I'm so sorry. I should've known something was wrong when you showed up at my house. I could tell you'd been crying, but I was too drunk to think straight. I'm so fucking sorry! I should've asked you what was wrong. I should've talked to you instead of just getting you to party with us. I can't say sorry enough.

What I should've said to you was how strong you are, how special. How much I look up to you, admire you. I've always wished I had as much confidence as you. I always wished I could be as brave as you, go after my dreams like you went after yours. You are so talented. Yes—ARE—I will never think of you as gone. I know you're still around, at least in spirit. I believe that. I know you do too, and I hope you can see what I've written, know how I feel.

Ever since we first met in middle school, I've always considered you a best friend. Always. Even though we've grown apart over the past few years. I didn't come around often lately because I knew you were so busy with the band, writing, college, work, your mom, Jordan. And truthfully, I knew you didn't like a lot of the people I hang with. I didn't want to put you in the position to feel bad about turning down invitations to hang out. But, looking back, I now realize YOU are who I wish I'd been hanging out with. You've always been such a good influence, always encouraging me to use my creativity to better my life. You are a ray of sunshine. Always trying to make people feel better. Always helping people. You always give the best advice. And, best of all, you always listen. Really listen. Not many people do that anymore. But you, you always…I really wish you didn't do what you did! I miss you and love you so fucking much!!!!

Love Your Best Friend and Party Pal Always,

Beth

P.S.

When I was writing this letter to you, a water droplet fell on the page. As I was about to shut my journal and go inside, I looked up into the cloudless, colorful, twilight sky. Another droplet fell. And another.

It wasn't raining.

Confused, I looked around.

The scent of patchouli drifted through the air, surrounding me like a hug.

Then, out of nowhere, I felt a light touch on my shoulder. Then a soft, cool breeze.

Tears filled my eyes, but it made me smile.

I blew a kiss to the setting sun. To you, Dahlia. I know that was you.

Thank you for always listening…

even in death.

♫ ∎ ♪

The correct choice was to call the cops. Turn to page 23.

As we step through the office door to make the call, I try to smile, but my eyes sting and my face refuses to comply with my effort. Dealing with this crap is the last thing I want to have to do. My life is a mess right now, and psycho Satan has nothing better to do than go and compound it with her hatred and jealousy. Man, I wish she would disappear.

I really need a drink right now. Smoke a bowl. Something to escape all this bullshit.

I feel a warm touch on my shoulder.

"Maybe sit and take a minute…Decide what you're gonna say." Jack's concern is palpable.

Two minutes pass. I remain standing. Steel-toe boot *tap-tap-tapping*.

Relaxation isn't in my wheelhouse of skills.

And dealing with cops right now…

Rage threatens to bubble to the surface as I reach for the office phone. I close my eyes, take a deep breath, and form a fist around the receiver. My mind flashes back to freshman year of high school.

I was on the payphone between classes talking to my then-boyfriend Aiden, when a group of seven senior girls surrounded me. My quarter's worth of a call was not yet up. But that didn't matter to them. They started taunting me with "Hurry up, slut!" and "End the call, whore" and "Cunt, it's our turn." I tried ignoring them so I could just finish my conversation before the bell rang for my next class. If I didn't check in with Aiden throughout the school day, he immediately accused me of cheating on him or hiding shit from him. This phone call check-in protected me from a potential argument and assault after school. But what happened next changed the course of my entire freshman year, as well as the rest of my high school years.

Cara stepped out of the group of harassment surrounding me, walked right up to the payphone, and slammed her hand down on the hangup lever. "Enough of this shit already," she said. With her face merely six inches from mine, she smugly stared down at me.

I stood there in shock. Disbelief. All I could think was, *this bitch I don't even know has the nerve to hang up my phone call? Now she's right in my face. What the hell does she plan on doing next?*

My hand squeezed the black phone receiver tighter, worried about whatever else she might do. Without thinking, I punched her in the face—with the hand still holding the phone receiver.

Cara instantly covered her face with her hands. Blood oozed through her fingers and gushed down her chin. She blinked away a tear. Then she grabbed my hair, yanked my head back, and we fell to the floor.

After a quick blur of wrestling to get her out from behind me and remove my hair from her grasp, I kicked my legs up and over my head, backward somersaulting myself over her. Then, I wrapped my arm around her throat from behind and squeezed as tight as I could.

I wanted to fucking end her, or at least scare her enough to get her and her bully buddies to never mess with me again.

I squeezed tighter and tighter. She tried telling her friends she couldn't breathe.

With my mouth right beside her ear, I shouted, "How the fuck do you like me now, bitch?"

A gasp later, all six senior girls pounced on the five-foot-two, 100-pound freshman me and started punching repeatedly. I covered my head and face with my arms, blocking their blows as rage ignited within me. Finally, the assistant principle, Mr. B., and the school's police officer, Deputy Brown, broke it up.

As Deputy Brown led me to the principal's office, my besties Beth and Allie came scurrying around the corner, eyes bugging out, worried, asking what happened. I couldn't even shrug as the officer man-handled me away from them and shoved me through the office door out of sight. Like I was the aggressor. Like I was the bully. Like I had started all of this.

Mr. B suspended me. No one else received so much as a detention. I suppose since Cara came away bloody with a broken nose and a fractured cheekbone, and I came away unscathed—at least physically—I must've been the one who started it. Right? Even after I was acquitted in court after Cara's parents tried to charge me with aggravated assault, not one of the girls who bullied me were ever disciplined.

I dropped out of school.

Returning to school my sophomore year, I paid that unfair school administration back by making the honor roll every semester of the three years it took me to earn my high school diploma.

People should never underestimate my resolve.

Sitting in the cemetery office with the old-school phone receiver held to my ear, I await the inevitable.

The 911 dispatcher answers, and I report the vandalism to my truck, making sure I don't leave out the detail of Jack and me seeing who did it.

An hour after the call ends, an officer arrives at my work. The police station is less a mile away. Officer Delany, a husky man with pale skin and a freckled face, asks us a handful of questions.

"What time did the incident occur?"

"Where were you two when it happened?"

"What did the car look like?"

"Did you touch any pieces of the broken mug?"

"How did you two respond?"

How did we respond?

What type of question is that?

Does he not see and hear us standing here reporting the crime to him? Does he not realize the time of the incident and the time of my 911 call were within minutes of each other?

Officer Delaney—or should I say Deputy Brown—stares at me, unblinking, as though waiting for me to slip up with my "story." As though analyzing every one of my words. As though I'm the one who broke my own truck window with a fucking Christmas mug.

Hey, but I did the right thing. Didn't I?

Man, I should've just left work, called Beth, and got drunk to forget all this bullshit.

Well, looks like Satan's going to get away with all the torment she's been dishing out on me.

It's a week after the Christmas mug incident, and the cops still haven't pressed any charges against her. They say they can't prove she did it. I called bullshit on that and told them to get prints off the mug since our witness statements obviously mean nothing. They told me they only got partials, not enough for a conclusive ID. If I had caught it on camera, they told me that would've helped. I could only laugh at that.

How was I supposed to know someone was going to vandalize my vehicle? Should I just walk around with my phone at the ready 24/7? Plus, I'm a gravedigger and groundskeeper; if I carried my phone around at work, it would get damaged. And this small-town cemetery certainly can't afford CCTV.

Idiots!

They also couldn't bust her lapdog husband last month when I caught him on my CCTV outside my house stealing one of my medical marijuana plants.

They told me the hood he wore masked too much of his face, and they didn't get a close enough shot of his license plate. The fact that I had just served Satan the day before with a restraining order for physically attacking me *on my property* and for leaving numerous death threats against me on Mom's answering machine didn't seem to have any sway in their ability to at least get a search warrant.

I don't understand what those small-town cops even do around here. Not their jobs, obviously.

And that little hooded weasel stole my medication! I can't afford to buy it, which is why I grow it. Dammit! If it wasn't for Mom and Jack loaning me money to fix my truck window, I wouldn't have a vehicle to drive right now because of that psycho.

What good are the cops in this town if they can't bust career criminals the police department is always receiving complaints about, and not just complaints from me? Satan's neighbors have filed numerous complaints, her sister-in-law has filed complaints, parents from her youngest daughter's sporting events have also complained. These so-called cops need to stop that menace before she causes even more harm.

And the theft of my band's gear—the Portland PD hasn't busted anyone for that little crime either. Our gear has probably already been sold to the highest bidder or traded for pain pills and cocaine.

We just landed a recurring monthly gig at Geno's, the best rock club in Portland—possibly in all of Maine—and now we need to somehow find a way to replace our gear before that first gig gets here. And the studio session next week…Dammit!

Just when something good finally happens, Satan swoops in and crushes it. Story of my life. If it wasn't her, I'm certain it would've been something else getting in the way. I have no idea how I'm supposed to replace my Mesa Boogie the company no longer makes. Even if I bought a different amp, the pay at my cemetery job isn't enough for me to buy new gear, especially not a Mesa. I scored that kickass amp on a wicked used gear sale at Buckdancer's Choice seven years ago.

At least they didn't nab my guitar. I always carry that with me, and Ronnie and I took my Jimmy to that gig.

Ronnie. There's another fucked-up situation I've landed myself in.

When he jumped on Satan's trunk, as crazy as that was, my drunk ass took it as a sign that he was the one—the one to stick by me no matter what, the one to do anything in his power to try to fix a terrible situation. But oh, how quickly that changed. A change I didn't want to mention to Jack because he would just get on my case even more about Ronnie. I already know how fucked up this is. I don't need the reminder. I just need more time to figure this shit out.

After Ronnie noticed the wink Mike gave me at the diner that night, Ronnie keeps accusing me of having a three-way with Mike and his wife. A fucking three-way?! I'm not even into that shit, and I certainly wouldn't do that with Mike behind Ronnie's back. We're in a goddamn band together! And our band is hot right now. I don't want to screw that up. But his accusatory bullshit is starting to make me wonder about that since it's triggered him to have delusions of *"proof"* he says confirms I'm lying. He's apparently gone a bit nutty on me. Plus, once I give him the boot from my apartment—since I never invited him to move in in the first place—he'll probably get the guys to boot *me* from the band anyway.

I need to time this out just right.

My grad school project includes my band going into the studio to record three songs about sympathetic villains to include with my essay, my PowerPoint presentation, and my novel manuscript for my thesis. As soon as I get that CD in hand, I can give Ronnie the boot, preferably with my steel-toe boot. If I do it sooner, my project is screwed. No, my project is *not* why I started dating him—that didn't happen until after I joined the band and after Jordan kicked me in the head with his five-year lie.

Dammit, why did I add the musical part to my project? Why do I have to reach so high, always trying to go above and beyond? Just so I can fall flat on my face? But if Jordan didn't abandon me, this never would've happened. Well, I guess he didn't make the decision for me to start dating Ronnie. But still…

Man, desperation is a fucking bitch! Pushed me right into the arms of a paranoid and jealous shadow, who knew exactly what to say and when to say it.

My life sucks!

Vulnerability and desperation, man.

If Jordan hadn't flaked out on me and lied to me all those years, this never would've happened.

Sure as shit—I blame it all on him.

Yeah, maybe I don't always make the smartest choices, but…

My biological clock is ticking louder than machinegun fire and speeding up as fast as a crazy train with Casey Jones driving that bitch. With the shitty family I've got, I need to make my own, choose my own, get the hell away from the ones trying to drag me down and ruin my life.

To hell with my family! Mom is my only family. Shit, she's my best friend.

Living in the apartment above Mom's unattached garage has been a gift. Makes it easier to help her out with her big, old house and large property she can no longer take care of by herself. Paying her rent rather than some slum lord also helps her pay her bills since waitressing and bartending most of her life didn't leave her with a retirement plan. Plus, I get to see her almost every day. Yeah, sometimes she gets a bit annoying with the multiple calls a day when

I'm trying to get my writing done or work on school assignments or practice music. But I can deal with that. I don't know how much time she has left, and I want to remain as close to her as I can until that dreaded day arrives.

Thank goodness Ronnie works third shift. Maybe now I can smoke enough ganga to sleep like I'm in a coma and forget about all the crap swirling around me. Looking around my apartment and seeing all his belongings now where Jordan's once were feels unnatural, unsettling. What did I ever see in him to begin with? Yeah, he said all the right things at the right time, and we do seem to have a lot in common: we love the same music, we both love horror, we've both been in a number of bands and gigged out a lot over the years, we both love to go hiking and spend time in nature. But he tries so hard to be like Jordan, it makes me wonder if he knows who he really is himself. He even plays the same instrument and loves the same metal bands. It's strange. But their personalities are miles-apart different.

Pulling open the desk drawer below my laptop, I see the corner of my favorite picture sticking out from under the packages of Sticky Notes. I slide aside the notepads to get a better look. The photo shows Jordan, our nieces Zoe and Nat, and me at a Christmas celebration at my mom's. We're all wearing ugly matching Christmas sweaters and performing "I Wish It Was Christmas Today" from the old Saturday Night Live skit with Jimmy Fallon, Tracy Morgan, Horatio Sanz, and Chris Kattan. Jordan's holding a keyboard while Zoe plays the melody I'd taught her. I'm singing and playing acoustic guitar, and Nat stands stone-faced, though trying so hard to keep a straight face, while swaying along in Tracy Morgan's role. We barely made it through the whole song without laughing our asses off. So much fun! I miss those days.

I tuck the picture back under the Sticky Notes and close the drawer.

Jordan always tries to make people laugh. Always has a funny joke or story to tell. Always tries to help my mom any way he can. Always dependable. Nothing like Ronnie's serious and paranoid ways. Always trying to be better than others. Always wondering what others think of him, what they think of our band. Always remaking himself. Always on edge, ready to pop like an overinflated balloon. Why didn't I notice all this about him sooner? Just because we have some of the same interests doesn't mean we should be a couple. And him jumping on Satan's car was probably only for the sake of getting the band's gear back, not to do something to help me. Why was I so blind? Did all his promises of making my dreams of having a family come true and his promises of how devoted of a family man he'd be create rose-colored glasses for me?

All bullshit. Phony people stick to me like those spikey seed pods from the pricker bushes I accidentally ran through when I was a kid. Those things tore the flesh on my legs to a bloody, painful mess. I miss being a kid. Just playing and having fun. No worries. No phonies and liars.

Phony people hover around me like junkies pining for a fix.

This isn't how my life was supposed to turn out. Growing old together with Jordan, finally having that son I thought we were *both* dreaming about, watching that son grow up and take on the world, and Jordan and I making music together until our dying breaths—*that* was the plan.

But my plans always seem to go haywire.

After clicking save on the story I've been writing for the past five hours, I shut down my laptop. Good thing I took that stroll through the trails out back in the woods earlier. Spending time out there always fills me with inspiration. My story's almost submission-ready. That'll make my third story submission this month. Hopefully one of the publishers bites. It's been over six months since I subbed my first novel—to five different indie publishers—and I *still* haven't heard a peep! Feels like rejections to me.

And it sure does amp up my Imposter Syndrome. Big time. They probably never read my book. Why would they? I'm a nobody.

If I chose the wrong direction with grad school, I'm completely screwed.

I grab a drink from my practically empty fridge, pick up a packed-full bowl from the coffee table, and head to my bedroom. Ronnie's two bass guitars hang on the wall next to Jordan's side of the bed, right where Jordan's Jamaican wood-carved masks once hung. Masks we bought in Negril when we got married ten years ago. The TV remote taunts me from my nightstand. I grab it, click to the Chiller channel, and settle back against my pillow.

Underworld is playing for the umpteenth time this month. Great movie, but I can recite it almost line-by-line. With a couple more clicks, a *Supernatural* rerun appears on the screen. Yeah, I can recite every episode of this show line-by-line too, but the characters comfort me. Feels like chosen family, or best friends I've had forever.

After a few tokes and half a mimosa, I crash, fast asleep, and find myself entrenched in a nightmare-memory—part memory, *all* nightmare—unable to escape.

Down in Aiden's underground hideaway-escape-hatch under his grandmother's trailer, the trapdoor creaks open overhead. Aiden's sinister grin peers over the edge. The beer stench reeks on his breath as he laughs.

Instant monster—just add beer.

With a guitar string wrapped around one of his hands—the low e—he jumps down into the tunnel-hole beside me. Stroking my long, tangled hair, he leans close and whispers into my ear. His beer breath sets my nerves on fire.

"My perfect little angel. So pure. So innocent. You think you know best? You think you're better than me?" His voice changes to a growl and increases in volume when he says, "Think you can flush my kilo and get away with it? Think again, wench!"

Grabbing a clump of my hair, he yanks my head back and tries to make out with me. I force my lips into a tight, flat line, refusing to let him in. I try to wiggle free, try to pull away, though I have nowhere to go to get away. In the dream, there's no secret tunnel leading out to the backyard like in real life.

He's so much bigger and stronger than me, fighting him is futile. I've tried many times before, only to have it end in more pain for me. I've tried numerous times to leave him, but all attempts ended with him causing harm to my friends and family. With his cunning ways, he has evaded arrest so many times I've lost count. All these real-life-thoughts swirl round my nightmare-mind.

When he stops slobbering all over my face, he releases my hair and wraps the guitar string around my neck.

"How do you like that? Strangled to death by the string from the thing that takes all your time away from me."

His lurid laughter makes my ears bleed.

He yanks the string so hard, so tight, dizziness consumes me.

"This is called poetic justice, my perfect little angel."

The phone rings, saving me from nightmare-murder. Drenched in sweat, heart racing so fast and so hard it pounds in my head, I open my eyes and look at the clock.

Three A.M.

I hope Mom's okay!

As soon as I grab the cordless phone, I see Ronnie's cell number displayed on the caller ID.

What's so important he needs to call me from work this early in the morning? Doesn't he have some cinnamon rolls to bake?

Dammit! I just want to get some rest for a change.

"Hey, Ronnie. Everything okay?" I cough, take a sip of my drink.

"Hi. What do you mean? Why wouldn't everything be okay?"

"Uh...I don't know. Maybe because you're calling me from work at three in the morning."

"So. You're usually up at this time writing or doing schoolwork. Do you have company or something? Who's there?"

"What? It's three in the morning. No one's here except Sam and Dean Winchester."

"What the fuck!? You've got *two* guys over there?! I fucking knew..."

"Whoa...Slow down. I'm watching TV. *Supernatural.* They're characters on the show. No one's here. *Jesus.* Enough with the accusations. What do you need? Why are you calling me from work?"

Jordan would've laughed at my Sam and Dean reference. He knows who they are. This is our show.

"Some guy just threw a trash can through the front door of the bakery and smashed out the glass. Cops just left. I had to fill out a statement and everything."

My glass bowl tumbles onto the floor, spilling ganga everywhere, as I sit up bolt straight. "Holy shit! No way? Seriously? Are you okay?"

Wait. Another broken window? What the hell is going on? Could it be Satan again? But he said it was a guy.

Aiden?

"Did you see what he looks like? Did he come in? What did he want? Did the cops get him?"

"Yeah, it's all good now. They're gone. I called my boss, told her. But that's not why I'm calling."

Why does he sound so calm? Some freak just smashed out the front door of the bakery where he works alone all night. Something like that would normally freak *anyone* out.

"Oh…Okay. Happy to hear you're alright. What's up? Is your car acting up again? Do you need me to pick you up in the morning?"

"No. Car's fine. I just…One of the cops…One of those fucking pigs is related to your ex-husband. Did *you* send him here? Are you trying to fuck with me?"

I fling the covers off and jump out of bed, heat rising, face flush. "What the hell are you talking about?" Groggy and confused as a motherfucker, I start pacing my small apartment. Bedroom to living room to kitchen and back. "Jordan doesn't have any cops in his family. What the fuck?!"

"Yeah, well this guy looked just like him but without long hair. And his name was Officer Jordan. He's your fucking brother-in-law. Just admit it. Jordan sent him here to fuck with me. Why the fuck won't he just go away already?"

"Um…Hate to break it to ya, Ronnie, but my brother-in-law is a fucking math teacher not a cop. And *Jordan* is that cop's *last* name. They go by last names not first names. I wouldn't be Officer Dahlia. And why would Jordan's brother have the same name as him. His name is Corey. What the hell is *really* going on? Did some guy really smash out the front door? Why are you calling me? I need to get up for work soon."

"Yeah, well, I was listening to the radio before that guy showed up, and the DJ kept telling me Jordan was coming, Jordan was watching me, and I needed to call the cops before the glass shatters. Oh, and I ordered Rosetta Stone for you."

"Wait. What? The DJ was talking to you? They were talking to you about Jordan?" I shake my head, rub my forehead. What the hell is this nutjob talking about? It's too freaking early in the morning to deal with this shit. What kind of game is he playing with me? Is he trying to get me to slip up, thinking I'm cheating on him, got some guy over here while he's at work? Maybe he thinks Jordan is here. "And you bought me Rosetta Stone? Why?"

"Yeah. I ordered it from an infomercial. I had the little TV on before the radio. The commercial came on. They kept telling me I needed to buy it. It's for you. That will make you happy, right? You said you've always wanted to learn Italian. So, I ordered it for you. Aren't you excited?"

What the hell is going on? Am I still dreaming? Is this really happening right now?

Releasing an irritated sigh, I step over to the window and pull the tapestry aside, look out into the driveway. My truck, with all the bumper stickers on the back window, is parked in front of the garage. Mom's pickup truck is parked in front of the walkway to her front door. No one else is here. The towering trees surrounding the property sway in the moonlight. Their shadows dance, wave, and shiver.

"Well, thank you for thinking of me, but Ronnie, you know money is tight right now. You told me yesterday you're behind on your car payment. You shouldn't've bought that for me. You need to return it. Call them back, cancel your order." I plop down on the bench in front of the window. "And what about the door of your work? Is the whole front of the bakery open to the outside? Is your boss coming to seal it up?"

"It's all boarded up. She already sent her husband to cover it."

Scratching my head, I stand and walk back to my bedroom. This shit isn't adding up. What's really going on over there? At my bureau, I pull out some clothes.

"Well, I can't imagine they'll be opening with that busted front door. Why are you still working? Why haven't they sent you home yet?"

"Time to make the donuts." Ronnie's sing-song voice sounds flat. He laughs a tight, un-humored chuckle at the retro reference to the old Dunkin' Donuts commercials. "Okay, I'll call and cancel my order. But I thought you wanted to learn Italian? Aren't you happy?"

Holy shit! What is he talking about? Why does he not sound concerned about what happened with that guy smashing out the window of the door? Something weird is going on.

"Happy? Honestly…I'm half asleep and trying to figure out what is going on over there. So, you still have to finish your shift? The bakery is still opening at six? Even though the front door is all smashed to shit? Or are you heading out soon?"

He laughs again but still doesn't sound amused. "You just said it yourself…I'm behind on my car payments. I can't leave work early. I need to get my hours." *Clinking* and *clanging* drift through the phone. "I've got three huge pans of cinnamon rolls to put in the oven. Of course I'm working. I'll cancel the Rosetta Stone. So, no one's over there with you?"

As I'm pulling on a pair of jeans, I balance the cordless phone on my shoulder. "*No*, Ronnie. I'm alone. The only one here with me is Sam and Dean *on the TV*. Mom's next door, sleeping, I assume. It *is* fucking three in the morning." Shifting the phone to my other shoulder, I pull open another drawer and grab a hoodie. "Ronnie, if you're alright, I really need to go to bed. Four o' clock comes real fucking early."

"Four? Why you gettin' up so early?"

"You already know why—I get up early to do more writing before work. I still need to polish up my manuscript before it's due at my last school residency in a few months." I stuff my feet into my Docs beside the front door. "Goodnight, Ronnie. Get back to work. I need to go to sleep. I'll see you later."

We hang up.

That studio session can't get here quick enough. I really can't take his shit anymore. This is fucking crazy!

I grab my truck keys off the hook beside the door, thunder down the stairs, and march out into the crisp October night.

My drive to the bakery flashes by in blur of confusion and exhaustion.

The twinkle of the red streetlight shimmers across the black hood of my SUV. All the parking lots of The Maine Mall and the shopping plazas around it sit empty. No customers. No employees. No one.

It's three-thirty in the morning.

I yawn. I guess no writing for me this morning. I'm immersed in Crazy Town instead.

The bakery where Ronnie works is only two more streetlights away. If that front door window isn't really broken, we're going to have a serious issue.

Rather than pulling into the front parking lot of the bakery, I shut off my headlights and turn left just before it and circle around the back.

Getting only a partial look at the front door, I don't see any plywood covering the window. But it's dark, and I didn't get a clear view. Only a couple dim interior security lights are on. I need to get closer.

I pull into the parking lot of the plaza behind Ronnie's work. His little red car sits parked beside the backdoor of the bakery.

Hiding under the hood of my black sweatshirt, I quietly open my door, step outside, and ease the door closed. Sticking close to the outside wall of his work, I circle around to the front of the building. I step up onto the sidewalk leading to the patio tables and chairs and the front door, and I now confirm that no plywood covers the door of the bakery. But a window *is* shattered.

Not the window of the front door.

The large window beside the door is gone, busted right out.

Shattered glass is everywhere out here. All over the tables and chairs and cement, reaching all the way to the tarmac of the lot.

What the hell is going on? Why is there so much glass outside if the guy threw the trashcan into the bakery?

Maybe that's possible. I don't know.

I need to move closer to get a better look. If I can find whatever he threw, find the trashcan—because obviously nothing was cleaned up after the incident for some reason—then I'll know for sure if he's lying. But with all these big windows out front, he'll probably see me sneaking around. The untrusting girlfriend.

Oh shit. A dining room light turned on.

I slip back away from the sidewalk, hide around the corner from the front patio. Ronnie must be coming out of the back kitchen. What if he's coming outside to finally clean up this mess? A mess he said was already cleaned up.

Isn't that what he said? Maybe he said his boss *was sending* her husband over, not that she *already sent* him over. I'm so freaking tired, maybe I heard him wrong? Or I'm remembering wrong? Whatever he said, it still doesn't make any sense.

Dammit!

I need to get out of here before he sees me.

Four-thirty in the morning, my fingers *clickety clack* across the keyboard at a rapid speed. With no time or ability to sleep after checking on Ronnie's sketchy story and seeing the broken window, I threw myself into my writing when I got back home. I can't afford to call out of work, and I need to get ready at 6:00. That gives me an hour and a half to bleed across the page.

Better than bleeding across the floor from slicing my wrists or blowing my brains out. Razor blades and bullets: great song title!

But nope. I chose door number three.

Write.

Maybe I'll put that song title to use when I get home from work tonight.

Checking up on my multiple novel submissions could've waited. That ate up fifteen minutes of my limited time this morning. Don't know why I did that before diving into my writing. Always makes me anxious, sometimes defeated. Still no replies. Waiting for replies is agonizing! Don't publishers realize they're holding onto our children, our creations, while we're left worried if those children will ever have the chance to become part of the world?

The wait time's so long, I might die before ever hearing back.

Dramatic much, Dahl? Suck it up. You chose this path. This is how the game's played.

I at least need to stay alive long enough to get to the bottom of Ronnie's story. It's driving me mad with confusion! Yeah, I could've called the police, *again*, about the broken window, try to figure this out right now, but I don't have time for Ronnie's mindfuck games. He can deal with that. It's his workplace, and he's a grownup. I have to go to work and get my school work done.

Smashing my head against the wall repeatedly also crossed my mind after getting home from the bakery and realizing Ronnie isn't just paranoid, jealous, and confused about his identity.

He's playing mind games with me. Trying to catch me in a lie. His behavior reminds me so much of Aiden's from back in my teens it makes me sick to my stomach.

Did I unwittingly let another Aiden into my life?

All Ronnie's belongings surround me as I just keep writing.

The manipulative sonofabitch lives with me!

I'm in a band with him.

A band that's scheduled to record in the studio next week.

A band who's helping me finish my grad school thesis project.

A project that's due in six weeks.

What the hell have I gotten myself into this time?

♫ ▮ ♪

"Well, look what the cat dragged in. You look like dogshit, Dahl. You alright?" Jack stands beside the Gator with the motor running and all the burial equipment loaded into the back. Smoke trails up from the end of the cancer stick hanging from the corner of his mouth.

I always wonder how he keeps that nail-for-his-coffin from torching his long beard and mustache.

"Didn't sleep. Ronnie's fucking with my head. I worked on my thesis early this morning. Don't ask any more questions. I don't have the energy to talk about it right now." I grab my travel coffee mug from the cup holder and my work gloves off the passenger's seat.

After slamming my truck door, I jump behind the wheel of the Gator. "Let's go dig this fucking grave and bury someone already."

Thirty minutes later, shovel in hand, I smash the tip of the spade into the dirt wall of the open grave over and over, imaging all that dirt and rocks I heave over my shoulder is all the bullshit from my life that keeps dragging me down and holding me back and clogging my brain.

"Why the frig is your sister hanging out with Aiden? That's what I want to know." Jack jumps down from the seat of the backhoe-excavator combo and grabs another shovel from the back of the Gator.

I pause, swipe my arm across my sweaty forehead, then roll my eyes up to look at Jack standing on the edge of the open grave, smoke curling up into the cloudless azure sky from another cigarette hanging from his lips.

"*Stop* calling that psycho my sister. And yeah, great question. Probably a new coke customer for her and her loser husband. Anything for money with those shysters." I slam the shovel into a clump of rocks and dirt. Clanging metal rings out as sharp pain shoots up both of my arms. "Damn rocks!" I pause again and lean on the handle of the spade. "Leave it to her to buddy up with another psycho *and* the abusive dickhead from the worst time of my life. That psycho thought he could ruin me?" An irritated laugh shoots out of me as I start digging again. "Fuckface never should've underestimated me. Thought I was his 'little angel'? Ha! He never really knew me *at all*."

"Why the hell the cops can't get a search warrant to see if your gear is at her house or his blows my mind. Especially since everyone in your band saw her car *and* her license plate."

"Jack, we fucking *chased* them to her car. So, the guys also *saw* both of them, not just the car. Plain as fucking day. Yeah, Aiden thought his hood would hide him, but running made that thing fall right off. We all saw him. The guys may not know who he is, but they all gave the same description to the police: long, reddish-auburn hair, burly build, about five-foot-eleven. There shouldn't be *anything* holding up the fucking pigs from finding our gear before those assholes sell it. But...here we are." I stop digging, lean the shovel against my thigh, and hold my arms out to the side. "Don't forget who I am. Shit always goes wrong for me. Nothing ever happens as it should in my life. If there's a way for shit to go haywire, even the *slimmest* chance, it will."

With a fling of my arm, I toss the shovel up out of the hole. Grabbing the grassy edge of the open grave, I jab the steel toe of my work boot into the rocky wall and haul my ass up and out. After I grab my iced coffee from the cup holder of the Gator, I plop down on the grass next to the pile of gravel beside the grave. "Man, it's smoldering hot today for freaking October." I shake my head. "I guess Hell *has* finally risen." Sweat trickles down my temples. "Man, Maine and its bipolar seasons…Wanna know what the weather's gonna be for the day? Step outside and find out."

I tip my mug toward Jack, who pauses from digging and looks at me with concern creased across his forehead. "Speaking of psychos and Hell—Have you told Ronnie to get the fuck out of your apartment and go back to his own place yet?"

"Damn it, Jack! I want to. Believe me. I need to find our gear and get the band's studio session over with next week. I *need* those tunes to finish my presentation for my thesis." Leaning to the side, I reach over and clean out the leaves from around the headstone beside the grave we've been digging.

"Is it so important that you'll risk your own safety and wellbeing?" Jack heaves another shovel full of dirt out of the grave.

"What do you mean 'safety'?" I sit back upright, take a haul off my coffee, and stare at him.

What is he talking about? I never told him about what happened last night with the call from Ronnie and what I saw when I drove to his work. I don't want to even think about it, let alone talk about it. It's too maddening. And I have too much on my plate right now. My mind can't handle more. I texted my bestie, Allie, before I came in, but she's busy pulling a double with her job and doing an overnight caring for her disabled brother. Hopefully she'll have time to get back to me later. And Beth's out of town, going to a metal show down in Worcester. Now I'm just too tired to deal with any of this. I just want to forget about it. Give my mind a break.

Jack shakes his head and keeps digging, shaping the perimeter of the hole to fit the cement vault for the casket. "Dahl, I'm a guy. I know his type. You're not safe with him. I worry about you." He stops and looks up at me. "You *need* to get him out of your place as soon as possible."

"Shit. You sound just like my mother."

His eyebrows arch up over his safety sunglasses. "Oh, so your mom doesn't think you're safe either?"

I laugh, though I'm not amused. Looking down, I pick at the grass while I tell him, "A couple weeks ago when I told her Ronnie was taking me to Salem for my annual fall visit, she made me write down the make and model of his car and the license plate number." I glance at him over my sunglasses. "She was worried he wouldn't bring me back. I just laughed at her. But now…I don't know." I turn away, keep picking at the grass and fallen leaves.

"What? You think she was on to something, don't you?"

No words come out of me.

"What aren't you telling me, Dahl? Has he hurt you? If that motherfucker lays a hand on you, I'll…"

"Hell no, Jack! No one lays a freaking hand on me and gets away with it! I learned my lesson the hard way. Aiden trained me well; I'll give him that. I will *never* take abuse like that ever again." I look away again, start cleaning more leaves out from around the headstone next to me. "It's just that…something really messed up happened last night, woke me right out of a recurring nightmare." I tell him what happened with Ronnie's phone call and me driving to his work to check up on his story.

"Holy shit, Dahl! He's fucking crazy! You really need to get him out of your place. *Now*."

"Yeah, but Jack…that's never happened before. He's nothing like that normally. I think he was just so exhausted from working third shift and getting no sleep. I think it's really messing with him and…"

"Stop making excuses for him. He's a freaking psycho and you know…"

A little red car pulls up on the gravel road beside the family plot we're working in. It pulls closer and the window rolls down.

"Hey, Dahl." Ronnie holds up a big, freshly baked cinnamon roll. "Can you take a break? I brought your favorite." A warm smile spreads across his pale face.

I turn toward Jack and cock my head. "See?" Standing up, I brush dirt off my jeans and grab my coffee. "I'm going to take a fifteen. Cool?"

Jack nods, turns away, goes back to shaping the newly dug grave.

♬🪦♪

Sitting in Ronnie's passenger seat in the back of the cemetery behind the old crypt where they used to keep the bodies stored before the burials, back before refrigeration and all the luxuries of the modern age, I pick and peel apart the huge, warm cinnamon roll while Ronnie talks band logistics. Though the sweet, gooey pastry smells and tastes delicious, it's hard to digest. After receiving Ronnie's phone call and discovering what I saw at his work, I've felt sick to my stomach.

I haven't even heard a word he's said. Well, I've *heard* him, but I haven't actually *listened*. Shock and confusion consume my mind as I wonder how he's able to act so casual, like nothing weird happened earlier this morning. Just another night at the bakery, making tasty treats to distract people from his mind games. To distract *me* is more like it. But I haven't forgotten. How can I? It's too messed up to drop it and forget.

"Ronnie, I gotta ask you something," I say in the middle of him still speaking about the upcoming studio session or gig or something. "What the hell really happened at your work last night? Did some guy really smash out the door window with a trashcan? Did you really have to call the cops and fill out a statement?"

"What? Did someone really bust out the door? Yeah, it happened just like I told you." He says this like whatever happened is a common occurrence I should have no reason to question, while his expression remains blank and difficult to read. His eyes look everywhere but at me. "Why would I lie about that?" He looks out the driver's side window, fusses with his long bangs.

"Well, you're acting all calm, like you're not concerned about it. Like it's not unusual or anything." Trying to will him to turn around and face me, I watch for any telltale signs of him lying.

He has already displayed common signs of someone who might be lying: answering a question with a question; not giving any details; refusing to look me in the eyes; shifty eye movements; turning away from me; fussing with his hair. But that's not proof. I need proof.

Screw this!

"Ronnie, *look* at me."

He turns toward me, still wearing a blank expression. But he looks past me out the passenger side window behind my head.

Shit. Should I tell him I drove to his work to see if he was making shit up last night? If I do, he'll think I don't trust him.

But I don't trust him!

No. It's best to bide my time before telling him. I need to do more digging, figure this shit out.

"What did the cops do when they showed up at your work? Did your boss come in too? Who cleaned up the mess? You said someone boarded up the door?"

"Wow. That's a lot of questions all at once." Ronnie turns away, looks down, appearing distraught. "I'm trying not to think too much about it." After a pause, he turns to me and looks me straight in the eyes. "I was really freaked out last night. *Not* something I want to remember." The sunlight shimmers in his eyes, making it look as though he might cry. He grasps my hand and gives it a gentle squeeze. "Getting to see you this morning really helps calm me down." Reaching his other hand over, he wipes icing off my cheek, licks his finger, then leans in and kisses the same spot. "Now you taste extra sweet." A timid, childlike smile emerges as he pulls away.

Maybe he is telling the truth. Maybe I took what I saw out of context and made unfair assumptions about the uncanny event. Plus, I was in a dead sleep when he called, so maybe I'm remembering the conversation wrong. Or maybe I heard him wrong. I was so confused and exhausted.

He reaches into his pants pocket and pulls out an envelope. "I forgot to tell you last night." After unsealing the envelope, he pulls out two tickets. "I got us tickets to go see *Sweeny Todd* on stage in Portsmouth this weekend." Waving them in the air, his smile widens and his eyes twinkle.

Quite the change in demeanor. Maybe a date night will be good for us. Give us a chance to forget about all the crazy bullshit surrounding us lately.

But what about his overdue car payment and his gear he might need to replace? Those tickets must've been expensive. But he looks so happy. I don't want to ruin his mood by bringing up bills and boring responsibilities.

I grab the tickets. "No way! That is freaking awesome! I had no idea that play was even going on. How did you know I'd love to see this?"

"You're a horror girl. Duh." He gets playful, laughing and shaking his head all willy-nilly. Then he sticks his tongue out, like he'd be crazy for not knowing I'd love to go see this play. "Plus, you love plays. It was a no-brainer."

Yes, both great points.

But wait.

How does he know I love plays? I've never told him that.

Oh well. He's in a good mood, not acting all jealous and accusey. And it's a relief he's not still accusing Jordan of having a cop-brother and sending him to his work to mess with him. I'll take it. Maybe in the chaos of the moment he really did think it was Jordan's brother? Afterall, he hasn't brought that part up again, even though he was so mad about it when he had called. He might realize how wrong he was and just wants to forget he made that mistake, and he might feel embarrassed about it. The poor guy never gets enough sleep working third shift; it's no wonder why he sometimes can't think straight. I don't want to make him feel bad by bringing it up again. And maybe I did mention I like plays and just forget about it. It's time to have some fun and forget about my problems. I lean over, hug him.

"Thank you for being so thoughtful. I'm wicked excited!"

Yes, the idea of seeing the play excites me, but going with Ronnie…The surprise *is* thoughtful, but something feels off.

Whatever. More craziness is not what I want to dig up. Maybe I need to lighten up and have some fun.

I lean back, peel another piece from the cinnamon roll, start eating again. My break is almost over, and it's close to the end of my short cemetery shift too. Wish I could get more hours. I've been begging Jack to schedule me for more, but the old sexist millionaire prick who heads the board of directors doesn't want "the girl" working fulltime. We're too delicate and weak to perform too much *man*-ual labor. Yeah, he's another motherfucker who can kiss my fed-up ass. But that's a whole other problem I don't have the energy to deal with right now.

I wish I hadn't lost my teaching job back in June. Working as a long-term sub and teaching creative writing was great, until I advocated for a student who was wronged by the principal, not allowed to win *Student of the Month* even though all the teachers had voted for him. I was hoping that gig was going to turn into a permanent teaching position, but I guess that's what I get for speaking up for what's right. This cemetery gig fell into my lap right when I was desperate for a job; with Jordan moved out, I didn't have the luxury of having time to go without a paycheck while searching for something better. And the cemetery is only five minutes from my house. I'd love to find a better gig, but that takes time, and time is in short supply at the moment. I just need to last a few more months until graduation, then I can get a better job. I just need to hang on a little longer. Hopefully I can land a good job before my damn student loan payments kick in six months after graduation. Damn you, Jordan, for putting me in this position! I never would've signed up for this if I'd known you were going to flake on me.

Ronnie mentions something about trying to find our gear, or looking for used gear, or something. I don't know. We'll figure something out. Maybe Jack's pawn shop idea. With everything going on, my thoughts keep swirling, making it hard to focus.

Why does drama surround me everywhere I turn? And I'm starting to see a common denominator in each situation—men. Well, except for Satan. But she *did* pull in a man from my past to help her torment me. So, yeah…men suck! At least the ones I've met.

A tightness forms in the pit of my stomach and the middle of my chest. Slight nausea gurgles in my gut. An ache radiates from the base of my neck down my back, shooting out tendrils of tension and needle-like pain through my limbs. My head feels like an echo chamber, muffled and tinny, ringing in my ears. A vision hits me, one looking down at us sitting in this car right now, like an out of body vision. The sudden need to escape fills me. A rapid pounding knocks against the inside of my skull. What the fuck is happening? Is this what an anxiety attack feels like?

I shake my head and roll the window down. "Whew, it's stuffy in here." I take in a deep breath of fresh air.

Man, going home and losing myself in my school project sounds like a great idea to help pull me out of this, make me forget all my troubles. More research and writing about sympathetic villains…Ha! Maybe that will help me figure out Ronnie, if in fact he is a villain. Or maybe I'm just paranoid from all my studies about this type of character, not to mention my past with lunatic-Aiden.

Hmm…No wonder why I have a fascination with the character type I'm writing about.

Well, I also need to practice for our studio session next week— that should certainly help me relieve some of this stress, shake off this weirdness, and release some pent-up rage. And now I've got that new song idea: Razor Blades and Bullets needs to come to life. Good thing Jordan bought that small practice amp for my last birthday.

Thankfully, Ronnie won't be at my place. His mom's working today, so he'll probably go to his parents' house to watch their dog.

"Well, don't forget, if you want to have a baby, we need to get all the date nights in that we can before that happens." With a beaming smile, he reaches over and squeezes my knee.

A sudden vise-grip sensation hits my whole body, making it hard to swallow the bite of pastry in my mouth. My stomach churns.

I *do* want a baby. And at 37, I'm running out of freaking time. But…

Jordan.

All my visions of my family, my future, even my music—Jordan appears in every one of them.

My excited mood to go to the play crashes. I stuff it down deep, smile, and say, "I've really gotta get back to work now. Break's over."

He leans over, kisses my cheek again. "Yeah, I gotta get to my folks' place and walk Toby. I'll be home for dinner before my shift tonight." His warm expression grows gushy and overly emotional as he says, "*Our* home." A manic smile spreads wide across his sunken-in cheeks, clashing with his watery puppy dog eyes.

In my mind, those eyes bulge and swirl in chaotic spirals as his head lolls around in a crazy, trippy manner *Clockwork Orange* style.

Holy shit, what have I gotten myself into? Is this really happening?

I turn away, blink a few times, brush away the image from my spiraling thoughts.

His puppy dog eyes remain riveted on me when I turn back to face him.

I need space.

I need to get away.

I don't want to be here anymore.

This cemetery shift can't get over with soon enough. I need to get back into a creative space, my shedding-shadows space. Write a new tune, crank my guitar, and release some tension. Escape all the crazy for a bit. But focusing on anything right now…I don't know.

A sick, suffocating feeling overwhelms me. An emptiness at my core, hollow. How can emptiness hurt like this?

Thoughts spin.

Before sunrise at Ronnie's work. Shattered glass, like thousands of shiny lies, strewn across the pavement.

My last fight with Jordan. Yelling. Crying. Pain in my chest. Dreams, like raging tidal waves, crashing down around me.

How could he do this to me? After 10 years married, 15 together. How could he?

Today. Tuesday. Jordan's day off.

That motherfucker's five-year lie pushed me right into this mess.

I can't focus.

Man, I really need a drink.

Once Jack and I finish prepping this grave, I'm beelining it to…

Have a drink and give Jordan a piece of my mind. Turn to page 71.

Go release my rage through music. Turn to page 108.

Time to pack Ronnie's shit and get it the hell out of here. Hopefully some relief comes once it's out of sight.

I toss the straight razor back into the drawer. On my way out of the bathroom and into the bedroom, I glance over at the purple Paul Reed Smith still lying on the couch.

Such a beauty!

I shake my head and move on.

In the bedroom, I kick Ronnie's hardshell bass case out of my path, trip, catch myself on the bed, feel my big toe screaming and swelling. Jesus, I can't even pack his stuff without fucking shit up. On the wall beside the bed hang his two basses. I grab one, seal it in the case, grab the second one, slip it into his gig bag that's leaning against the nightstand. Then I haul them both down to the garage. An old box for the air conditioner Jordan bought last year sits on a shelf beside the hallway door. I grab it, bring it upstairs.

Well, two things are moved, his most prized possessions, and I still feel shitty, shittier than before, still want to end it all. Maybe the mood-lift won't hit me until it's *all* out of my sight.

But then there's the graffiti everywhere and the smashed-up surveillance system.

Dammit. I hate this.

Fuck this life!

I drag myself back into the bedroom, haul Ronnie's clothes off the two shelves built into the wall, and toss them into the box. Packing his stuff makes me realize he doesn't really have many belongings here after all: a week-worth of clothes, hygiene products in the bathroom, his two basses, a small practice amp, a stack of old *Bass Player* magazines.

Doesn't matter. Seeing his stuff here has made me queasy ever since he first showed up with it.

Jordan's stuff belongs here, not Ronnie's.

I turn to the nightstand on Jordan's side of the bed—no, it was never Ronnie's side—and pull open the drawer. Underwear and socks. I wouldn't be surprised to find hidden porno mags at the bottom. I've often seen him rifle around in here. Not sure what the hell he's looking for if it's only for his underwear and socks. *Must* be nudie mags.

Fucking perv!

Just the thought of him makes my stomach turn. Or maybe that's all the Dr.s I drank. Whatever. Equal ick.

As I grab the handful of socks and skivvies, I hear what sounds like a maraca.

Weird.

When I move everything to the box, a prescription pill bottle falls to the floor. Two, actually. They roll under the bed.

What the…

Something else he's been keeping from me?

I reach down, pick them up.

One, of course, is filled with magic blue pills.

That *is* shocking. The way his dick grew stiffer even after the cops barged in earlier, I'd think he'd have no need for those. But he is a fucking drunk, so it makes sense.

On to the second bottle.

OxyContin. 60 milligrams each. At least thirty or so pills inside.

Why does he need these?

Another thought hits me.

Pill bottle in hand, I head to the kitchen.

Dammit! I finished the Dr. McGillicuddy's.

I open the fridge, grab a bottle of iced tea.

Most people might think the best place to fall asleep forever is in your own bed.

But not me.

Not now.

It smells like Ronnie in there. And after what happened earlier tonight, the graffiti too…

The couch welcomes me. I sit beside the sleek purple body of Paul Reed, wet my palate with a sip of tea—too bad it's not liquor, but I still feel the Dr. doing its work—and rest back against the plush Poe pillow. A handful of pills in my palm, then down my gullet.

I grab the purple and turquoise chenille blanket, curl up in the corner of the couch, get cozy, and wait for everything to fade to black.

♫ ▮ ♪

"I never thought this day would come so soon, but here I stand, looking out at all of you and grieving over the death of Dahlia, the love of my life. I don't even know where to start. Dahl was…"

Jordan's voice catches in his throat. Hearing himself say *was* drives the reality of this situation to his core, like a stake in the heart. He looks away, wipes his eyes, and tries his best to continue.

"Let's try that again, shall we." He clears his throat and continues. "Dahlia *is* and always will be my angel, though she didn't like it when I called her that. I guess she didn't see it in herself. But I did. She lifted me up and helped me in so many ways, though I don't think she ever realized how much I needed her, how much I loved her. We joked around a lot, as many of you know, and she would always joke about how badly she wanted wings, but what she never knew was she already had them. With those wings, she lifted up everyone she came in contact with, not just me. Whether it was as simple as a smile—and hers lights up any and every room she ever graces with her presence—or kind words, or sharing her stories and her songs, she knew how to make people feel seen, heard, cared about. And caring…Dahlia has the biggest, most open heart of anyone I've ever known. I often told her it was her big heart that always got her into trouble. It got her mixed up with people who wanted to take from her, take all that light that shines so brightly and keep it for themselves, leaving her feeling down and used. And," he pauses, tries to contain his tears, smooth his tone, "if I'm really being honest here, I, too, took that light from her, though I never knew I was doing it at the time. I took that light, and now she's gone, and it's all my fault."

Whispers and murmurs ripple through the crowd gathered in the cemetery.

Sitting in the front row beside the open grave, Penny leans forward, oxygen tank at her feet, and says just loud enough for Jordan to hear, "It's not your fault, hun. It's *not*."

He refuses to look at her. He knows if he sees the grief on the face of his mother-in-law over the loss of her baby girl he will be soon to follow in Dahlia's footsteps.

"I wish I could give it all back to her. I wish I could give her the life I promised her but then took away without warning. I wish I could hold her and tell her everything is going to be alright, but I can't. And now…"

His words trail off as he sees Penny's tears, the open grave, the bouquets of lilies and orchids and sunflowers everywhere. But the one thing that brings it all down—seeing the portrait of Dahlia, the one his longtime best friend, Joey—also taken by suicide—drew for Jordan for their eighth wedding anniversary. She stands barefoot on the white sandy beach of Negril, Jamaica in her white bikini and turquoise sarong, holding a bouquet of lilies and orchids on their wedding day.

That smile. Those blue eyes I could drown in. That long, silky hair I could wrap myself in forever.

As the tears pour down his face, Jordan takes off, leaves the burial site, the cemetery and…

By the time Penny returns home from her baby girl's funeral, she hears the news.

Jordan took his own life with a bullet to the head only thirty minutes after giving his eulogy for Dahlia, the love of his life, his angel.

A deluge of fresh tears pours down Penny's flush cheeks. Overwhelmed, she struggles to breathe, adjusts her nasal cannula, and turns up her oxygen.

Try again on page 107.

Good thing I brought the blanket out with me. It's chilly outside. The cool night air's refreshing against my angry-hot skin. I don't think I'll doze during this impromptu writing session, that's for sure—as long as Ronnie doesn't wake up and come ruin my time alone because if that happens, I'll be sure to make myself fall asleep to not have to deal with him.

I should've brought a flashlight out with me so I could walk the trails in the woods and do some writing at the old tree fort. But no, maybe that wouldn't be a good idea. Just reminds me of when Jordan and I built the fort with our nieces, Nat and Zoe. Plus, I love this swing. Maybe I'll go walk the trails tomorrow, climb some trees, pretend I'm a kid again. That sounds pretty freaking awesome!

I love the woods, the trees.

I miss being a kid. Carefree. No stress. No worries.

Curled up in the corner of the bench swing, I affix the booklight to the top of my notebook, take a sip from my mimosa, and put pen to paper. With the waxing gibbous moon so bright overhead, the shadow of a tree branch sways and shimmies across the page, dancing around with my pen strokes. A barred owl calls out through the trees. Its hoots sound almost like it's saying, "Who cooks for you? Who cooks for you all?"

Not hungry at all, neighbor. Rage and despair have my stomach tied in knots.

Maybe I should journal a bit first, or write lyrics or poetry. Something to help me process everything going on. I don't know. Whatever flows, flows. I won't force it.

Mimosa, good friend that she is, pours all my thoughts out of my mind to splash across the pages, uninhibited. The fault lines of my internal earthquake split and crack, releasing demons from deep within. These creatures of darkness run amuck, moving my pen at their will, like a session of automatic writing.

But what is my question?

My subconsciousness already knows the question, I'm sure, even if it's not written down. I know of many questions I need answers for. But are any of those the correct question, *the* question?

Will I ever start making the right choices for my life? Am I on the right path? Will this hellscape I call "My Life" ever lead to peace and happiness besides that which comes with death? That baby boy who comes to me in dreams, will he ever come into this world as my son? Will we ever build sandcastles together, climb trees and build forts together, read books and play music together, like in the visions that dance across the backs of my eyelids? Am I meant to have a child, a family? Will I ever finish grad school? Will I ever stop struggling financially? Will I ever be treated as an equal, not just in the world and in my work, but as a partner? Are there any men who don't lie, cheat, and abuse their partners? Is anyone really trustworthy? Or are most people scum? What will…

Before I read the words I wrote in my notebook, the bell chime hanging on my front door jingles and clatters against steal.

"What the fuck?" Ronnie's groggy voice carries to the backyard from the driveway. "Where the hell is she?"

I shift on the swing, trying to stay quiet, trying to stay hidden, but my foot kicks over my empty mimosa glass. It lands on a stepping stone in the flower garden and shatters.

My life is that glass.

♫ ▌ ♪

"Yeah, no vocal isolation booth or laying down guitar solos after. We do strictly live recordings here at Rock Coast Studio." Ryan, the audio engineer, reiterates the recording procedure as he props open the door at the top of the loading ramp in the back parking lot of the studio.

"Cool. *We're* a live band, so we're all good." Mike hauls his Marshall cab out of the hearse and sets it down next to Kyle's two bass drums.

"Sounds good." I try to not make eye contact with Mike unless absolutely necessary. With Ronnie acting weird lately, I also make sure not to get too chummy with Kyle, even though he's never gotten all accusatory about Kyle and me. I wonder why. Maybe Ronnie and Mike had some sort of beef between them from before I joined the band. Whatever it is, I stick to an all-business-and-nothing-but-business vibe with the guys. I need this session to go smoothly. No drama. No setbacks. Finish it for my school project and move on. Professional is my middle name.

As I open the back door of my SUV and grab my backpack with my guitar pedals inside, I see Kyle pulling out pieces of his kit from the hearse. No way in hell is Ronnie's jealousy going to make me not offer to help Kyle carry in his kit. That's like an unspoken rule for all non-drummers of a band—at least in my book it is.

"Here, let me grab something for you." I step over and grab the high-hat stand and the double bass drum pedal.

As he turns away with a bass drum in his hands, Kyle says, "Thanks." He doesn't look at me at all and heads toward the loading ramp of the studio.

Huh…That's odd. Kyle normally shows a lot of appreciation every time I help him, and he always tells me I don't have to help.

Come to think of it, neither Mike or Kyle have spoken to me much since I arrived. Just simple acknowledgements of my arrival and one- or two-word responses to anything I've said. I wonder if Ronnie has gotten all accusatory with Kyle too and just hasn't laid into me about it yet? Or maybe they're just pissed off about all our gear getting stolen by people I know.

Hey, at least I was the one who hunted our gear down and got it all back in time for our studio session. Whatever. Either way, I foresee an uncomfortable recording session ahead.

Just remember—breathe, stay calm, stay professional.

This recording session can't get over with soon enough. I need this piece of my thesis done, so I can finish digging into how the hell Ronnie knows a bunch of stuff about me that I've never told him. Besides the fact that he stalked my Facebook page. I didn't have the energy to confront him about it after he came outside and found me writing on the swing the other night. I needed sleep, not more stress. Recurring arguments and tension, sandpaper scraping away my psyche, are wearing on me, muddling my mind.

But, man, I also want to find out what really happened at his work the other night with that broken window and the weird phone call from him. It was all so strange. Or is that just my obsessive find-out-who-dunnit mind speaking? Or is it my try-to-fix-them-and-make-them-happy people-pleaser side?

Why does all that matter anyway? Why does anything really matter? He's been driving me mad! Every time I see him now, I'm trying to find out if he's lied to me about something.

What if that's on me though? What if my history of dealing with liars and psychos is making me turn everyone into liars and psychos even when they're not like that?

Whatever. I don't care. I need the madness to end.

Once this session ends, kicking him out of my apartment won't affect my project, my thesis. And I have a sinking feeling *that* is the *only* ending that will fit this mysterious tale.

Yeah, kicking him out of my place will most likely lead to me getting kicked out of the band, but I can always find another band to join. Or better yet, I'll quit this band and start my own fucking band! But that entails starting from scratch *all over again*. This is the fifth band I've been in already.

Why is it so fucking difficult to keep a gigging band together?

Once our gear is loaded in and we get all set up, we sound check. Playing our longest song helps us get our levels set and gives us a warmup before hitting that record button. No one says anything to one another when the song ends.

"All right. Sounds great! I've got a good mix back here," Ryan says through our headphones. "If everyone's ready, and if no one needs to use the bathroom, you can go ahead and play all three songs. You can repeat any if you're not happy with the first go-through. We'll wait until the end to have a listen and see if we need any more takes."

"Sounds good," I say into my mic. No one else in the band says a word. I turn and look at each of them when I say, "Does anyone need to use the bathroom before that red light goes on?" No one looks at me except Ronnie. Mike and Kyle both say, "No," as they tinker with their instruments. Such obvious displays of avoidance, I feel like calling them out about it on the spot, but I don't want to rock the boat in the studio, setting an even more negative vibe than the one I've already been feeling. I need to get good takes for my school project.

Ronnie's eyes remain riveted on me.

"How about you? Need to go before…"

"Nope." Wearing a blank expression, he stares at me for a few uncomfortable seconds. Then he thumps a few notes on his bass and says, "Let's roll," as he turns away.

I nod and turn back to my mic. "Looks like we're ready whenever you are, Ryan."

We pound out our three tracks. Tracks one and two take three go-throughs, but we nail them both on the third go-round. Once the mistake-free second take of the third song ends, we've got plenty of time for a listen in the control room and a few audio tweaks to level everything out. And we'll still have about twenty minutes left on our time slot to break down, pack up, and load our vehicles.

Ryan continues working on the tracks while we clean out.

In the back parking lot, we pack our vehicles in silence. No one says anything. Nothing about how the session went. Nothing about practicing for our next Geno's gig. Nothing.

"Here you go, guys and gals." Ryan's walking down the loading ramp of the studio with four CDs in his hand and a USB drive. "I burned the tunes to a CD for each of you. I also sent them to you through Dropbox, but I thought you'd like to have something in-hand when you leave."

I rush over, anxious to get the tunes in my possession. "Hey, thanks a lot, dude. Much appreciated!" I pocket the USB drive.

We shake. He waves to the rest of the guys, who are still loading their gear. They all wave and shout, "Thanks." Then Ryan heads back into the studio and shuts the back door.

After passing out the CDs to the guys, I help Kyle load the last of his cymbal stands into the hearse. After he flings the back door shut, I turn toward my SUV and see Mike and Ronnie standing nearby. No one's talking.

I step over to the guys and hold up my CD. "I can't wait to crank this baby on the way home. Great job in there, guys!" Throwing a smile to each one of them, I wait to hear what they think about how our session went.

"Yeah, same." Standing beside me, Ronnie tucks his CD into the front pocket of his pullover hoodie.

Mike and Kyle share a look I can't read. Then Mike looks at me, then at Ronnie.

"Yeah, well, I hate to say this, but I'm done. The band is done."

His blunt words hit me like a punch in the gut.

Speechless, I glance at Kyle. Stone-faced, he just nods.

Then I turn toward Ronnie, who looks as shocked as I feel.

I turn back to Mike. "Okay. Well, I'm real sorry to hear that. I thought the session went pretty fucking awesome, but…"

"It's not that…" Mike stops short before elaborating, looking as though he's trying to figure out how to say what he wants to say.

Before Mike gets another word out, Ronnie hauls his arm back and punches him in the mouth. "I know you've been fucking my girl!"

I jump out of the way.

Kyle takes a step back and looks as though he's assessing the situation before reacting.

"What the fuck…Motherfucker…" Mike touches his jaw, wiggles it side-to-side. He turns toward Ronnie, eyes ablaze, and then wraps his arm around his neck. Mike gets him in a head lock, and a full-on brawl takes place right there in the parking lot of the studio.

Punches and kicks start swinging. Mike throws punch after punch against the side of Ronnie's head. A swift leg swipe from Ronnie takes Mike's feet out from under him, releases his headlock grip, and sends him to the pavement. Ronnie dives on top of his friend and bandmate and throws a couple jabs at his face. Blood and spittle fly everywhere.

But the beatdown doesn't last long.

Kyle, the biggest guy out of all three, at six-three three hundred pounds, steps in and pulls each one of them off each other like they're grade school kids in a playground tussle. "Whoa now. Let's all calm down and get a grip on ourselves. The band's just breaking up. No need for overreactions."

The brawlers each step away from each other, wiping their faces, straightening out their hair and clothes.

"I never fucked *'your girl,'* you insecure fucking prick! We've only been bandmates."

Ouch! I thought we were friends too. Guess not. Business only.

"This…" Mike points back and forth at Ronnie and me. "Your obsession over her is why this band is fucking done. You stalked her online for years until you saw just the right time to invite her into our band. Then you swooped in when her marriage went south, promising all sorts of bullshit you have no intentions of delivering on just so you can get into her pants. Now this? Fuck this is bullshit! We're out." He waves at Kyle to follow him to the hearse.

Kyle looks at us and shrugs, then follows Mike.

So, it's true? And they both knew all this time? And no one told me? What the fuck? I guess we were never really friends.

Dumfounded, I stare at Ronnie. He's wiping blood from the corner of his lip, looking like a wounded puppy dog, all apologetic eyes, obviously wanting sympathy.

In the final words of Mike…

Fuck this bullshit! I'm out.

My suspicions were just confirmed.

I turn away, open the door of my SUV, hop in, and drive away.

Without a damn clue how to calm my boiling rage, I gun-it down Forest Avenue. Weaving in and out of traffic, I head straight toward I-295, punching the steering wheel and screaming obscenities the whole way. Flames of fury engulf my head. Pounding pain throbs at my temples, and my cheeks feel scorching hot. Not to mention the bolts of lightning shooting painful jolts down both my forearms and ricocheting around my wrists like a billion tiny needles. Please, don't tell me I'm going to need carpal tunnel surgery on top of everything else I'm dealing with.

Son of a bitch! I can't deal with any of this right now. It all needs to go away, vanish.

Why do I have to exist at all?

Sometimes I wish I were never born.

Disappear me, oh great magic from beyond the stars. Reach down from the cosmos and wipe me out of existence, please. Toss me into a black hole, or whatever it takes to wipe it all away and strip me of the torment of all the heaviness.

Maybe going for a drive and blasting some tunes will calm me down. Or maybe I can find a very large, old Mr. Oak to clear my slate, eliminate the madness for me.

Man, I could really use one of Jordan's amazing massages.

No! To hell with Jordan, the scared, little lying man-boy that he is. I do still have that Nine Stones gift card he gave me for my birthday though. But I need to get my gear home. I don't want to get ripped off again. For all I know, some psycho could be following me.

What if Ronnie goes right back to my place? His face is the last thing I want to see.

Nope, I don't want to go home right now.

I need to get away, to escape.

♬ ▮ ♪

Blast some tunes and go for a drive to calm down. Turn to page 61.

Take my Nine Stones gift card and go get a massage. Turn to page 80.

A long, sketchy road ahead. Scattered broken dreams behind. And all I can think to do is die.

Tears flood my eyes and drench my face as lyrics from one of my songs rattle around my brain.

Dammit! This drive is supposed to help clear my head, make me feel better.

The road in front of me appears blurry and washed out through the windshield. With the push of a button, I switch from the demo CD we just recorded to Soundgarden's *Superunknown.* "Fell On Black Days" blasts from the stereo speakers. Jordan has always said I have a searchlight soul as bright as the sun, but it sure as hell doesn't help me navigate through my horror-stricken life. He also tells me my heart is too big and always gets me into trouble. Yeah, that one might be spot-on.

Images from my shitty life flash through my mind.

Crying muddy rivers and screaming for help down in the hidden hole under Aiden's trailer. Aiden' s beady eyes glaring down at me while he rapes me. Jordan admitting his five-year lie. The last fight I had with Jordan. A hooded Aiden lurking in the dark corner of Geno's, stalking me. Chasing Satan and Aiden through the streets of Portland to get my stolen gear back. Ronnie glaring at me every time I talk to Mike. The broken window of my Jimmy and Satan's middle finger waving out her car window. Ronnie's three A.M. phone call filled with accusations and delusions. Mike ending the band and revealing Ronnie's secret game plan. Mike and Ronnie's bloody scuffle. Satan's death threats screaming through the phone while Mom's head bleeds.

"Fuck. Fuck. Fuck!" My fists pound the steering wheel over and over, punctuating every word I scream as my foot presses harder on the gas pedal.

I hate my life.

Every door I've opened to create the life I've dreamed about has slammed in my face.

All my fears have come to life, as though my fearing them attracted them to me. Everything I fight to keep away from moves closer, lurking in the shadows, hiding in every dark corner, waiting to hit me, kick me on my ass right when something good comes my way. Though not much good comes my way these days.

What is it about me that brings on all this chaos, all this pain, all this torment?

Did I do something bad that I don't remember, and karma's making me pay?

Is it a past life mistake coming back to haunt me?

Hard luck and trouble's been holding my hand since I began to crawl. Was I born under a bad sign?

Is there something about me that attracts psychos and nutjobs?

Or am I just that shitty of a decision maker?

My mind reels with possibility after possibility. How can anyone explain the bad luck of my existence? Just when it seems like everything is moving in the right direction, a curveball whacks me upside the head. Just like the old saying goes, if it wasn't for bad luck…

Dammit! I need find a way to stop these snowballing thoughts.

I head toward the Saco River, hoping the sound of flowing water will ease my mind. It's not far from my house. I take the long way there, zooming down little side roads that wind this way and that, twisting the wheel around curves, watching the blackened trees veiled by night whip past like towering Shadow People.

The need to get away from everything tugs at me.

Getting away from Satan involves moving away from Mom. But I have no money to move. And if I move away from Mom, I won't be next door and readily available to help her. She has no one. Only me.

And she once had Jordan.

Another person I don't want to think about.

All the plans we had for after my grad school graduation flew out the window when he finally revealed his 5-year lie. Now I'm left picking up the pieces of my shattered life. Alone. In the dark. Barely hanging on.

At least when I write, I'm the only one to blame if it all goes wrong. And I'm the only one who can fix it. But life…

Creating a fulfilling life doesn't involve *only* solitary endeavors, at least not for me. Afterall, humans are social creatures. And creating a family takes more than one person. It takes a relationship. A trusting partnership. Two people working together toward a common goal.

I *thought* we had a common goal.

Now I'm alone.

And here I am about to earn my MFA in Creative Writing. Not a great degree guaranteed to earn me a sustainable income. But when I signed up, Jordan had my back, encouraged me. I can't quit now; the money's been spent—or rather, borrowed. I still need to pay that shit back somehow!

Living alone is near impossible, unless you make a ton of money or live in a one room shack or efficiency apartment—or have a partner, a friend, or a roommate you can trust.

I have none of that.

No family.

No partner.

No friends.

And now I have no band to create with.

Music has been my life since I was a young child. I could start a solo project, but acoustic guitar players populate that niche. Acoustic is fun but not really my jam. I prefer loud and crunchy grooves.

There's writing. I still have that.

But it's not enough.

It can't hold my hand, kiss me gently. It can't hold me close, keep me safe. It can't tuck my hair behind my ear, tell me everything's going to be all right. It can't create a family with me.

My head, my chest, my entire body feels gripped in a vise as my sobs turn to screams. I punch the dash, the door, the ceiling, the steering wheel. Knuckles bloody. Throat scratchy. Overdriven heartbeat pounding in my head like a death metal blast beat. I scream and scream.

Nothing I do makes a positive change. I have no control over anything in my life. I have no control over my own mind. I have no control over anything.

It's maddening.

I want it all to stop.

I just want it to fucking end.

Now!

The next road runs along the river, leading toward the park where the rope swing hangs. In the daylight, the view of each passing yard has always left me in awe. To live with the view and sound of flowing water outside your window…I wish I had that luxury to help calm my mind, help me sleep at night.

A calm mind.

What is that?

It's a feeling I haven't felt in far too long.

My foot presses harder against the gas pedal. My next scream shoots out louder than the last one. The road on the left just before the bridge leads to the park.

I hesitate to make that turn.

I need the bridge to cross me over to another life.

Nonexistent time weighs heavy on my shoulders.

Tears flow faster.

My foot floors the gas.

I fly past the road on the left, speed onto the bridge.

I cut the wheel sharp.

Metal crunches against concrete as the front end of my Jimmy slams into the railing of the bridge, then flips up and over, sending me and it airborne.

In this river, my mind fades to black. No coming back.

Penny hears a loud knocking on the window of her front door.

Who the hell could that be at this hour?

Maybe Dahl. But why?

She looks at the clock on the stove. 11:30 P.M.

Her lights were on when I pulled in. Maybe she wrote a new story and saw me come home late, and she can't wait for me to read it and add it to my collection.

After slipping on her bathrobe, Penny untangles the long hose connected to her oxygen tank and slowly makes her way to the front door. She jumps as another knock sounds against the glass.

"I'm coming, Dahl," she says as she rounds the corner into the foyer.

But when she flips on the front porch light and looks out the window, it's not her daughter knocking.

A tall, husky police officer stands on the other side of the glass, hat held to his chest.

"Officer Palisano?" Penny's heart drops and her breathing grows labored. She adjusts her nasal cannula. "I wasn't expecting to see *you* when I opened the door. What's going on? What's wrong?" She worries her worst nightmare may have come true. Ronnie must've done something horrible to her daughter, her baby girl.

"Hello, Penny. Sorry to bother you so late, but I have some bad news." He pauses, clears his throat.

Penny loses her balance, grasps hold of the doorframe, using it like a crutch as her breathing grows more labored and shallower.

"It's Dahlia."

"My Dahl? Is she alright? What did that motherfucker do to her? Where is she?"

"I'm sorry, Penny, but rescue services just pulled Dahlia out of the Saco River. Her SUV went off the Salmon Falls Bridge. She was alone. And I'm sorry to say, she didn't make it out alive."

Penny mouths the word "No," but no sound comes out. A shortened breath later, as tears fall and crash down her reddened cheeks, she faints. Officer Palisano catches her and radios for an ambulance.

The correct choice was to take my Nine Stones gift card and get a massage. Turn to page 80.

Drowning my sorrows in a bubble bath should be a great way to end this night, end the pain and anger swirling within me like raging storms. Warm water to envelope me in a total-body hug. Maybe not the hug I want the most, but someone ripped that hug away from me, and now I'm left feeling discarded, a piece of trash thrown away and forgotten about. A piece of trash not good enough to create a family with. Loneliness spreads like a cancer, sinking deep into my bones, deep into every cell within my body.

I attempt to alter my thinking, try to come up with solutions to improve my life, but only empty options ricochet around my mind. Distant friends, out of reach. Much too late to make the calls. A text sent to my lost love mocks me on the screen of my cell. I know he won't respond. But at least he'll have one last thing to remember me by. Though he probably doesn't care.

I accidentally catch a glimpse of my reflection in the mirror above the sink. Not a sight I want to see. Flush cheeks. Puffy, black-smudged eyes. Obsidian rivers running rampant.

Amplified pain.

Thudding migraine.

Chest so tight it might burst.

I clench my fist and punch the wall. Sheetrock indents and rips. Bones snap and pop upon impact.

Shit. Did I just wake the sleeping stalker?

Nah. He was lit by the time the play ended, passed out before trying to make any moves on me, thank goodness.

I turn away. My leg bumps an open drawer. The overhead light twinkles on something shiny inside. I reach in, pull out Ronnie's straight razor. The shimmer on my left palm calls to me.

Twisted words swirl around my head.

I've scraped and clawed ten thousand miles. Been kicked and stomped ten thousand more. Broke through walls to prove I can, then mud-dragged 'round and 'round again.

I've bled on strings, wove words with songs, carved my story on the wall. But tragedy ends every tale, and all I seem to do is fail. No matter what I do I lose. Just like the saying goes—

Born to lose.

Only cold resides inside me.

My bloodied knuckles throb and sting.

My fingertips cling to the edge of sanity.

And all I can think to do is die.

Time to slip into a bath and leave it all behind.

I lean down toward the tub, turn the water on, and step inside. After undressing, I lie down on the hard, white porcelain, rest my head back against the tub's edge.

My mind's a haze of grief and regret, anger and hate. The pieces of my dreams lie scattered, never to form a whole.

I'm done trying.

Warm water rises around me. The warmth envelops me like a comforting hug.

Straight razor in hand, I ease out the blade. The overhead light reflects on the stainless-steel surface, mocking my darkness. With the cool, sharp edge against the flesh of my pulsing wrist, I close my eyes, unable to watch as I push down, break the skin, feel the sting, and drag the blade up my forearm to the crook of my elbow. To make this stick, I need to do the other arm too. But I don't want to look.

I place the blade in my left hand. My weak fingers curl around the cool steel, but I can't make a fist, can't hold tight. Searing pain screams up my arm, surges through my body. The chill of the blade slips from my palm, plops in the water, thuds against the tub. My head lolls to the right, mind grows foggy.

An image of Jordan, Mom, a baby boy, sunlight.

But wait. I don't want to.

I just want to hold you all...

Forever.

207-699-5464

2:43 A.M.

Jordan: Great to hear from you! I wanted to call you but didn't think you wanted to hear from me I miss you been reconsidering a lot of stuff Can I see you?

Penny pulls into the driveway and sees a couple of Dahlia's apartment lights still on. *My workaholic girl...must be up late writing her thesis. I'm so proud of her.* A smile spreads wide.

She parks her pickup and adjusts her nasal cannula, wondering why she can't get a good draw of oxygen. The interior light pops on when she opens the door. As she steps onto the gravel driveway and pulls her travel oxygen tank off the seat, she notices the oxygen level just hit zero.

I'll be fine. It's not far to get inside to my other tank.

She slings the strap of the oxygen tank's travel bag over her shoulder, shuts the truck door.

The light at the end of the walkway illuminates the steps leading down to the driveway. Penny takes each step slowly, making sure she doesn't increase her breathing rate too high. At the top, she pauses before making her way to the front porch steps.

She readies herself to progress the rest of the way to the house, but she cusses herself out first. "Damn it! You forgot to leave the porch light on, you space cadet." Taking in the deepest breath she can, she shakes her head and steps forward.

The fading path of light trails ahead of her as she slowly shuffles up the walkway. At the porch, she grabs the railing and pauses to catch her breath before taking the first step.

As she lifts her foot to head up the stairs, she feels something graze her ankle. Figuring it's only the fallen leaves, she ignores it, only thinking of her need to go inside and get hooked up to her oxygen tank. Just as she takes that second step, whatever grazed her ankle pulls tight and trips her. As she reaches for the railing, she realizes, *Dammit. I forgot to get rid of the old dog leash.* She falls down on the stairs, left hip hitting the edge of the step hard.

"Ow," she screams.

Still holding the railing, she tries to pull herself up. Excruciating pain radiates from her left hip all through her body. Tears fill her eyes.

Son of a bitch! I think I broke my fucking hip.

Reflexively, she opens her mouth to yell for Dahlia but stops herself. That'll take too much breath—breath she doesn't have.

Instead, she reaches her hand into the side pocket of the oxygen tank's travel bag and pulls out a bicycle horn. Dahlia gave it to her should Penny ever need to call for her help when she's out in the yard since she *still* refuses to own a cell phone.

She squeezes the rubber ball. The horn blares through the yard and the woods all around.

But Dahlia never comes to her window to look outside for her mother. She never comes out of her apartment to make sure her mother is all right.

This is the first time Penny has ever wished to not live in such a secluded location.

She squeezes the horn again.

Nothing. No Dahlia.

What is she doing? Maybe she fell asleep.

Penny's breathing turns to wheezing.

She squeezes the horn again.

Still no Dahlia.

Please, wake up, Dahlia. I really need you right now, sweetie.

She squeezes the horn again and again and…

Her breathing turns into short, spread-out gasps. Gurgling in her throat.

All energy to blast the horn again seeps out of her with her last few short gasps for breath.

Hovering just above the ground beside my mother, I reach for her over and over, trying to help her up and bring her to her oxygen tank inside the house.

"I'm here, Mom. Please, hold on. I'll help you. Please, stay with me."

But every time my ethereal hand grasps for Mom's arm, it permeates through, grabs hold of nothing, as though the image of my dying mother is nothing but a bad dream. A horrible nightmare, the very thing I wanted to escape.

"Noooooo!" I scream into the dark, starry sky like a wolf howling in the moonlight.

I can't even check her pulse to see if she's still hanging on.

I try reaching for her again, but once more, my hand moves through Mom's motionless, unbreathing body.

One more time, my inner wolf howls, trying to save the only family I have left. *"Help! Someone* please, *help!"* Screaming and screaming, I pray some distant neighbor hears my cries. But then I realize…

No one hears the cries of a ghost screaming into the night.

"This can't be happening." My hands cover my face to catch and swipe away tears, but no tears fall.

Ghosts can't cry.

Hollow and empty.

I wanted to escape this loneliness. But now…

Settling my ethereal form on the ground beside Mom's body, I want so desperately to hug her once more but can't. I can never feel the warm embrace of a loved one's hug again.

"What the hell have I done?"

The correct choice was to take a notebook and a pen to write.
Turn to page 53.

Going against all I had expected, he answered my text. And quickly. In less than five minutes.

Me: *Are you home? Can we talk? Is it okay for me to come over?*

Jordan: *Yep come on over I'm here alone*

You know where rick lives right

Me: *Yes, I do. I'll head over in about ten minutes. See you soon.*

One last shot of Dr. McGillicuddy's minty goodness down my gullet, and I slip on my boots and pocket my phone.

Not bothering to clean myself up at all after arriving home from my grimy cemetery shift, I grab my keys and head back downstairs to my Jimmy. On my way out the door, I grab the empty bottle of Dr. I just finished off and toss it in the recycle box in the garage before I step outside. I can't count on anyone else to make sure it gets recycled after I'm gone.

Jordan may have said it was okay for me to come over, but I know nothing will change his mind about his decision. He made that quite clear last time we talked. Right now, he probably thinks he might be able to get a piece of ass without any commitment.

Delusional prick!

Making Jordan know—*NO!* Making him *feel* how much he screwed me over and fucked up my life sits at the forefront of my mind.

I jump in my Jimmy and tear up dirt and rocks all the way up my long dirt driveway. Tires squeal as I turn the wheel and speed out onto the road.

Our last counseling session replays over and over in my mind. Jordan yelling at me after I told him how I felt. The unexpressive look on his face when I poured my heart out about wanting to grow old together, have grandchildren.

Really? Do my feelings mean nothing to him?

And his reaction to me talking about our future plans…I can't shake the image of his deer-in-headlights expression. Like he was shocked about my hopes to build a family together. He *knew*. We've been planning this *together* for five years. Why did he look so shocked?

Or maybe I read that wrong. Maybe that was the look of a criminal caught in the spotlight of an approaching police officer. His five-year lie revealed for the whole world to see. For *me* to see.

How could he not feel bad about what he did to me? Why didn't he shed a tear over all of this? Did I mean so little to him that he can just move on like our fifteen years together never happened?

Seven minutes later—seven minutes of crying, screaming, punching my steering wheel, and damning Jordan to Hell—I see Rick's house in the distance. The front porch light illuminates the walkway. The living room light shines through the picture window. Jordan stands beside the small lamp on the sill, looking out toward the driveway. Perfect location to watch my memorable arrival.

The driveway is not where I'm headed.

The tall, wide, two-hundred-year-old oak tree stands tall, sturdy, and unyielding like a sentry at the front border of the yard.

I love trees.

I once loved Jordan.

Before he betrayed my trust and crushed my world.

He's going to wish he'd made a different decision. I'm going to make sure of that.

You think you can crush my world and move on like it's nothing?

Just you wait.

I'm about to fuck you up for life.

Love you too, hun!

My foot presses harder on the gas pedal. High beams light my way.

Just as I reach the roadway in front of the yard, I lose my breath, thoughts scatter.

What am I doing? I can't do this to him. I don't really want to hurt him. I love him so fucking much, it hurts to even think about him, to see him, to try to talk to him.

But he threw me away like I meant nothing to him. Threw me away like a dessert wrapper, like garbage after he had his fill. Like our time together was all for nothing.

Sobbing, unsure what to do, I punch the gas. Speed past the tall oak standing guard in the front yard. Road barely visible through the torrent of tears.

I need to get out of here. I need to get away. I need to make this pain stop.

About a mile flies by. Maybe more. My headlights reflect off an upcoming *Stop* sign. Main Street traffic of the neighboring town zooms along beyond. With no more big trees near enough, I gun it toward the intersection. The speedometer hits sixty, sixty-five, seventy. The *Stop* sign zooms up fast.

A tractor trailer truck approaches, followed by a box truck, another tractor trailer truck, and a line of cars.

I zip past the stop into the onslaught of traffic and close my eyes.

The sound of squealing tires and honking horns fills my head. Crunching metal shoves me, throws me aside.

Then everything disappears.

The grave hangs open like a pit ready to engulf him as he stands there sobbing and holding one lily and one orchid. A gentle hand lands on his shuddering shoulder. He doesn't need to look to know who it is.

"I can't believe I did this to her." His stuttered words escape his lips in a whisper.

"It's not your fault, Jordan. She chose her own path. *She* did this to *herself*." Dahlia's mother, Penny, says through tears. She wraps her arm around his shoulders, hugs him. "I can't believe she did this instead of…" A double breath from her crying interrupts her before she says, "Instead of talking to one of us."

"Well, in her defense, last time she tried to talk to me, I was kind of a stubborn, insensitive prick, hiding from my shame." He shakes his head, wipes his eyes. "But this time…this time was going to be different. I was so happy to receive that text from her that night. I didn't think she ever wanted to see or hear from me again after our last fight. Then that sound, that chime on my phone—Music to my ears." He turns and looks at his second mother. "She had no idea...I was going to ask for her forgiveness. Ask her to take me back. Ask her to make a family with me."

"Oh, Jordan..." Penny's sobs cut her words short as she embraces her son-in-law.

The two stand together hugging and staring down at the black and silver casket. No more words. Only tears.

The lily and the orchid drop from Jordan's trembling hands and land gently in the open grave.

The correct choice was to release my rage through music.
Turn to page 108.

A gentle breeze blows through the trees, sending melodic whispers through the leaves. Branches scritch and squeak, a musical accompaniment.

I stand and listen, half-filled bowl of weed and a lighter in hand. The need to mellow my mood pounds in my head. The mesmerizing shimmer of that stainless steel razor blade calls to me.

Just push that image away and breathe.

I try to let the soft sounds sooth my mind, my mood, my spirit as I stand with the soft glow of the front porch light at my back.

The coolness of the late-night air chills my tear-soaked cheeks. I wipe it all away only to make room for more. My lips taste salty.

The wind picks up. The bench swing hanging from my back deck creaks as it sways to the night's music. I wander toward the sound.

I sit on the old, splintery wood of the bench and sway along with the night-song. With the need to lift my mood, I raise the bowl to my lips and repeatedly try to take a toke. The wind keeps blowing out the lighter. I give up trying.

Nothing can rid me of this mood.

The small, rectangular piece of cedar Jordan had cut to size and drilled holes into to make another swing for me lies on the ground near the flower garden pathway in front of me. The long ropes to hang it lie in two coiled mounds like a couple snakes on the ground beside the wooden seat. I kick one mound with my toes, stirring up pine needles and fallen leaves. There are better ways to use that rope.

I stand up, place my bowl and lighter on the bench swing, and reach for the snakes.

Time to eliminate all my troubles, return to where I came from.

Bare feet crunch along the leaf-covered ground as I enter the woods, escape the world.

"Hi, Jordan, it's Penny. I hope I'm not bothering you." Penny scratches the peach fuzz growing back on the bald spot on the side of her head while holding the cordless phone to her ear. "Have you heard from Dahl?"

"Hi, Mom…I mean Penny. No, I haven't heard from her at all. Why do you ask?"

"I can't get a hold of her, and I'm worried about her. She always looks exhausted, bags under her eyes. She's gotten real skinny lately too, like she's not eating, and she barely smiles anymore. I miss that smile. But now…she always seems angry or upset about something."

"I hope everything's okay," says Jordan. "Have you called her cell?"

"Yep, tried calling her multiple times, both phones. Goes to voicemail every time. I left messages. But I'm her mom; she might not want to talk to me about whatever's eatin' at her."

"Huh, maybe. But it's not like her to not answer her phone."

"That's exactly what I thought. It's weird. Her truck's here, and the lights are on in the apartment. I just don't have the breath to climb all those stairs to see if she's home or out with that psycho from her band."

"Huh…Yeah, that psycho. Is he still coming around?"

"I haven't seen his car in the driveway recently. I hope he hasn't taken her somewhere and done something horrible to her. I *told* her I don't trust him." She pauses, takes her nasal cannula out of her nose, takes a drag off her cigarette. "Is there any chance you could swing by and go see if she's in her apartment? I'm hoping she's just locked herself away to get her schoolwork done. Her graduation's coming right up."

"Not sure she'll want to see me, but yeah, I can do that. I can get there in about half an hour. Does that work?"

"Yes, that would be wonderful. Thank you, hun. You're the best." She stubs out her cigarette, puts her oxygen back on, takes a deep breath. "You know, Jordan, I really wish you two could work things out, but I don't want to butt my nose in."

"Yeah, me too. But I'm pretty sure she hates me now. See you soon, Mom."

"Sounds good, hun."

♫ 🪦 ♪

With the front door flung open, Penny stands waiting at the bottom of Dahlia's front hall stairs, small travel oxygen tank hanging from her shoulder, nasal cannula attached to her nose. She hears Jordan's footsteps scuffing and clomping across the floors upstairs as he checks up on her daughter. He finishes his search about three minutes later.

"She's not here. And there's *graffiti* all over the walls and shit…Weird." He shakes his head.

"Graffiti?"

"Yeah. Doesn't look like she did it."

"Probly that idiot from her band. He betta repaint my fucking walls…that lowlife!"

Jordan just huffs in response.

"Looks like she just up and left. Nothing's put away. Lights're all on. Her cell's on the coffee table." His brow furrows as he adds, "It's just not like her to leave all her lights on and take off without her cell. You know?"

They stand side by side in silence for a moment.

"Now that I think of it…sometimes she takes her writing outside or takes a walk through the trails in the woods. Says it helps with inspiration. That could explain why she left her cell behind." Jordan glances around the side of the garage toward the backyard.

"Yeah, she does that sometimes. You think…" Penny stops short when she sees Jordan start walking toward the backyard. Slowly, she follows.

At the bench swing, Jordan stops. "Her bowl…" He points at it. "She was here. Not like her to leave this behind. Unless…" He looks at the ground. "What's this?" He scoots down and touches a trail through the fallen leaves and pine needles. It leads to the woods. "Wait." He glances around. "Maybe…" As he stands up, he looks under the back deck at the pile of scrap wood. His brow furrows. He turns around, looks out into the woods. "The old fort…"

"What about it?"

He points to the trail along the ground leading into the woods. "Looks like she might've dragged some wood out to work on the tree fort. She used to joke about building a tree fort writing sanctuary in place of that dilapidated old thing we built with the girls."

"You really think she'd take the time to do that?"

"I have no idea. But it's someplace to start." With a shrug he adds, "Penny, wait here. I'm gonna go check it out. If she's not there, I can check a couple of the trails. Be back soon."

Penny grabs Dahlia's bowl and lighter, places it on a stepping stone in the garden, and sits on the bench swing. "Okay. I could use a rest anyway." She sets her oxygen tank beside her.

♫ ∎ ♪

The trail on the ground near the garden looks like a drag mark. And he was right. As he follows it into the woods, it leads him toward the old tree fort they'd made years ago with their nieces. Though he knows Dahlia's great at climbing trees, he knows he took his drill with him when he moved out; he wonders if she's using nails instead of screws like he had warned her against. Screws hold up better, and they're safer, a sturdier hold.

I hope she doesn't fall right through the second story she wanted to add trying to use nails.

But he doesn't wonder about that for long.

Though he's never been much of a runner, Jordan sprints through the trees when he sees the tree fort and…

Dahlia dangling, swinging from a noose tied to the fat oak branch jutting out from under the floor of the fort.

"Dahl…Noooooooooo!"

He rushes up to her, out of breath. With nothing to cut her down with, he grabs around her thighs and lifts, lightening the weight, hoping he's not too late. Hoping he can save her life. Hoping…

"Jordan?" Penny yells in her raspy smoker's voice from back at the bench swing. "What is it, Jordan?"

"No no no no no…" He hugs her legs close, still lifting, still hoping, crying. But she's cold. Colder than the cool autumn air blowing through the leaves. Autumn, her favorite time of year.

In the cold air, he sweats, hyperventilating. The pain and pressure on his head and chest overwhelm him. Unbearable, like hammer hits bashing him senseless, like punches knocking the wind out of him.

A sliver of sunlight slices through the trees, illuminating Dahlia's pale face and empty eyes.

Those blue eyes he will never gaze into again.

Through breathless stutters, he speaks to his lost love.

"Why, Dahl? Why didn't you call me? I would've answered. I would always answer a call from you. Always."

Try again on page 107.

"I know this is last minute, so anyone who has an opening is fine by me." I take the next exit off I-295 and head back in town toward The Old Port. "Shanelle in twenty minutes sounds great! Thank you!"

Wow! I can't believe someone's available. Navigating through downtown traffic and finding a parking space will eat up most of the twenty-minute wait. As anxious, stressed, and depressed as I feel, the prospect of a massage fills me with excitement. I've only had a professional massage once before, and that, too, came as a birthday gift quite a few years ago. Spa treatments fit like a square peg in the small circle of my tight budget. Plus, I've never really been a spa-type girl. Poor artists like me have better things to spend our pennies on, like books and guitar effects pedals and weed medibles.

The CD from today's studio session screams at me from the passenger seat. Our songs run about four to five minutes in length, so I'll be able to listen to a couple songs on my drive to Nine Stones. I stop at the next red light and pop the CD into the stereo.

"Medicated Zombification" is the first track. As the light turns green and I step on the gas, I anticipate hearing Kyle's kickass drum opening, but instead, I'm greeted with Kyle counting us in and hitting his sticks together with each beat of his four-count.

What the hell? Why didn't this part get cut? We're not supposed to hear the drummer counting the band into the song on a studio mix. What the fuck kind of hack engineering job is this?

I need to present this to a whole audience-filled room in a couple months, not to mention my thesis advisor, my writing mentor, and the director of the graduate program.

Okay, just try to calm down and listen to how the rest of the recording came out. Afterall, I'm in a creative writing program, not a music program, so maybe this won't matter.

But it matters to me! This is my music! I wrote it! A lot of people are going to hear this. I want it to sound good. Plus, this session cost money, money I could've certainly used for fuel this winter instead of a shitty recording.

I hit the back arrow to start the song over. An uncomfortable cringe surges through me when I hear Kyle counting us in again, but I push through it and focus on the rest of the song as I turn left onto Congress Street.

The rest of the song sounds pretty freaking killer!

Oops. Maybe not.

Between the second chorus and the solo comes a click sound, like the engineer punched-in the solo section. Did he take the solo from one recording and paste it into another? If so, why? And why do I hear the punch-in?

Another click-sound-punch-in comes after the chorus too, dammit!

Man, I might've wasted my limited funds on a hack of a studio with a shitty engineer. But don't get ahead of yourself. Maybe it's just this song.

During Ronnie's short bass line interlude before the last chorus, an image of his manic smile and swirling crazy-eyes flash across my mind. I push it away as best I can as I make the last turn onto India Street to find a parking space near the spa.

Shit! Now I'm going to be late for my damn appointment. Bumper-to-bumper parked cars line both sides of India. Parking in Portland sucks! If I didn't just make the appointment, I might be able to call and reschedule. But I need this *now*. If I cancel without a 24-hour notice, I still have to pay, and if I'm too late and waste my gift card, I can't afford to make another appointment. My Jimmy moves at a turtle's pace as I scour the street for some place to park. That's when I hear it.

Between track one and track two, I hear Kyle say, "Which song next?" Then my voice comes through the speakers. "How about 'Dead Inside', and then we go right into 'Bury Yourself'. Cool?"

And again, I clearly hear Kyle counting us in with his voice and his drumstick hits.

What the fuck type of shit-ass recording did I just blow my fucking money on? I'm embarrassed to have to share this when I present my thesis at my senior residency in a couple months. I don't know how to fix this myself, and I have no more money to put toward another recording session at a different studio.

Plus, I don't have a band anymore.

Dammit! If I were tech savvy at all and had a DAW program on my computer, maybe I could fix this myself. But if I had tech skills and recording gear, I wouldn't've had to pay for a studio session—I would've done it all myself like all the younger musicians are doing these days. Fuuuuuuuuck!

I hit the back arrow to listen to all the mistakes again. Probably a bad idea at the moment, but I do it anyway. It's a waste of time, though, because I'm more focused on finding a parking space than listening to this suck-ass recording.

"Dead Inside" plays as I circle around the block to find parking. My revved-up heart rate pounds in my head, pain throbbing in my temples, when I realize I have to circle the block *again*. Shit! The *tic-tic-ticking* of the clock in my head knocks against my skull. I *am* going to be late. Can I get anything right? I can't even get to a fucking appointment on time, an appointment I just made ten minutes away from the place! Heat rises from under my shirt collar as stress sweat breaks out around my neck. When I find an empty space on the opposite corner of the block from the spa, I realize I didn't pay attention to "Dead Inside" at all. When I cut the engine, I'm already ten minutes late. Man, just trying to get to this freaking appointment has made me more stressed than when I called to book it—if that's even possible.

What a fucking pathetic freak I am if I can't even handle looking for parking space and running a few minutes late for an appointment.

Holy crap I need this massage!

I grab the blanket off my back seat and the towel from the floor and spread them over my gear in the way-way back to hide it all as best I can. I don't want to take any chances of getting ripped off again. With shaky hands, I clip my keys to my purse and book it down the sidewalk to my appointment.

After arriving and giving my gift card to the teenage girl working the front counter, a twenty-something woman, wearing a warm smile, strolls around the corner, greets me, and leads me down the sea green hallway toward a tea station.

Twenty minutes late and counting.

Great. And when I leave here, I have the joy of listening to a shitty studio mix of my former band's demo while I drive home to face Ronnie, the guy who's been stalking me for who the hell knows how long and is living in my apartment.

Lovely.

It doesn't matter how long this massage lasts. It could go on for two hours or more, but it won't make a difference. Nothing will.

Rage, anxiety, and depression fill my entire being, clinging to me like a fungus, eating me from the inside out.

So much for a relaxing and refreshing massage. I'm more wound the hell up now than I was before. My body should feel better, and yeah, it did during the massage, but my screwed-up life still has me all tied in knots. I can't get out of my head! At least the wind blowing through the open car window feels good. I take in a deep breath of fresh air, hoping it will help clear my head.

Maybe I should've driven home in silence instead of listening to the shitty mix of our tunes. That, of course, made me think about how embarrassed I'm going to be when I present this with my thesis in a couple months. Even the levels are all wonky, the reverb's way overdone, and the vocals are buried in the mix. It sounds worse than when we all listened to it together before packing up. Maybe my professors, the director, and my writing mentor won't care about that part. But *I* care. There'll be an audience listening to that crappy mix. This recording was also supposed to be our demo—the first of our tunes to be recorded. Tunes we could share online and with venues we haven't performed at yet. Not that *that* part matters now that the band split up. But still…Maybe I'm being too much of a perfectionist. But I paid for a good recording, for Christ's sake, and that's what I should've walked away with.

Maybe that's not it. Maybe it's…I don't know…Just hearing the tunes I wrote with that band puts Ronnie's crazed face into my headspace. Not a pleasant sight.

And now, there's my mailbox up ahead. I hope Ronnie's not already at my place.

No, it will never be "his place." He'll be gone soon. Very soon.

As I pull down my long driveway, the urge to spark a joint and pour myself a drink intensifies.

But wait.

What the hell?

Son of a bitch, what the fuck am I arriving home to?

Looks like that toke and drink won't happen soon enough.

Jesus Christ! Can I ever catch a fucking break from the insanity?

The front door to my apartment is ajar. No vehicles in the driveway. Not even Mom's truck.

Guess my gear will have to stay in the Jimmy for now. No idea what the hell I'm about to walk into. I hope no one's still inside my place!

After shifting to park, I slip out my boot knife from inside my tall Doc Marten before easing myself out of my vehicle. The surveillance camera above my front door dangles from the cord, smashed. I hold my cell phone up to record that and whatever else I find, then shoulder the front door open further. That's when I notice the open door at the top of the hallway stairs. Looks like someone kicked it open. A partial tread from a shoe marks the center of the bottom half.

Walking up the stairs quietly proves difficult in my heavy-clomping boots, but I try. Knife at my side, phone held out in front and facing forward, I step inside and turn the corner to see…

A total fucking mess. Graffiti everywhere.

Graffiti I recognize.

The signature pointy knife-like lettering, red paint dripping like blood. Wings. Roses. Skulls.

My heart sinks.

He knows where I live. Knows when I'm not home.

But I was supposed to be home. The massage was a last-minute decision.

Has he been stalking me again?

I search my apartment. As I move through the living room, I navigate around bits and pieces of the smashed-up DVR I use for my surveillance system. I check closets and under the bed but find no one, just a mess and more graffiti. Skulls. Demons. Daggers. More red dripping paint. Bureau drawers all emptied, clothes thrown around. Mattress stripped and flipped. Then I see the huge black wings spread wide across the wall at the head of my bed, red paint dripping as though the wings were severed and now bleeding. Pointy, knife-like lettering with drips of red paint arches over the top: *Angel Baby.*

Motherfucker. It *was* him!

After a complete go-round with my cell, capturing all the damage on video, a memory from my teens hits me. When Aiden snuck in through my second-floor bedroom window after he'd been watching the house from the woods to see if I'd brought home a guy friend from school, whom I had previously mentioned wanted to start a band with me. My uninvited company proceeded to smack me around and raped me just for making him worry I'd brought a guy home from school. That was the day he first started threatening to harm my friends and family if I ever reported his abuse or attempted to leave him.

Attempting to shake off the memory with a shake of my head, I set down my boot knife and grab the buck knife—bigger and deadlier—from beside my small Marshall practice amp and unsheathe it. Good thing I keep a knife hidden in every room. With a life like mine—gotta stay armed. After a peek out the music room window and no sight of anyone lurking around outside, I scurry to check out all the other windows.

When I make it to the second set of windows in the living room, I turn left toward the kitchen and realize how visible I am from the outside. To my right—the tall, double windows beside the couch that I just looked out of. To my left—the sliding glass door leading out to the back deck, back yard, and the woods. The last window for me to check.

I hesitate.

Tightening my grip on the hilt of the knife, I drop to the floor and crawl toward the door, making myself a smaller target. Aiden never owned guns back when I dated him, but who knows how he's changed since then. Everyone and their fucking Grandmother owns at least one gun, if not more, these days. Maybe he does too.

Or maybe I'm just paranoid as all hell.

Rightfully so after finding my apartment vandalized.

I wish I owned a gun right now.

Lying flat on my stomach with my head near the bottom edge of the doorframe, I peer out into the back yard and the woods beyond. Vibrations from my blast beat heart rate pounds against the tile floor. Sweat tickles at my temples. Breath holds tight and shallow, tensing every muscle.

No one on the deck or in the back yard.

My eyes move further out toward the tree line.

The bottom branch of a hemlock sways slightly.

Maybe a bird?

A shallow breath later, the patch of ferns between that tree and the oak beside it, leaves rustling.

A squirrel…maybe?

Higher branches on the hemlock bounce and sway. Then I see it.

A foot. Then another. Read and black. Maybe sneakers? Higher branches bounce as the feet move out of sight. Shit! Why am I still watching? Someone's in the fucking tree outside my back door!

Someone?

No. There's only one person that can be. And after the graffiti…

Call the fucking cops already, you amateur sleuth!

I backward shimmy away from the door and across the kitchen floor. Once I make it to the living room, I jump to my feet, grab the landline, and call 911. While telling them why I need them to send help, I scurry back through the kitchen to lock the front doors. First, the one at the bottom of the stairs. Going down the stairs sets my heart rate soaring. Then, back up the stairs to lock the apartment door behind me.

Oh, shit. Can't lock this one. The psycho kicked it in, dammit!

I crouch down in the far corner of the living room near the big closet door where I'm hidden from every window in the place.

Shaking.

Sweating.

Knife and cell in hand, landline sitting beside me.

I wait.

And wait.

And wait.

Thirty minutes later, a cruiser finally arrives. I hear it pull in, see its flashing blue lights reflect through the front windows and shine across the wall. The police department is five minutes from my house, and my small town employs ten officers. Not sure what takes them so long, but Officer Palisano finally shows up, alone.

I guess they don't think I'm in danger.

That means they have no idea who did this or who's out in that tree. Well, after those lights flashing down my driveway, *whoever* I saw in that tree is probably hightailing it right out of here.

"Came home and found it like this. Didn't touch anything except closet doorknobs when I searched. Looks like nothing was stolen, though I couldn't do a thorough search without touching stuff. So, I waited for you. But I saw someone out back in that tree right there. See? That big hemlock." I point out the sliding glass door. "Red and black shoes. I think maybe sneakers." I lean closer to the glass. "I don't see anyone now, but that tree's bushy, and now with your lights…I don't know. Maybe they're gone now, but still…Can you please check there first? It's freaking me out.

"Sure thing." Officer Palisano leans close to the window and peers out into the trees as he unlocks the slider. Grabbing his flashlight from his belt, he aims it toward the tree's thick branches as he steps outside and then conducts a search around the hemlock and the whole back yard.

I stand by the slider, white-knuckling my buck knife, and wait.

Five minutes later, he climbs the back steps and comes back inside.

"No one's out there. Saw a bunch of footprints around the base of that hemlock, along with a few cigarette butts." On the palm of his gloved hand, he shows me five stubbed-out cancer sticks. "American Spirits. Know anyone who smokes those?"

"Huh, yeah, at least one, but that was years ago. But that's exactly who I suspect did this," I say, sweeping my hand through the air, motioning to the graffiti, "and that's who I suspect I saw in that tree."

Nodding, he pulls out a baggy, inserts the cigarette butts, seals it, and repockets it.

He takes a step closer to the kitchen cabinets to inspect the free artwork I received while away from home.

"Hmm…Yeah, I recognize this handiwork. The signature tag. Officers have seen this around town. Spotted around Portland and Westbrook too." He points to a little squiggly, psychedelic image near the lower left corner of a cabinet door covered in skulls. Not an actual signature of a name, but a graffiti tag. Aiden used to practice creating his own tag back in our teens. He covered his bedroom walls in graffiti art, as well as a ton of street signs and business signs around town.

I tell Palisano the time I got home and how long I've been gone, though I can't speak for my mom next door.

The whole visit is short and quite uneventful.

After strolling through the apartment and snapping some pictures and dusting for prints, Palisano stands beside the door at the top of the hallway stairs. "Well, I, too, have my suspicions who may have done this." He's no stranger to Aiden's criminal history. Afterall, Aiden grew up in this town where Palisano has been an officer for twenty-five years.

"I'd say, 'Check my surveillance,' but they smashed my equipment, my DVR." I point to the living room floor.

"It's not sent to your phone?" He looks confused.

I shake my head. "Haven't had the money to update it since my husband left earlier this year."

He nods. "Aha," is all he says. He holds up the little briefcase-like box in his hand. "If I can make a match to these prints, hopefully I can find him and make an arrest. Maybe forensics can get something off the cigarettes. Maybe not. We'll see. You can touch stuff now, and make sure to contact me if you find anything's been stolen or if you suspect someone's trespassing again." Palisano talks like he's already convinced who did this. "In the meantime, see if a friend can stay with you, or better yet, see if you can stay with someone else until you get that surveillance updated."

"Will do. Thanks."

Officer Palisano's heavy footsteps clomp down my stairs as I turn toward the mess I need to clean.

Trying to unwind and calm down with a fat bowl of ganga, smoke wafting out from between my lips, I make sure the Dr. is on hand—McGillicuddy's that is. The frosty bottle and shot glass sit on the coffee table in front of me. Cleaning that mess was a bitch! Then hauling my gear up here after…I am fucking beat! Unfortunately, I'm stuck with the graffiti until I can repaint. Need to see if I can borrow money from Mom to add a few deadbolts to my doors. I pour a shot.

Thankfully Ronnie didn't show up here before I pulled in. I dread his reaction to the graffiti, the break-in, but fuck him. Him and his shit will be out of here by tomorrow, or the next day at the latest. If I had it in me to act as vindictive as some girlfriends do, then I'd throw all his shit out the window and change my locks now. But it's late, I have no energy left to move his stuff and no money to buy new locks. And honestly, I don't want to stoop to his level. Knowing me, I'd feel bad about it after.

Guilt is a heaviness I refuse to carry.

But, man oh man, it feels damn fucking good fantasizing about it. Getting him the hell out of my life can't happen soon enough. I've been fuming about his bullshit since peeling out of the studio parking lot. Our demo sucks *and* Mike confirmed my suspicions.

On top of everything I've been dealing with, Ronnie, that jealous freak, *has* been stalking me. And here I had actually considered I was paranoid thinking that.

Nope.

Ronnie planned this whole thing. Right down to swooping in when I was vulnerable and separated from my husband. Promised to treat me like a queen, make the metal band I've dreamed of, make the family I've dreamed of, be the father I always imagined Jordan to be, or what I had thought Jordan *wanted* to be. And then I find out Ronnie's had a vasectomy and never told me. *Everything* was a fucking lie!

All his lies are exactly why he tries to buy my happiness. Like our *Sweeny Todd* night. No fun, though the actors put on one hell of a performance. I can't even believe I still went out with him that night. But I really wanted to see that fucking play! It's not like I can afford that shit with my part-time cemetery job.

And now this break-in?

I wonder if Mike and Kyle ever really wanted me in the band or if Ronnie just convinced them, in his manipulative way, to agree. He does have a way of talking big and putting stars in people's eyes, the ego-stroker that he is. He probably promised them I'd be the next Maria Brink or Lzzy Hale or Alissa White-Gluz. Probably promised them we'd be the next Arch Enemy or some bullshit star-studded lie.

I don't play music for recognition and fame. I play music because it courses through my veins. It's in my blood. It makes my soul sing. Music equals life.

Yeah, that last one…Not so sure now.

My life is a total fucking mess. The only good thing going for me right now—grad school. But now I'm stuck with a shitty recording to go with my project. Why can't I stop stressing about that? Yeah, maybe embarrassment will wash over me when I play that for the audience at my presentation, but it probably won't affect my grade. But it still sucks! My whole goal of going above and beyond to combine both of my passions to create a unique thesis project flew right out the fucking window. Going to grad school never seemed achievable for me, coming from a low-income, single-mom family with more than one kid. And now that I made it this far, I wanted to go big and finish with a bang. Now, that goal's been squashed. *And* I wasted my time and my money! That's how it typically goes for me, one disappointment after the other.

Just look at the shit-storm flying through my life, making it harder and harder to concentrate on polishing my thesis. Up until now, working on my project has helped me hide away from all my problems, bury my head in my work and forget about my crumbling life.

Now I find out that not only was my marriage based on lies, but so is this new relationship, the band, the studio engineer's recording abilities, my family. Everything is a fucking lie! I don't even know what's real anymore.

Psycho Satan's running around all buddy-buddy-criminal-co-conspirator with Aiden, the maniac who left nightmare scars on my brain, causing night terrors and me waking with the sweat-drenched shakes almost daily. Now he's crashed through my door again, literally. And who knows how often he's hidden in the trees, spying on me, stalking me. Yeah, maybe today was the first time, but knowing him, I highly doubt it.

How will I ever get a good night's sleep again?

My mother and best friend is knocking on heaven's door, barely holding on with her oxygen tank and her cigarettes and scratching bald spots on her head from all the stress caused by Satan.

And friends? I'd love to call on a friend right now. I wish I could talk to Allie, my bestie, but she's an "in-the-moment" chick who doesn't keep her cell on her all the time. I always have a hard time getting a hold of her. She works her fingers to the bone, then spends her off time caring for her aging parents and disabled brother. She's a fucking angel. Most of my other friends have turned into drunks or drug addicts, always looking for the next party. There's Beth, but she's probably at a concert or a party. She's always on the go, always hanging with a group of people I don't care to hang out with. My other two friends who haven't turned into drunks or drug addicts are always so busy with their careers and their families I have a hard time getting them to return my texts. I don't blame them though. Good for them for having their shit together. I'm happy for them.

As for me…

No matter how hard I work to make my life what I've dreamed it could be, everything falls apart. Everyone leaves or abuses or lies or steals or berates or sabotages all I've worked so hard to build and create.

And family, that's what I tried to have with Jordan. Been planning together for the past five years. We even thought of names for the little boy I see when I close my eyes. Then Jordan smacked me in the face with, *"Oh, sorry, I really don't want kids. I just didn't know how to tell you."*

A five-year-fucking-lie! Motherfucker!

And then there's Ronnie, not just a liar and jealous freak, but a stalker too.

Why do I have such a bad habit of allowing the worst people into my life, people who tear me down and stomp on me, people who hold me back, pull me down, and crush all my hopes and dreams? Why do I…

Oh, shit.

Here he comes.

The thud of Ronnie's footsteps stomping up the front hall stairs makes my muscles tense and my stomach turn.

I really need to get him out of my place and change my fucking locks. But dammit…What if Aiden comes back tonight? And I'm home alone? Even if Mom's home and that happens, there's not much she can do but call the cops. And by the time they get here, who knows what Aiden could do to me by then? To Mom? Maybe I should wait until tomorrow to kick Ronnie out…just in case.

This suuuuucks!

Not sure if I'm ready for this, but here goes.

"Where's my metal Goddess? Got great news!" Ronnie sing-songs his words as he saunters into the kitchen with a huge bouquet of lilies and sunflowers, two of my favorites. Again.

The ick-shivers run through me. I don't even try to force a smile. Even if I try, I know it will look fake.

Why didn't I see through his manipulative crap sooner? I need to burn those rose-colored glasses and tell him to fuck off.

Bide your time, Dahl, just make it through tonight. You can get rid of his ass tomorrow. One. More. Night. I shudder at the thought.

His squeaking sneaker announces the sudden halt in his steps when he notices the graffiti across the cupboards. "What the fuck is that?"

As a fresh hit wafts out from between my lips, I turn toward him and say, "I'm doing some redecorating. I call it 'Punk Rock Life'. Like it?" A sigh-laugh tumbles out of me, though I'm not amused.

He sits the large vase of flowers next to my Dr. on the coffee table in front of me. "Seriously?" He glances around. "Never knew you were into graffiti art, but that's cool."

What? Does he really believe my story? Damn. Maybe it's my turn to lie, at least to avoid more accusations I know he'll throw at me if I tell him the truth.

The thought of turning into a liar makes me cringe. I despise liars. But…

Fuck it! The truth can wait. For now.

I shrug. "The mood just hit me. What do you think?" I roll with it.

He smiles. "Maybe you can do our album cover art."

"We no longer have a band. Remember?"

"No worries. I already talked to some buddies. Got a new lead guitarist and drummer swinging by here tomorrow to talk about forming a new one." He sits down beside me on the couch, big smile, doe-eyes.

What the fuck is *this* all about? Does he not remember what happened about three hours ago?

Speechless, I stare at him.

I set down the bowl and lighter and replace them with another shot of Dr. McGillicuddy's. Weed mellows me too much, might make me lose my nerve to address the mammoth in the room. And I do *not* plan on remaining mellow. Not now. Not with him.

He leans toward me, aiming for a kiss.

I turn away, look straight ahead. Then I tip my shot back, enjoy the flavor, the invigoration.

Do you think he takes the hint?

Nope.

Out of my peripheral, I see him leaning closer and reaching toward me, as though to brush my hair aside, whisper sweet bullshit into my ear.

"Mmm, you smell so good. The smell of your patchouli always gets me going."

I can't take it anymore. I refuse!

Abrupt, I stand and push the coffee table out of my way, walk away from the couch.

He laughs. "Whoa! What's got your panties in a bunch?" He stands, steps toward me.

"Really? Am I the only one here who remembers what went down after our studio session?"

Stepping right up beside me, he loops his arm around my waist and pulls me so close our bodies press together. I pull my head away. He starts kissing my neck and breathing heavy in my ear.

"Come on. It's been too long." He squeezes my ass.

I shove him away. "What the fuck, Dude? You accuse me of fucking Mike, which I'm sure is what broke up the band, then you punch him in the face over your delusion? Now you think I want to fuck you? Man, you need to get a grip."

He reaches for my waist again, but I back further away, go over to the coffee table, pour myself another shot, tip it back, slam the glass on the table. Man, sure wish I could handle the hard stuff, so it would hit me quicker.

"And what about at your work, the crazy guy who broke the window? Did that even happen, or was that just an excuse to call me in the middle of the night to check up on me?"

Ronnie's face goes blank. Then a smile forms that I can't quite read. "What guy? What broken window?" He steps up beside me and rests his hand on my shoulder. "What is this all about? Are you drunk?"

My arm flies up, knocks his hand away. "Another fucking liar!" As I stomp away, I growl and grab my hair in frustration. Heat rises to my face so quickly it feels like flames engulfing me.

Do they *all* lie?

After taking a deep breath, I say, "Dude, I saw the broken window. I drove to your work right after you called. Glass all over the sidewalk and parking lot, broken window, no cops. What is *up* with you? What the hell is going on?"

"Hey, I have another surprise." He smiles wide. "I went to Buckdancer's Choice before I came here." Turning away, he heads toward the front door. "I'll be right back."

Thundering footfalls speed down the stairs.

What the hell?

So shocked I can feel my eyes bugging out, I stand alone in the middle of the living room. Wanting to go to the roof and scream at the world, I go back to the coffee table instead, reach for my bowl and lighter. I want to calm down. But if I calm down, I might not do what needs to be done. I set it all back down, reach for the bottle, tip it back, take a gulp. Fuck the glass!

Ronnie walks back in carrying a coffin-shaped hardshell guitar case. He lies it across the kitchen island, unclips the locks, opens the lid. As his head tips down toward what hides inside, Ronnie's eyes roll up to look at me. A manic smile appears. "My metal Goddess deserves nothing but the best."

He spins the case so I can see what's inside.

The Paul Allender, lead guitarist for Cradle of Filth, signature purple maple-top Paul Reed Smith with the bat inlays up the fretboard shimmers under the ceiling fan light. The guitar I've dreamt about but can never play with my tiny hands and that wide fretboard.

"What? How the hell did you pay for this? And why? You're behind on your car payments *and* your mortgage." Refusing to indulge his mania, I remain in the living room.

Ronnie stays silent. He pulls the axe out of its velvet-lined coffin and brings it to me. A Jimi Hendrix guitar strap dangles from the purple body. He lifts the strap and tries to loop it over my head for me to try it.

I step back, put my hands out, reject the offer. "No. You need to return that. This shit going on between us, a bouquet of flowers and my dream guitar will not fix or make me forget. What the hell is going on?"

His elated expression falls away, face pales, and his eyes widen. "Jimi's 'Purple Haze' came on the radio. *He* told me to get this for you, told me you needed it for the new band. Are you saying I should ignore Jimi's advice? Isn't he your hero?"

My mouth drops open and my eyes practically pop out of my skull. He actually thinks Jimi Hendrix talked to him through the radio? This is way more serious than I ever suspected. He's far beyond whatever I can do to help him.

Shit. What am I supposed to do?

With the guitar held out to his side, Ronnie sidles up beside me and wraps his arm around my waist again. I pull away, but he holds on tight and pulls me closer. Though I lean my head back, trying not to get too close, he leans in and whispers in my ear. "You'll look so hot with this sexy beast strapped across your body. Come on. You know you want to hold her. I want to see you hold her." He sticks his tongue in my ear.

I shove him away as hard as I can. "*Ronnie*, back the fuck off! This is serious. You're spending money you don't have to make me happy. You said *Jimi Hendrix* talked to you through the radio? Then there's the broken window at your work, the story about the guy who broke it, the cop you thought was Jordan's brother, and then the fight with Mike over your accusations of us sleeping together. I think you need to…"

"Facts! *Not* accusations." Rage paints his face; rage I've never seen from him since we met ten months ago. Worse than his fight with Mike. He tosses the PRS onto the couch. "Come on. You think I haven't seen the signs. You live in the woods. Then a month after you join the band, Mike says his family is shopping for houses out of the city with lots of woods for his boys to ride their dirt bikes. Then suddenly his wife hates you. The way he stares at your ass on stage. The way he has his nephew take all those pictures at practice. The way he changes his songwriting to please you. Come on. It's freaking obvious. You've been fucking! Stop lying about it!"

Me, a liar? This motherfucker just called me a liar? Oh man, it's on.

Fury bubbles up inside. The shakes surge through me. More heat rises to my face.

"Dude, if I wanted to fuck Mike, why the hell would I date you?"

"Great question. You tell me."

"First of all, I've only met his wife twice. And last time you accused me of fucking him, you said I was having a three-way with him *and his wife*. Now you tell me she hates me. Why does your story keep changing. And how can she hate me when she doesn't even know me?"

"Duh. She hates you because you're fucking her husband."

"No. I. Am. Not! Mike's not my type *at all*. He's a redneck, who loves to hunt. I'm a fucking vegetarian!"

"So what. That don't prove shit."

"The only time I've ever hung out with Mike has been with the band. He doesn't even know where I live! He knows what town, but that's it. And if you think I've been sneaking him over here, all you had to do was ask to see my surveillance footage."

A derisive laugh shoots out of him. "Yeah, you erased all *that* footage. I'm not an idiot, Dahl." As he shakes his head, a smartass smile appears on his psycho face.

A fucking smile!

I want to smack that smug look right off him! But I refuse to resort to violence. That will only work against me here.

I go on and on with more reasons why me fucking Mike is a batshit insane idea, but Ronnie has a rebuttal, albeit delusional rebuttals, for everything I say. Unable to contain my anger, I stomp off into the bedroom to get some space.

He follows me, yelling on and on about me hiding the affair.

As calmly as I can, I say, "Please, stop. Just give me some space."

He doesn't.

He moves toward me, uncomfortably close, spewing more insane reasons why he knows I'm lying. "You're a pothead, and now Mike smokes more weed than before you joined the band. He jumps on all your song ideas like you..."

The hanging shoe rack I've only half put together rests against the wall. I grab it, raise it over my head, then smash it against the floor with each word I shout. "I. Don't. Lie!" I drop the remaining broken pieces. "I'm not fucking Mike! This shit's fucking crazy. *You're* fucking crazy! Do you *hear* yourself? You. Sound. Crazy!"

Ronnie jumps back. Fear washes over his face. He scurries out of the bedroom, goes into the music room.

I'm relieved he walked away, leaving me alone to calm myself down. But then I wonder what he's doing near my music gear.

I go to the music room door and peer inside. Ronnie's crouched down in the back corner, shaking and looking like a scared little puppy. The closer I get to him, I notice he's crying.

Shit. Now I feel bad for flipping out with that shoe rack. But damn it, he wouldn't back off. I didn't know what to do. He's obviously having some sort of psychotic break or some shit. I don't know. What if he tried to hurt me? Wouldn't be the first time some dude cornered me and smacked me around, had their way with me. Nope. Not letting that happen again.

But now look at him.

I step over to him, reach my hand out to console him. He flinches. Fear fills his eyes.

"Ronnie, I'm not going to hurt you. You wouldn't listen or give me space. I just wanted you to stop." I reach toward him again. He doesn't pull away.

As I rub his shoulder to help him feel safe, he starts sobbing.

"What's going on? *Please*, tell me." I gently squeeze his shoulder, lift his chin so he'll look at me.

"I'm not crazy." His words come out stuttered. "I'm *not*." He buries his head in his knees.

I lean in, give him a hug.

Why am I like this? Why can't I stop myself from trying to help someone who treats me like shit?

"Your heart's too big, always gets you into trouble." Jordan's words bounce around my brain.

"Ronnie, I really think you need to go speak with someone, someone who can help you."

"I'm not crazy." The words come out choppy as he shakes his head, refusing to look at me.

"Let's call the crisis center, get you in to speak with someone. I'll drive you there. I'll be right there with you the whole time. Come on." I squeeze his shoulder and give it a slight pull to nudge him up off the floor to come with me.

He shoves me away, jumps to his feet. "No fucking way! Don't try to turn this all on me! I don't need some head doc telling me I'm crazy just to make *you* look right," he screams in my face, spittle flying.

It's like I flicked a switch.

He grasps my upper arms, picks me up off the ground, and carries me to the bedroom. A twisted creeper-grin emerges on his sweaty face.

A memory flashes across my mind—an image of Aiden straddling me, my shirt torn open, knife to my throat.

"Never again!" I kick and scream, trying to squirm free, but Ronnie is much taller, stronger, and filled with psychotic rage.

Another flashback flickers across my mind: Aiden, picking me up, carrying me to his bedroom, shoving me through the trapdoor in the floor into his hideaway-hole/escape-hatch under his trailer. The memory flies from my mind as Ronnie throws me onto the bed. He unzips his pants, hauls his stiff dick out.

Why the hell is he aroused right now?

He jumps up onto the mattress and tries to straddle me.

At least this psycho doesn't have a knife to my throat.

Wish I had my knife right now.

Maybe this time I can get away.

My knee flies up and nails him in the balls. As he grunts and falls to the side, cradling his crotch, I start scooting off the bed.

But I don't get far before he grabs a handful of my long hair and shoves my face between his legs.

"Time to soothe the pain with those soft lips of yours." Rubbing his shaft, he shoves his dick in my face. "Wrap your lips around this, baby. You know you want to."

I start screaming, "No! Stop! Please, stop! Someone help!"

"No one can hear you out here in the woods, sweety." He wraps his hand tighter in my hair, getting closer to the scalp. It feels like my flesh is tearing open.

Struggling to get away, I kick and scream, knock everything off the nightstand. The lamp crashes to the floor. The alarm clock falls off the edge, hanging by its cord. Notebooks and loose papers scatter everywhere. A couple more kicks and the clock radio blares to life. Sting's "Every Breath You Take" blasts through static. I grab for my cell teetering on the edge of the table. Though I can't see what I'm doing, I squeeze the side buttons, signaling an emergency, fumble with the SOS slide, try contacting 911. *Hope* it's contacting 911. I've never done this before.

Ronnie yanks my hair. My cell slips from my hand. The more I wrestle to get away, the tighter he latches on.

How's this skinny asshole so fucking strong?

"Get your fucking hands off me, *psycho*!"

He keeps grabbing at me, yanking my head closer, trying to get me to suck his dick, but I keep fighting back.

He doesn't give up.

As much as it disgusts me to even be this close to him, I finally open my mouth, insert his cock, and bite down as hard as I can.

"Arrrrrrrgh!" His scream pierces my eardrums. He immediately releases my hair and backhands me upside the head. I fall to the floor.

I shake it off, reach under the mattress, retrieve my knife.

"You stupid whore!" Cradling his dick in his palm, he drops his legs over the side of the bed to get up. As soon as his feet touch the floor, I drive the blade into his left leg just above the knee.

"Motherfucker!"

He winces, backhands me across the face, and shoves me to the ground. My ass hits the floor. He wraps his hands around the hilt of the blade, grunts as he yanks it out, then throws it across the room. A crimson river runs down his calf, dripping onto the hardwood floor. He still stands up.

Towering over me, he steps closer, appears barely phased by the injury.

Just like psycho Aiden, who still fought off my protectors after they beat him in the head with nunchucks.

I bury the memory—*again.*

Ronnie glares down at me with his red-rage face, sweat-drenched hair, and bugged-out eyes.

Crab-crawling away, I grab my cell, yell down at the screen, "Help! Someone, help me! Please, someone…"

"You're not as smart as you think you are, cunt! No one can hear you!" Leaning down, he grasps my ankle, pulls me under him. "But *I'll* help you." That last line comes out creepy-calm, almost soothing. But I know better, know where it's coming from. Grabbing my other ankle, he twists my legs, flips me onto my stomach.

I reach out, grasp at the floor, trying to pull myself away. Making it only as far as the doorway, I feel Ronnie lower himself on top of me. His knees tighten around my hips, freeze me in place. Warm moisture soaks through my jeans on my left hip. The copper scent fills my nostrils, making me gag. Though I keep reaching and pulling at the doorframe, I can't pull free from his leghold. His stiff cock presses against my ass.

Leaning down against my back, he flattens me to the floor and slowly lowers his face beside my ear. His beer breath makes me want to retch as he whispers, "Now I know you like it rough. No more teasing. Take it like the whore you are."

He reaches underneath me, fumbles for the zipper of my jeans.

Sirens blare outside my windows.

Wow! That was fast. Thank God!

A few more fumbles with my zipper and more kicks from me. The sirens grow louder and the blue lights swirl and flash across the walls beside the living room windows.

"Help! Up here! Please, help me!"

Ronnie's knee-grip on my hips loosens, and I pull away, hair all disheveled and sticking to my sweaty face and neck. I scrabble across the living room floor toward the kitchen.

Multiple footfalls thunder up the hallway stairs. The front door flies open, smashes against the wall.

Just as I make it to the kitchen and start lifting myself to my feet, crying and sniffling, two police officers rush in, guns raised.

I turn in the direction of their aimed guns and see Ronnie, stiff dick in his hands, blood river running down his leg, staining my authentic, handwoven Navajo rug from Arizona.

"Freeze!"

"Stop right there!"

Ronnie's hands fly up into the air, face flush, shaggy hair sticking to his drenched forehead. His erection hangs out of his unzipped jeans, and for some bizarre reason, it looks like it's stiffening even more.

What the hell is wrong with this freak?

The taller, female cop rushes toward Ronnie, gun aimed. "Put your dick in your pants, then turn around with your hands behind your back!" She ignores the knife wound, not bothering to ask if he's okay.

Ha! I like this chick!

Ronnie complies, slowly.

The older, male officer, the one who's worked for the town's PD since I was a teen, steps over to me, gun still aimed at Ronnie. His salt-and-pepper hair sticks out a little from under his hat. "Dahlia, are you okay? Do you need medical services?"

Shaking my head, I look down at my rumpled clothes, run my hand down my front to straighten myself out. I don't want to look back up. I don't want to look him in the face. I don't want to make eye contact.

I'm fucking mortified.

This isn't the first time Officer Frank Palisano has saved me from a psycho boyfriend.

How the hell do I get myself into situations like this?

As I try to control my sobbing, I wipe the tears and snot from my face, attempt to neaten my hair. That's when I notice Ronnie's reddened handprints on both of my upper arms, one already starting to bruise. And the blood stain on my favorite jeans. A couple stuttered attempts at deep breaths later, and now I'm fucking pissed. My shoulders hike up to my ears as I breath in one more time and look up at the female cop cuffing Ronnie. My words come out as calm as I can manage. "Get that fucking psycho out of my house, please."

Officer Palisano steps over to them and nods at his partner. She steps back and lets Palisano take it from here. And he doesn't take it easy.

Palisano glances down at the leg wound. "Looks like she needs to practice her aim." His eyes roll up and glare at Ronnie.

He yanks Ronnie's arms back, makes him wince, shoves him toward the door. As they pass by me, Palisano looks down at me, attempts a smile, though it's more of a smirk. "I'll take care of this creep for you." He side-eyes the graffiti on the cupboards. "You *really* should have someone stay with you tonight."

It's hard to talk. It's hard to look him in the eyes, but I do. And all I can bring myself to say is, "I really know how to pick 'em, huh?"

Palisano's smirk remains as he slowly nods and then looks back toward Ronnie. Just before he shoves him toward the stairs, Palisano says, "There ain't no smacking me around like you did to this young woman. You're done, asshole."

Alone at home in the woods at midnight, with no one to stay with me and no place else to stay, my head pounds, my entire body aches, and the deluge of tears hasn't let up. I texted Beth. I texted Allie. I received the *"Notifications silenced"* message both times. Still no return texts. Still no calls. I sent those texts an hour ago. But it's late, so I guess I understand. Still sucks. I could go sleep at Mom's. But she isn't even home yet. Her blackened windows look ominous. I'd still be alone inside there. And I have no idea where she is. She refuses to own a cell phone, so I can't call or text her.

So, I sit on the bench in front of the living room window and gaze out at the night sky, stars twinkling, full moon shining bright, whip-o-wills filling the air with their songs, bats swooping over the yard as they feast and soar. My Jimmy sits parked in the driveway in front of the garage. Mom's parking space is still empty. Jordan's parking space is empty. My bottle of Dr. McGillicuddy's is now empty. And I feel empty.

How could I be such a fool? How did I let another psycho rapist and abuser into my life? How am I thirty-seven years old, on the verge of divorce, no kids, no house, no career, still going to college, still an amateur writer, still no publications, still living in my mother's garage apartment, still dealing with psycho Satan, still driving an unreliable vehicle, still broke as shit, and still struggling to keep a gigging band together? This is not how I'd imagined my life would turn out. This is not where I want to be. This is not the life I chose. This is not the life I dreamed about as a child, but still, somehow, I'm here. Alone. Broken, beaten and scarred. No one to confide in. No one to cry to. No one to hold. No one to tell me everything is going to be all right. Because everything is *not* going to be all right. The sun may rise tomorrow, but *I* don't want to. I don't want this life. I don't want this fucked up bullshit. I can't deal with it anymore. I'm tired and fed up with every*thing* and every*one*.

It's not like I have time to meet someone new, get to know them, cultivate a relationship, grow to love and trust them, and then conceive the child I've dreamed about, start the family I've been planning—alone—for years. I'm fucking thirty-seven! I'm running out of time.

The moment Ronnie showed up in my driveway with his car packed and ready to move into my place without even asking, I should've immediately said, "No way in hell," and got rid of his psycho ass then.

Woulda, shoulda, coulda. Always living with regret of my stupid-ass decisions.

What is wrong with me? How do I get myself into messed up shit like this? As much as I try to make the right decisions, I keep fucking up over and over again. Why can't I get my shit together? Why do all these horrible people flock to me like I'm fire and they're moths? I can't make it stop. It's maddening!

Little, white crumpled clouds of cotton cover the floor around me. Like I'm in the sky. But no. I'm out of tissues again. I don't have the energy to move to go get more. It's like a weight is on me, pressing me down, making me feel…heavy.

Like that old painting: *The Nightmare.* The incubus on the sleeping woman. A perfect depiction of my life, how I feel. Depression. Like a monster holding me down. Preying upon my life force, my essence, my soul.

How is it that I feel so low, so alone, so lost, when I've worked so hard my whole life, worked so hard for the things I want, worked so hard to make my dreams come true, only to end up living a fucking nightmare?

All I want to do is escape, get away from all this bullshit, get away from all that keeps dragging me down. All I want to do is sleep. Close my eyes…forever.

My bowl sits on top of the stereo speaker beside the bench. No matter how much I smoke, it does nothing to make me relaxed or happy or calm. If only I did heroin instead. Then I could just nod off, wrapped in a velvety soft opiate blanket, and drift away.

My head pounds like a hammer to the skull, thundering through my whole achy body. My upper arms throb, heart in a crushing vise-grip, teeth grind, jaw tense.

The bench creaks under my weight as I stand up. Joints protest as I hesitantly put one foot in front of the other. Dizzying anxiety makes my movements slow and choppy. Once I get to the bathroom, I refuse to look in the mirror. I can't stand to see the mess I've become. When I open the drawer next to the sink, Ronnie's straight razor shimmers under the overhead light. I reach for it, pull it out, flip it open, and sob.

It won't take much effort to make it all stop. Right here. Right now.

The cold steel feels refreshing against the clammy skin of my palm.

My shoulders bounce along with my sobs. My head feels like it might burst from the pressure. My tears fall, crashing around me. The salty rivers flow down my cheeks nonstop. I don't know what the fuck to do with myself anymore. I'm a fucking wreck!

I could call Jordan, confide in him, see if he'll reconsider coming back, reconsider creating a family with me, the family we've *talked about* creating for the past five years. But I don't want to sound desperate, and I don't want to make him think I'm only calling because Ronnie went psycho on me. Plus, Jordan made it clear during our last fight he no longer wants to talk to me about this subject.

If I call one of my other friends, they probably won't answer this late. Plus, I don't want to be the Debbie Downer, bringing them down with all my life's boo-hooing woes. Squashing other people's happiness and contentment is the last thing I want to do. It's bad enough for me to deal with. I don't want to dump my shit on anyone else, especially not my loved ones.

But I really need someone right now. I could use a shoulder. An ear. A hug would be fucking wonderful. Where the hell is Mom? She gives the best hugs! Why isn't she home yet? This is so weird. I don't remember the last time she stayed the night somewhere else. And of all the nights she doesn't come home…Why tonight? When I need her the most?

I feel selfish even thinking that. She deserves to have a social life. At least someone around here does.

I grab my cell. Make sure the volume's turned up. Check my texts.

Still nothing.

I toss it aside, sink deep into the couch.

I'm alone. Empty. Hanging onto the frayed ends of sanity by my fingertips. And slipping.

Maybe if I pack Ronnie's shit and move it to the garage, a wave of closure will wash over me, lift my spirits.

Or maybe I just need to go outside, get some fresh air, listen to the leaves sing in the wind.

I don't know.

What I do know—there's no way in hell I'll be able to rest and fall asleep right now.

I have no idea what the hell to do with myself, how to get out of my head full of spiraling out of control thoughts. Why can't I find a way to make them all stop, or at least mellow out?

I wish so desperately to talk to someone.

I wish Mom was home. But her house sits dark and empty. Like me. And though she'd talk my ear off most nights, if I brought these feelings to her, she'd urge me to get help, call Opportunity Alliance, the crisis center. Call the suicide prevention hotline. Call the professionals.

But a stranger? Why would I want to dump my shit on a stranger? Though that is their job. They get paid to listen to people like me boo-hoo and piss and moan.

Man, I feel so pathetic. What a fucking weak loser I am. I just want to feel better. Please, just make it all stop! How can I make it all go away?

Pack Ronnie's shit, and hope it brings some relief. Turn to page 49.

Go outside for some fresh air and get lost in nature. Turn to page 75.

Call the suicide prevention hot line. Turn to page 126.

Under the strange heat of the October sun, I empty my mind and jump back into the open grave.

Jack turns around and looks at me, mouth parted, about to speak. I hold up my hand.

"Let's just forget about him and get back to work."

He clamps his lips shut and nods. "You got it."

As I slam the spade over and over again into the walls of this final resting place for bones, digging out rocks and hucking them over my shoulder, muscles aching and screaming, sweat drenches every inch of my body. It seeps out of my pores, and every swipe across my forehead feels like I'm wiping away my worries. I refuse to think about any of it right now.

Just move.

Mind blank.

Breathe the fresh air.

Feel the sun on my skin.

And keep moving.

Two straight hours of intense physical labor later, I punch the clock and head on home.

After a quick shower to wash away the day, I take my landline phone off the hook, shut off my cell's notifications, do a few stretches, and go to my music room. Still no return call from Allie, which really sucks. I could definitely use someone to talk to. Mom's not home to lend an ear either. But at least I have music to help me escape, and…

No distractions.

The setting sun shimmers through the window above my practice amp. Orange and fuchsia paint the sky around wisps of gossamer clouds. Lengthening shadows of tree branch arms stretch and reach and wave across the ground. Standing in a beam of sunshine, breathing in the light, I try imaging that light filling me with positive energy.

I strap on my guitar, tune up, plug in, flip the switch and start noodling. "Razor Blades and Bullets" tumbles around my mind, chasing rhythms, searching for a melody to weave into song. As I ride a wave of a catchy riff, lyrics begin forming on the tip of my tongue, sailing on the notes spilling from the tips of my fingers.

> Razor blades and bullets, weaponry of the mind
> Tripping through life, always wanting to hide
> Razor blades and bullets, weaponry of the mind
> Battling shadows, always follow behind
> Razor blades and bullets, no longer part of the hive
> Razor blades and bullets…

> Word after word,
> Line after line,
> Verse after verse,
> Riff after riff,
> Scene after scene,
> I write.

I lose myself in the music of each line, the poetry, the actions, the story. The only things occupying my mind.

After recording a rough idea on my phone's voice memo, I jot down lyrics, chord changes, and a melody line in my songbook. My pen dances across the pages, filling each staff of music with my visions.

Songs: stories set to music.

My sore neck and wrists throb and ache by the time I finish and finally look up. The sky outside the window no longer shimmers with vibrant colors. The silvery sheen of the moon fills the forest around my home. Diamonds twinkle across the black canvas of the night sky. Tree shadows twirl and sway with the wind. Whip-o-wills sing their nighttime lullabies.

I yawn, click off by amp, set my guitar in its stand, and glance at my watch. It's long past dinner. Ronnie's work shift began over an hour ago. He must've eaten dinner at his parents' place. Probably left a ton of messages on my cell by now. But I refuse to check.

I shut off my phone and forbid myself from replacing the receiver of the landline back into its cradle.

The quiet embraces me.

I eat a small, healthy dinner, meditate, and go to bed, trying my hardest not to think about what horrors await me tomorrow. I close my eyes to darkness, hoping for a visit from the baby boy of my wanted future rather than nightmares from my haunted past and present.

♫ ▮ ♪

Determination to find our music equipment kicks me into gear and drives me through the day. Our studio session needs to go off without a hitch. Once that's past me, the time to clean out my dumpster fire of a life sets into motion.

After the third pawn shop of the day and traipsing along one cobblestone street after another, we've discovered not only my Mesa amp, but also three quarters of the rest of our band's gear that was stolen. Now, out on the sidewalk at Longfellow Square, I pull out the lead detective's business card, along with my cell, and dial him up.

"Yes, that's right. Not only are there signature flaws—dings and scratches—that we have documented in pictures matching the gear in these three shops, but we also double checked the serial numbers. Everything matches."

Mike's at my shoulder, his long beard brushing against my shoulder as he listens in on what Detective Blake says. His gear's also irreplaceable, at least not available brand new. Eagerness to retrieve our belongings surges through him as much as it does me, I'm sure. Buckdancer's Choice still sells Ronnie's and Kyle's gear, though needing to rebuy everything would take a while to save money for. Mike hangs on every word coming through the phone. I do too.

And, yep, there it is—Ronnie's giving me the stink eye.

Friendship running through a band helps hold the band together, at least that's what I've always believed. But Ronnie obviously thinks my friendship with the guys—specifically with Mike for some reason—runs deeper than platonic camaraderie. I don't understand. We only hangout when it involves the whole band. We're a crew. A team. Well, that's what I've hoped to build with these guys.

No doubt Ronnie's jealous streak links directly to the fact that he swooped in when my marriage was at its weakest point, when I was at my most vulnerable and desperate, and tried to steal me away. But I don't have time to deal with his bullshit right now. I need to get my fucking gear back!

With a huge smile and shooter-marble-sized eyes, Mike pulls away and slaps Kyle on the shoulder. "He's coming to get our shit back, man. Can you believe it?"

"Hell yeah, dude!" Kyle raises his hands and looks up to the clear sky. "I can't fucking believe it!"

Mike and Kyle high-five, fist bump, shoulder bump. All their excitement comes out in playful jabs at one another. Ronnie still stands staring at me, loaded eyes and tight expression. Why can't this guy take the win and be happy, at least for a moment?

I slap high-fives and pound fist bumps with Mike and Kyle. When I turn to Ronnie for more of the same, he turns away and starts reading flyers on the sidewalk billboard nearby. Tension tingles through me. Mine or his, I'm not sure.

Whatever. He can wallow in his misery all he wants. As for me, I'm on a mission his assholery cannot thwart. We've got tunes to record soon.

By dinner time, my gear sits in the back of my Jimmy as I'm heading home. At least one thing has worked out for me. Maybe now my life will take a turn toward better days.

♫ ▮ ♪

"Mom, what's going on? I thought you'd be excited about the news. *I* sure as hell am."

After unloading my amp and hauling it upstairs to my apartment, I ran next door to tell Mom the good news and to bring her the groceries she had called and asked me to pick up for her on my way home. I found her and her friend Jody sitting at the kitchen table, with a deck of tarot cards and a quartz crystal sitting in the middle, a coffee in front of both of them, each looking like *their* valuables got stolen. And Mom keeps scratching her head incessantly.

Were their tarot readings that depressing and foreboding?

I sit down between them. "What the hell's going on?" I turn toward Mom. "What's wrong with your head? Why do you keep scratching?" I lean closer. "Holy shit! You're bleeding! And there's a bald spot there?" I reach over and gently pull her hand away from her head. There's blood under her fingernails and on her fingertips. "Ma, you've gotta stop that." I gently place her hand on the table.

Jody hands me a napkin.

"I can't even believe what she's puttin' me through," Mom says without elaborating. She stubs out her cigarette butt in the ashtray, puts her nasal cannula back on, and takes a deep breath of pure oxygen.

I hand her the napkin. "What? Who?" I turn to Jody. "What's she talking about?"

"Ya sista. She sto'med in heah earlier when Alex and Dan were heah to give ya motha the receipts for the materials they bought to fix ya motha's apa'tment building. We were all just shootin' the shit ova coffees, then Sarah threw open the front door, swearing up a sto'm, then came into the kitchen and punched Alex in the face. Told ya motha the guys a'e rippin' her off and buying shit for themselves with her Home Depot credit cahd."

Tears threaten to fall from my mother's eyes. She starts scratching her head again and says, "Doesn't that idiot realize I get all the credit card statements? I'd know if they were ripping me off. She's still pissed off I hired them to do the work instead of letting her husband do it to work off the money they still owe me from loaning them the downpayment for their house *and* for bailing her out of jail for that fight she started at the bar a couple years ago." A derisive laugh escapes her. "No wonder why The Devil landed in the past for my reading. I never should've let them borrow all that money."

No surprise. Even Mom sees my former sibling as evil.

As I pull her hand away from her head again, I'm furious. "I hope you called the cops this time?"

"No, she didn't. I told her to. But she won't. You should heah all the horrible messages ya sista's left on the machine already. I think it's up to at least five by now." Jody gets up and goes to double-check the doors, making sure they're locked. "I already told ya motha I'm lockin' these damn doors every time I come ova to visit. I'm not lettin' that shithead do this to my friend anymore. The'e's not much I can do to stop her, but I can at least do that." She grabs a dish towel from the oven door handle, runs the corner under warm water at the sink, and comes back to wipe the blood from my mother's scalp. "Look what she's doing to ya, Penny. There's no need of this."

"If you're not going to do it, I'll call the fucking cops *right now*." I get up and head to the phone in the dining room. Before I grab the receiver, it rings. The caller ID displays Satan's number. "It's her. Should I answer it?"

"No…Yeah, go ahead. Let's see what she has to say for herself."

Over my shoulder, I see Mom grab her coffee mug with a shaky hand. Coffee spills over the edge, and Jody hands her another napkin to dry off the tablecloth.

"Hello."

"Why the fuck are *you* answering the phone? Put Ma on." Her venom shoots through the receiver, poisoning my ear.

"Hello to you too, *sis*."

"Just put the gullible traitor on the fucking phone."

"Um, do you realize Mom's over here scratching bald spots in her head because of what you're doing to her. This really needs to stop. *You* need to stop. She's your freaking mother. Treat her with some respe…"

"Fuck you, you stupid cunt! How dare you talk to me like that? I'll put you ten feet under if you even think of speaking to me like…"

It takes all my willpower to remain calm and keep an angry tone out of my voice. She wants me to stoop to her level, so she can put some sort of *blame* on me. I refuse. "Are you listening to yourself? Do you hear the insanity coming out of you? Mom can't deal with all this stress. You know she's been sick. Her freaking oxygen delivery's coming today, and here you are…"

"I'll fucking beat you senseless, you spoiled little bitch! Put *my* mother on the phone. *Now!*"

As she continues screaming into my ear, I hold the cordless receiver away from my head. Jody and Mom look at me, mouths agape. They can hear the craziness all the way in the kitchen. I look at them and shrug. Then, I hang up the phone.

Ten seconds later, the phone rings again. I let the answering machine take it. And, yep, it's her again. More screaming. More swearing. More venom. More threats to kill me. Nothing new.

No one answers it.

The phone rings again and again. At the end of every string of rings, the psycho leaves another message full of threats and name-calling. By the end of my twenty-minute visit with my mother, she has received fifteen calls and fifteen more nasty answering machine messages from the person people expect me to call my sister.

If she acted like a sister, if she'd never assaulted me, if she didn't steal from me, if she didn't try to destroy my property, if she treated Mom and me with respect, and if she didn't feel joy every time something bad happens to me—like when she smiled at the news of my separation from Jordan—maybe I would still call her sister like I used to. Like when we were close many years ago.

But no. I no longer call her my sister. I no longer call her by her given name.

She's Satan.

As I pull Mom's hand away from her head again, Jody hands her a clean, wet dishtowel to wash up the fresh blood.

"If you insist on *not* calling the police, at *least* take the damn phone off the hook so you don't have to listen to all those hateful messages that are obviously stressing you the hell out."

"I can't take it off the hook. I need to be available for my tenants. Rent is due, and only one has paid yet. I need to be available so I can get paid. I need some money to order oil and pay my contractors."

I have no idea why she only takes cash for the rent. But I'm not a landlord, so what do I know? Maybe because it's her retirement money she needs to live on. Maybe it's so she doesn't have to go to the bank when she needs cash. She refuses to learn how to use online banking, and she refuses to use a debit card to make purchases. I don't know why she does what she does. She's a woman stuck in her ways.

At a loss of what to do to better this situation, and needing to put in time on my thesis, I tell Mom, "If things get any worse, call me. I'll be home all night doing schoolwork." Leaning down, I give her a hug and a kiss on the cheek. "And stop that damn scratching before you're *completely* bald." With a playful bump to her shoulder, I laugh, trying to lighten the mood.

She looks up at me with teary eyes and smiles. "At least then I won't need to color the gray anymore."

We all laugh.

Mom thanks me for picking up some groceries for her and asks me to help with her laundry. Going up and down stairs weakens her and makes her short of breath, which is why I help take care of her house and do some chores. A big part of why I live in her garage apartment. And it's cheaper than owning a home while I finish grad school. Not that I could afford one now anyway, but still…Sacrifices, man. Gotta do what I gotta do. Plus, Mom needs my help. That's important to me.

Once I finish her request, I set the basket of warm clothes beside her chair. "If *she* doesn't call me," I say to Jody, "will you please call me if things get worse?"

Jody nods and smirks. "You *know* I will, sweetie."

As I walk across the driveway back to my apartment, I pray no crazy phone calls ring into my house later tonight.

Late Saturday afternoon, I step out of the shower after a long and unusually sweltering day of working a burial ceremony at the cemetery and see my living room filled with rose petals strewn across the hardwood floor and lit candles all around. After quickly drying off in the bathroom and taking my hair out of the towel wrapped around my head, I slip on my silk bathrobe and step out into my flower-filled apartment.

A vase of pink lilies, one of my favorites, stands perky and bright on the mantle. A potted purple orchid, another of my favorites, sits atop the stereo cabinet. And on the island in the kitchen sits a huge vase of at least two dozen red roses. It smells sweet and magical. I smile so wide my cheeks hurt.

I search my small two-bedroom apartment to find Ronnie, but he's nowhere. And I don't see his car anywhere out in the driveway. The only vehicles parked out there are mine and Mom's truck.

What the hell?

Still smiling, I shrug and start getting ready to go see *Sweeny Todd*.

By the time I'm dressed and have finished applying my armor—eyeliner and mascara—Ronnie pulls into the driveway and comes clomping up the stairs to my door. He clammers around in the kitchen for a few minutes, which gives me time to finish getting ready.

I step out into the living room just as he turns on the stereo. "Like a Stone" starts playing, and Ronnie spins around to face me with his hand held out, smile emerging, beckoning me for a dance. He knows how much I love Chris Cornell. He knows how much this music makes me happy.

I take his hand. He gently pulls me close.

We dance.

After a few moments, smiles still plastered on both of our faces, he tells me, "That baby you want so much could be coming sooner than you know."

My stomach drops.

What the hell is he talking about?

I pull my head away from his chest, look up at him. His smile is so huge he looks maniacal. A Joker's smile. Eyes wide, he continues twirling me through the dance.

"What are you talking about?" I try not to sound negative, but I already don't like where this is going.

First, he showed up at my house with his car filled with most of his belongings, insisting he's moving in. Then, he starts getting all accusey and jealous. And the sketchy bakery story? Now he's trying to rush having a kid with me. We haven't even been dating that long. My divorce isn't even final. I'm not even sure I want a divorce.

"Turns out I can reverse my vasectomy. I scheduled an appointment with a doctor to discuss the procedure."

Whoa! Vasectomy? That's news to me.

Yeah, maybe I'm not so sure I *really* want to have a kid with him, but he promised to give me the child I've been dreaming about. I know that sounds odd, but it's a matter of principle.

I halt the dance, let go of him, and step back a few feet. "What are you talking about? You had a vasectomy? When did you plan on telling me this?"

His expression morphs from manic to faux surprise. "Yeah, five years ago. I told you that. When I was dating Tanya. She didn't want kids, and I didn't want to wear a rubber, so I got fixed." He laughs like it's no big deal.

Yeah, it is a big fucking deal. He lied to me! Doesn't he remember why my husband and me got separated in the first place? Lies. Lies. Fucking lies!

That bakery story he dished out to me now sounds like a whole ton of lies.

And who gets a vasectomy just because they don't want to wear a rubber? Seems quite drastic to me. He only dated Tanya for a year, unless that's a lie too. But why lie about that?

Who the hell am I dating?

Flames instantly light my rage, setting my head on fire, flushing my cheeks. My heart's pounding so hard, so fast, it just might pop right out of my chest.

"You knew the reason why Jordan and I separated, and you rushed right up, trying to sweep me off my feet with the promise of the future I've dreamed about—knowing all the time that it would never happen? Really?" I turn away and walk to the kitchen, feeling the need to put distance between us before I rip his goddamn lying face off. What a fucking phony! I open the fridge, grab the pitcher of premixed mimosa, and pour myself a drink.

As I drop the second ice cube into the tumbler, Ronnie's warm hands slide around my waist from behind. He presses his body against mine and leans down to whisper in my ear. "You never asked. But I'm reversing it. I'm doing this for you. For *us*."

"I never *asked*?!" I pull apart his interlocked fingers, remove them from my stomach, shove him away with my elbow. I spin to face him. "That is a piss poor fucking answer. You realize that, right? What else have you *not* told me about? What else have you *lied* to me about? Might as well get it all out on the table now."

I pause, think about the bakery's broken window.

"Like…who the hell really busted out the window at your work? Who was it, Ronnie? Was it some tweaked out homeless junkie, was it the bitch who busted out my truck window, was it her hooded accomplice, or was it…" Biting my tongue on implying he broke it himself, I allow breathing room for him to step forward and admit—if my suspicion is in fact true.

Or…maybe it *was* Aiden, and all the crazy from my life is too much for Ronnie to handle. I don't even know how to deal with all of it myself. I mean, look what the hell it's doing to me. Nothing good, that's for sure.

Sometimes…I wish to not wake up in the morning.

Sometimes…I want to slit my wrists, let the pain and loneliness bleed out as I drift away into a forever peaceful sleep.

Sometimes…I want to drive right off a fucking bridge and pretend I'm flying, never to come down again. Just…fly away.

I need wings.

He steps back, leans against the counter opposite from me. "Why are you so hung up on that broken window? I've dealt with it. Now, let's move on."

Shock shakes my head. Trying to get a grasp on his nonchalant attitude about the crazy occurrence, I scramble for words to respond.

"Come on, Ronnie, that shit isn't normal. Stuff that that doesn't happen hardly ever, especially around here. This is Maine, one of the most mellow, peaceful states in the whole goddamned country, so, yeah, I'm hung up on the broken window. And why? Because *you* act like it's no big deal and keep avoiding talking about it. That is very fucking weird. What the hell? Stop spinning this to make it look like I'm making a big deal out of nothing. It isn't nothing! Who broke the window?"

Eyes wide, he stares me dead in the face. "Some sketched out junkie, I guess. I don't know. I only saw him running away. Portland's filled with 'em. Junkies everywhere. So, no, it's not unusual. And, yes, you are making a big deal out of a small problem, a problem I already took care of. I already told you…" Taking a long-legged step across the narrow kitchen, he comes up close to me again. He looks down and gently grasps my chin. "You have so much on your plate, so much stress to deal with about your sister and your schoolwork and taking care of your mother and, well, everything…" He pauses to kiss my overheated cheek. "I don't want to add to your stress with my problems. That's all." A smile spreads wide as he slips his arm around my waste.

Why does he sound so convincing? Is he really telling the truth? Am I so used to crazy that I see crazy everywhere, even when crazy isn't there? I don't know what to think anymore.

As he goes on and on about how deep his love for me goes and how he would do anything to make me happy, I remember his comment the day he showed me the *Sweeny Todd* tickets. *"I know how much you love plays."*

I know I never told him anything about my love of theatre. He doesn't seem like the type who would be into that at all. He's a poor punk rock boy who barely graduated high school and has played in punk and metal bands his whole adult life while working a variety of jobs to pay for his ramshackle house. Plus, I haven't even been to a play in over five years. It's not like the topic of theatre sits on the tip of my tongue to talk about.

My mind spins so fast I feel a bit dizzy. Where's an anchor when you need one? Rebuttals escape me as my tornado of thoughts swirls on.

Shit. I need a drink. Or a toke. Something to slow this storm down.

He keeps on talking, trying to convince me of his undying love, as I tip back my drink and think of all the other things I never told him but he somehow magically knows about: my love of old blues tunes, how I think saxophone is sexy, my secret desire to hang out in jazz clubs, the Arizona vacation Jordan and I took a few years ago, Jordan and me getting married in Jamaica.

How does he know about all of that?

A sneaking suspicion creeps into my muddled mind.

Has he been stalking me?

♫ ▌ ♪

Loneliness envelopes me like a shroud though I'm not alone. The desire for a warm hug and a comforting shoulder eats through my insides like maggots devouring me. A heaviness weighs down on my chest, pinning me to the bed. A demonic incubus feeding on my soul, piercing my heart with horns of malice. Tears of emptiness and frustration trail from the corners of my eyes, tickling my temples like tiny insects feeding on my sorrow. Fuseli's *The Nightmare* painting lives.

The pressure on my head pounds and aches, a vise crushing a grapefruit to pulp. How much did I drink to get me through the night? Maybe too much, but certainly not as much as Ronnie. He drank so much, I had to drive us back home.

His foot touches my leg again. I cringe and shift my body over to the edge of the mattress as far away from him as I can get without falling right off the damn bed. Sleep has evaded me for two hours already, subjecting me to the torture of hearing Ronnie breathe and smelling the scent of his nauseating cologne as it assaults my senses. It seems pointless to keep lying here trying to accomplish the impossible—having a peaceful night's sleep while lying next to my potential stalker.

Oh yeah, he did assure me earlier tonight during the drive to the *Sweeny Todd* play that he found out "all sorts of interesting things" about me by going through my Facebook posts and pictures when I mentioned I was interested in auditioning for his band. He also assured me that the doctor reversing his vasectomy told him he'll be able to have kids once the procedure is complete. But his assurance doesn't make me feel assured. I don't know shit about vasectomies— except they prevent the dude from having kids—or if what he's told me is true until I speak to a legit doctor. As for my love of plays and whatnot, he would've had to go way back to very old posts and pictures to find out some of the stuff he knows about me that I never told him about. I haven't been sharing much on social media in the past couple of years. And some of that stuff he mentioned I don't remember ever posting on social media.

Well, that's an easy tell. All I need do is check to see if some of the things he knows about me that I never told him can be found on my Facebook page. Easy-peasy.

The need to finally find the truth to *something* lifts some of the heaviness from my chest. With slow and steady movements, I ease myself out from under the covers and off the bed. I wipe my eyes on the sleeve of my T-shirt. My fuzzy socks allow me to slide my feet across the hardwood floor rather than make noisy footsteps out of the bedroom.

I snatch my phone from the kitchen counter, unplug the charger, and go hide in the bathroom.

And, yep, after thirty minutes of searching, I found one post from ten years ago with a couple pictures of my wedding with Jordan in Jamaica. Ronnie might be telling the truth about that one, though it's still a bit creepy seeing how far back he searched through my posts and pictures. Sure seems like a stalker move to me. But what about my love of plays?

After another thirty minutes of searching and finding no posts or pictures on my Facebook about my love of plays, or anything at all about me going to even one play, I revert to a general search through posts from around the time period when I remember attending the last play I had seen before tonight, *The Lion, the Witch, and the Wardrobe.* That was seven years ago. I thought it was only five years ago. My bad. But that's not the point. The point is—

In the only post on my Facebook with any mention of the play, I talk about taking my niece, Zoe, out for some "Me and Mini-Me Time". It says nothing in the post about taking her to see the play. A picture accompanies the post. It shows Zoe and me sitting at a patio table under a rainbow umbrella on a sunny day in front of The Cookie Jar, with each of us taking a messy bite from our huge raspberry bear claw. The detail about the play comes in the comments under the post.

My friend Beth had asked me in the comments about what brought us to The Cookie Jar, and my response told her we were in South Portland to see *The Lion, The Witch, and the Wardrobe* at The Portland Players Theater, which is close to the bakery. I also told her how happy I was that Zoe wanted to see the play because "*I absolutely love live theater performances*". Those two comments are buried amidst a sea of comments proclaiming how adorable my niece is and how much she looks like she could be my daughter.

How did Ronnie find that? He must've been searching every single post and picture and comment on my page to discover that detail about me. But why? What's the point? To try to play up the whole idea of "*Wow, I love plays too—we have so much in common.*"

Classic. Just like Henry Rollins sings about in "Liar."

After all this searching and wondering and speculating, my rising frustration and irritation scream for a drink. Plus, hiding in the bathroom for so long has made me cold and uncomfortable, and there's no need to keep searching. I found the proverbial needle. Now, what can I poke with it?

I go to the kitchen, pour myself a mimosa, and plop down on the couch with the silky chenille blanket wrapped around me. The first couple of sips taste sweet and refreshing. The third sip helps me melt into the cushions, and I rest my head back on my velvety Edgar Allen Poe throw pillow.

Why did Ronnie scour my social media page to find things out about me instead of just asking me about myself like a normal person when they want to get to know someone better? I swear social media has created a communication breakdown, making people forget how to communicate in person. Body language—what's that? Vocal intonation—what does that even mean? Tone of voice—why does that matter? What tech giants promote as progress for society I see as regression for humans. But that's a topic I don't have the brain power to think about right now. I'm too pissed off at *one* person. I don't have the energy for anger against a *whole group* of billionaire techies.

Whoa! This drink's already getting to me, pushing my mind right down the rabbit hole of outrage. Ronnie better watch out. At this rate, I just might stab him to death in his sleep. No, but really…I'll save that type of rage for my songwriting. But if he wakes up now, he's in for one hell of a fight. I'm so fucking irate! Why did I let him make me second-guess myself?

All this anger's got my body tied in knots. I zipped straight from a deep hole of lonely depression to fire-in-my-eyes fury! I don't know which is worse.

Both suck equal bags of donkey dicks.

Why can't I just make it all stop, disappear myself from the ugliness of life, say "Goodbye, cruel world" and drift away?

Man, I could really use a professional massage to help calm my nerves. If it wasn't so late, I'd call Nine Stones and put that birthday gift card I still haven't cashed in to good use right now.

I sink deeper into my pillow and pull the blanket up to my shoulders, trying to relax. But my hurricane of thoughts refuses to slow down, kicking up even more rage.

I don't care if Ronnie swears his vasectomy can be reversed. Yes, all the research he showed me before we left for the play backs up his claim, but those research findings also say, "The more time that passes between the vasectomy and the reversal, the lower the chances for success". He fails to see the importance of that statement. But that shit doesn't even matter. I don't care about the research! I don't care if the vasectomy can be reversed! What I freaking care about is he kept it from me! He not only kept an important piece of information from me, but he also knows so much about me I no longer feel comfortable around him.

Now that I'm thinking about it, I don't know if I've ever really felt *comfortable* with him. His jealousy puts me on edge, questioning everything I do, wondering if my behavior or what I say will somehow make me look suspicious of something and then push him to make accusations. Just when chatting with the guys in the band I find that I censor my wording and my actions to make sure I don't say or do anything Ronnie might take the wrong way.

Shit. My glass is empty. I need a refill. Gotta be quiet getting in the fridge. The last thing I want is for Ronnie to wake up and try talking to me. If I even see him or hear his voice right now, this glass will meet his face, hard. But first, refill it and drink it.

Ah…That's better. Back to my warm spot on the couch.

No, don't touch your phone again. No more scrolling. I already know. I already found it.

This is fucking insane! What the hell am I doing with my life?

Everything I try to accomplish fails. I had to drop out of the first college I went to because their tuition is too expensive, and I'm poor. I wasted five years of my life applying to a graduate program that refused to accept me, even though I graduated college in the top 10% of my class. Then Jordan encouraged me to follow my dreams, encouraged me to take my writing more seriously, encouraged me to go for my MFA and start a new path. Then, he abandons me when I'm in the thick of it and only working part-time. Now, finishing my master's degree may never happen at the rate I'm going with all my life's setbacks getting in the way. Every person I've ever had a relationship with has either physically abused me, mentally and emotionally abused me, cheated on me, or lied to me. Most of them did more than one of those things. After a ten-year marriage, my husband refuses to create a family with me, refuses to even talk to me about the possibility. Then there's Psycho Satan—the arsenic icing on my mountain-high shit cake—who attacks me in some way pretty much every other week, and her actions are pushing my mother closer and closer to an early grave. And Aiden, the worst memory from my past—the blood-filled cherry on top of my dessert of despair—has come back to torment me for whatever insane reason.

Dammit! I hate my shitty life! What's the point in trying to make it better? Every time I get two steps ahead, something or someone kicks me three steps back. Two steps ahead. Three steps back. Two steps ahead. Three steps back. Over and over again. I just can't deal with it anymore!

I wish I had the money to move away from it all, start over somewhere else, a place where nobody knows me.

Yeah, that doesn't sound lonely at all. Not one bit.

This apartment feels like a fucking cage, claustrophobic. I need to get out of here. Go somewhere. Get some fresh air or something.

Or maybe if I just *do* something, *any*thing. I gotta get out of my head, get out of these thoughts that won't stop bombarding me, dragging me down.

But where am I supposed to go at two in the morning? What the hell can I do at this hour that won't wake up the sleeping pile of lies on the other side of that door? I can't go next door to Mom's. The "I told you so" look on her face that I'm *certain* will appear is not what I need right now. She's still not home yet anyway, probably playing cards at her friend's house down the street. Plus, I need space to think. I need to figure this shit out on my own—like a big girl.

I could always do some writing. That's therapeutic, right? Take out my anger on some fictional characters maybe? No, but really— Writing is nice and quiet, especially if I take a notebook and pen outside to the porch swing. There is a section of my thesis I've been struggling with. Maybe I can step away and work on that. Nature's hug and freehand writing always help tap into the creative pathways of the psyche.

Or maybe a warm bubble bath to drown my sorrows, slip under and fade away, escape. As long as Ronnie doesn't wake up and try to join me. I'd rather slit my throat with Ronnie's damn straight razor than share a bath with him right now.

Take a bubble bath and drown my sorrows. Turn to page 66.
Take a notebook and a pen outside to write. Turn to page 53.

Cordless phone in my shaky hand, cell on the coffee table with the lit-up screen displaying the Maine Crisis Hotline, I dial 1-888-568…

Tears blur my vision. I wipe them away, see the rest of the phone number. My trembling finger hovers over the next number to press on the receiver. Chest heaves and shoulders bounce from my pathetic sobbing.

I can't do this.

I hang up.

Shit.

What a fucking mess I am.

Squeezing the receiver with a white-knuckle grip, a desperate scream erupts out of me. Tears waterfall down my steaming-hot cheeks.

Why can't I do this?

I *need* to do this.

I need to talk to *some*one.

If I don't let this out, it's sure as shit going to drown me, suffocate me, close my eyes forever, snuff me out of existence. That's a surefire way to never reach my goals, to never earn my graduate degree, to never have the family I dream about, to never meet the little boy who visits me while I sleep, to never see my work published, to not be around to help Mom, to never write and perform music again.

I.

Need.

To.

Do.

This.

Now!

Fuck it.

1-888-568-1112. Maine's Crisis Hotline rings into my ear.

"Maine Crisis…this…Holly. How…help…"

Out of breath and unable to stop crying, I catch only part of what the person on the other end is saying. I try to talk, but the double-breathing effect from my cries keeps words out of reach. I need to say something. What if they hang up?

"Hello?"

"Yes, sorry, someone's here. I'm here please don't hang up…I-I-I…" Sobs swallow my words. What am I supposed to say?

"It's okay. Take your time. Making this call isn't easy. But I'm here. I'm here as long as it takes you. I'm here to listen. And I look forward to hearing your story." The soft, calm voice rolls through the line, wrapping around me like a gentle hug, a warm blanket, a soft pillow to rest my head on.

My sobs intensify with the anticipation of dumping all my dirt into this stranger's ear. I grab a tissue from the roll of toilet paper sitting on the coffee table beside my cell, cover my mouth, and attempt to calm myself enough to talk.

As soon as I grow quieter, the voice on the phone says, "Are you calling for yourself or are you concerned about someone else?"

"Me. It's me," I manage to say.

"Alright. That's a good start. I am very concerned that you are so upset, and I want to help. I just need to ask you a few questions. Can you please give me your name and number just in case our call gets cut off, so I can call you back?"

My name and number?

I hesitate.

What the fuck is this all about? Is my name going to go into some database? A list of crazies to keep track of? A list of nutjobs to never hire for jobs or rent an apartment to or allow near children or…

"I want to assure you—our agency *never* traces *any* calls that come in to us, and we never share or sell your information to anyone or to any companies. This is a safe space. Sometimes cell calls get dropped or phones run out of battery, and I just want to make sure you are able to talk to me for as long as you need to."

"I'm on a landline, so I don't have to worry about that." My words come out choppy as I try to simmer down my crying. Giving her my name and number doesn't sit right with me, though her reasoning makes sense. But still…

"Are you calling from your home or someone else's? And is someone there with you or are you alone?"

"I'm at my home, alone." Though I hesitate, I give her my first name and phone number. Then I blurt out, "I don't *want* to be alone." My crying intensifies. Big time. I grab more tissues, try to calm down.

Why do I feel so out of control?

Before I realize what I'm doing, my dirty laundry spills from my mouth into the phone, starting with what happened tonight, Ronnie and the blade, the cops arresting him and hauling his ass out of here.

"Dahlia, you did the right thing calling the cops and reporting what Ronnie did to you. I am so sorry you had to go through that. And I imagine you must be hurting a lot right now, and it may seem like there is no way out, but I believe that I can help you, *if* you let me."

"That's not even everything. That's only what happened *t-t-tonight*. My life is a never-ending h-h-horror story." My breath hitches. I cover my mouth with a tissue, wanting to save her from listening to me cry more.

"Has Ronnie done this to you before?"

"No, n-n-nothing like that but…" An image of Jordan crosses my mind, which intensifies my crying, again.

"Dahlia, it's okay. Take your time." She waits while I quiet my sobs. Then she says, "Dahlia, I need you to tell me—have you put the straight razor away? And are there any other weapons you have that could harm you?"

"No, no more…weapons n-n-near me."

"Good. That's very good. Now, you said Ronnie's never done this to you before. What else have you been dealing with that makes you want to harm yourself?"

I jump back to the fight with Jordan, our separation, Satan's attacks, and work my way to pull all the story threads together to meet somewhere in the middle.

By the time I make it to the part about the studio session and the band breaking up, my one-way tale has turned into a mutual back-and-forth conversation, unfolding with much more ease than I had anticipated. A feeling of nostalgia surges through me, similar to déjà vu but stronger. The counselor's name is Holly, and for some odd reason, if feels like we've known each other longer than we've been on this call. After the first few minutes of talking with her, even the timbre and cadence of her voice started to sound familiar as though we've talked before. I'm not sure what to make of that. All I know is, the longer I talk, the easier it is to talk to someone about everything—even this stranger, who doesn't feel so much like a stranger anymore.

Our conversation lasts about twenty-five minutes or so. Depression and loneliness and feelings of betrayal still weigh heavy on my shoulders when I hang up the phone, but...

Now I have a plan.

And now I think sleep won't be as much of a problem as I'd thought before that much needed call.

I get up off the couch to return the phone receiver to the charger cradle and notice I'm no longer dizzy and off balance, no longer light-headed and brain-fogged. But when I glance into the bedroom and see Ronnie's two basses hanging on the wall and his clothes on the shelves and his blood on the floor, a knot forms in my stomach and nausea kicks in.

I take a deep breath and turn away.

The couch seems like a much better option for tonight.

Hey, did you really think one phone call would fix *every*thing?

Hell no!

All I can hope for is progress, improvement. One foot in front of the other, as the saying goes.

Oh, and not wanting to make myself bleed out of this life at a premature date—that's a pretty fucking big thing to hope for too.

The silky, chenille blanket on the couch calls to me. I plop my exhausted ass onto the sofa and see step one of my plan staring at me from beside my packed bowl and lighter. An appointment time with a counselor, scheduled for tomorrow, written on a purple Sticky Note. A few deep breaths help me melt back into the pillow. As I reach for my bowl and lighter to assist with falling asleep, my cell phone chimes. Is it Beth or Allie texting me back?

Nope.

The lit-up screen displays an email notification.

At this hour?

Probably some automated promotional bullshit.

But the odd timing piques my interest, and I can't stop myself from checking to see who it's from.

Philip Franco appears on the *Sender* line.

The name sounds familiar, but I can't place it. I click it open.

Is this real?

Did I just get spammed?

I open the "Submissions" folder in my Gmail account. Scanning past the recent submissions I've sent out that have not reached their submission deadline yet, I finally find the five novel submissions I sent out over six months ago.

There it is!

Philip Franco, Editor-in-Chief of the indie UK publisher Hallowed Ground Press.

No fucking way!

This does *not* feel real At. All.

They want to publish my novel!

Shit!

It's going to be really tough to fall asleep now.

But I'd much rather lose sleep from excitement than despair.

Maybe I *can* handle this thing called life after all.

Maybe.

Setting my phone aside, I grab the bowl of Indica and take a couple tokes. I hope this new counselor doesn't instantly want to put me on sleeping pills or antianxiety meds. Weed is much safer than those chemical concoctions.

My body feels relaxed now, but thinking about my novel acceptance sets my thoughts alight and sends them spinning. I need to tell someone the good news. But it's so late, no one will answer a text or a call at this hour.

Oh well, I can still send one.

Without thinking it through, I send a quick text to Jordan. I'm not sure why because I know he won't respond. I'm the last person he wants to hear from. As soon as the *Delivered* notification appears under my message, I lie down and close my eyes.

A text message chimes on my phone.

Why would Jordan be awake this late?

Probably a promotional text.

I reach out to shut off my phone, so I can sleep without interruptions. The screen lights up with the second text chime before I squeeze the buttons.

"Congratulations! I always knew you could do it babe I'm your biggest fan"

Jordan's text ends with a purple heart emoji.

The End

Read the Author's Note on page 225.

Try Not to Die: By Your Own Hand Survivor Version

Our band's last song wails and thunders across the fog-filled venue. The crowd jumps and thrashes against one another. I step up to the mic, spotlight hot against my skin, and belt out the second verse.

Sinking lower, they're dragging you down
Parallel plane, disappear in the dark.
Chains confine you, constricting movement,
Stealing your breath, silencing all your words.
Now stagnation threatens to bloom
As the flames lick at every inch of your skin.
Are you content to crawl with vermin, the bottom feeders,
Are you happy where you're at?

Just as we're about launch into the chorus, I peer out over the audience, trying to see if Beth showed up. She looks like a no-show, but there' a tall, burly hooded figure standing in the back corner, sweatshirt zipped up to their neck.

Alone.

Not moving.

Just staring.

Did we attract an A&R rep to our gig? We have been playing a ton of shows lately. Maybe word got out we've been attracting some big crowds. I *hope* it's a recruiter of some sort.

That must be why the person came alone. That must be why their hands are empty, no drink. That must be why they don't join in with the jumping and moshing.

Mike tears into his guitar solo. I step back from the mic, glance over at Ronnie on bass. Curiosity paints his face as he looks from the hood in the corner to me. I try to stay focused on playing guitar, but memories flash through my mind.

Aiden backhands me, shoves me into the dug-out hideaway-escape-hatch under his trailer and locks the trap door above my head.

Cuffed to the bedpost, tears stream down my temples as Aiden, with a knife held to my throat, straddles me while professing his undying love and tearing off my shirt. Above the bed, his graffiti art of me as an angel surrounded by roses and skulls stares back at me in violet, black, and crimson with drips like blood. Pointy, knife-like lettering arches over the top of it: *Angel Baby*. I try to pretend I'm somewhere else, somewhere peaceful.

With a few whips of my long hair, I headbang the horrors out of my thoughts. Turning back-to to the audience, I watch for the cue from our drummer, Kyle. Right after our synchronized stop, I spin back toward the mic and belt out the final chorus. Shivers run through me as I sing.

The hooded figure remains still, staring.

A sinking sensation hits me.

I can't help but feel like I'm the one he's staring at.

Our set ends. The audience goes nuts. Mike's best bud, Wally, jumps on stage to help break down our gear so we can clear the stage for the last band to set up.

We head to the bar.

The three drinks I had before our set make me trip as I walk up the steps leading to the pool table and bar area. I grab the railing, steady myself. Out of the corner of my eye I see the hood slowly swivel, following my every move. Stay with your people. Don't go anywhere alone. I bend down to adjust my pantleg, making sure my throwing knife's in place and at the ready. For some reason, the hope of an A&R scout checking out our band has shifted and twisted into nothing I want to consider.

At the top of the stairs I see Jen, lead singer from the opening band, Blood Rain. "Hell yeah! Here comes the growler."

We high-five.

"I still can't believe that big voice comes out of such a little lady." Gordon, Jen's lead guitarist, spiked bracelet around his wrist, throws me the metal horns.

I glance around, look over each shoulder, then turn back toward them. "What? Where's this 'lady' you're talking about?"

They laugh.

I smirk and walk over to the guys at the bar.

Harry, the bartender, already has my margarita waiting for me. I plop my ass in the stool between Mike and Ronnie and take a refreshing sip. With the cool glass against my lips and the tangy libation filling my mouth, I glance over to the corner of the mosh floor.

The hood's now watching the bar, face masked in shadow, reddish-auburn hair hanging down to their burly chest.

That final detail evaded my perception while on stage.

Now I don't need to see their face to know who it is.

My muscles tense. I take another sip, wash it away.

"So, another packed show," Harry says. "You guys really know how to tear people away from their computers and out of their houses. What do you cats say? Can I book you every third Friday of the month?"

The guys each bump their elbows into my arms, looking at me with excited expressions. Kyle, standing behind us, leans in and reaches his arm across the bar.

"Fuckin'-A-right we will!" Kyle fist bumps Harry, then throws looks to the guys and me. "What? Come on, I knew you'd all say yes."

We laugh, nod our heads, and say, "Yeah," in unison. We bump shoulders and sip our drinks, excited for regularly scheduled gigs.

Damn. It's only taken me all through my twenties and early thirties to finally get into a band dedicated enough to score recurring gigs at Geno's, Portland's legendary dive bar and rock club. Hell, recurring gigs period is freaking awesome. Man, why's it been so hard to keep a gigging band together? It's not like I'm gunning for fame. I just want to write tunes and perform. Now I've got it. This is freaking awesome!

After Harry walks off to go write us into the bar's gig schedule, I ask my bandmates, "Hey, did you guys notice that person all alone in the corner, hiding under their hood?"

Ronnie nods, is about to say something when Kyle says, "No. Where? What guy?"

Ronnie's eyes follow mine as I turn toward the dark corner in the back of the mosh floor. The corner is empty.

I jump off my stool and frantically search the crowd all around the bar and near the pool tables behind us, wondering if the guy followed me. I can't find him anywhere.

The fucker disappeared.

♫ ▮ ♪

At the 24-hour diner after the show, we sit at the corner booth next to the large front windows so we can see Mike's tricked-out hearse parked out front with most of our gear loaded in the back. It's pretty sweet he doesn't mind hauling my gig amp back to our practice space for me after our shows. Saves me a lot of time and hassle. But my guitar always stays with me.

Ronnie scooches over close to my side. Leaning toward my ear, he whispers, "So, the guy in the hood, I noticed he never took his eyes off you. Freaked you the fuck out, I could tell. Is this someone I need to take care of for you?"

With a shrug, I turn away, look out the window.

I don't want to think about it. Not. At. All. And I don't want to think about what will happen to Ronnie if he tries to take care of this problem for me. Nothing good, I know that, especially considering the psychotic who hid under that hood.

I wish Beth had been at the show. She'd have pointed that lunatic right out before I even stepped off the stage, her recognition pulling him out of the shadows, not allowing him to hide. She despises him *almost* as much as I do. Knows how much he ruined high school for me. Plus, he never liked me hanging out with her; we had too much fun together going to parties. If Jordan were still coming to my shows, he'd've pulled me off stage and ushered me right out of there. Jordan knows the nightmares I've dealt with because of that psycho.

"I'm not sure," is all I say as I open the menu.

Ronnie needs to stay out of this, or he'll end up in the hospital, or worse. Plus, I'd like to enjoy my buzz after the great show we just had. Recurring gigs at Geno's!

Turning his head, Ronnie throws me a squinty side-eye. "Hmm, why don't I believe you?"

I refuse to look at him. Lies—not my forte. The truth always clings to me like a second skin.

"Let's just enjoy some food, talk about it tomorrow. I don't wanna ruin this night." I glance up from my menu, look around our booth: Mike, Kyle, Wally, Ronnie. Dropping the menu, I pound the table with my fist. "Monthly gigs at Geno's, man! If that ain't sweet-ass fucking news I don't know what is. Now, let's order some grindage."

"Hell yeah!" They shout in unison.

Everyone in the diner, all ten customers and four employees, throws us dirty looks. We ignore them and pass high-fives and fist bumps around the table.

But the hood from the gig dominates my thoughts. Man, my head is swimming right now. I wish the diner sold booze.

After we order and our food arrives, Mike and Kyle keep the gig conversations going strong. Thank god. It allows me a breather from Ronnie's questions and my thoughts of the corner creeper.

"Now, if we can score monthly gigs down at the beach this summer, we'll be gold." Kyle stuffs a forkful of French toast into his mouth.

"Don't forget Lewiston. That city loves metal bands. And that shit ain't seasonally dependent. Recurring gigs up there, man, *that's* what we need." The scraping of Mike's steak knife against his plate as he carves his meat makes me cringe. That nails-on-chalkboard feeling, but deeper, darker. And the bloody red inside that rare steak makes this vegetarian want to gag.

"Shit. Don't dis the beach, man. That place is packed, and not just with locals. We can hit the fucking tourists too, dude."

As Kyle and Mike go back and forth, I sense Ronnie watching my every move. I try to ignore it. Pretend I don't notice.

My stomach flip-flops. Shoulders ache. My knee bounces so fast the booth shakes. After smothering my home fries with more ketchup, the bottle slips from my sweaty hand, hits the table hard, and topples over. The guys jump. Red pours out of the top of the bottle like blood oozing from an open wound.

Ronnie pulls a wad of napkins out of the dispenser and wipes up the spill as I stand the bottle back up and clean off the top.

"How many drinks did you have tonight, Growler?" Mike winks at me as he slices another chunk off his thin slab of steak.

"Not enough, that's for sure." I stuff a forkful of ketchup-smothered home fries into my mouth. Then I notice Ronnie wearing a strange expression as his eyes dart back and forth between Mike and me. Not sure what that's about, but I don't have long to ponder.

Wally points out the front window. "Guys…Some fuckers are stealing your gear!"

We bolt out of our booth, knocking silverware, napkins, and jelly packets onto the floor. The table wobbles, spilling our coffees all over the place, and sending the ketchup bottle splatting to the ground.

We rush toward the door.

"Hey, you haven't paid your bill!" A server waves a slip of paper in the air as we fly past.

"We'll be right back," I yell over my shoulder.

Platform boots make it difficult to run, but I sprint down the sidewalk with my bandmates. Nothing holds me back. The thieves are right there, not too far ahead. It's like I could almost reach out and grab them.

The distance grows between us. Maybe if we didn't drink so much at the show, we'd be able to catch up to these scumbags.

They toss our shit into the back seat of a car, jump in, and peel out.

Shit. Why didn't we just jump in one of our vehicles, dammit? It's too late to turn back now—the highway's so close I can practically spit on it.

The four of us—Wally stayed back with the car, and to hopefully call 911 and pay our bill—chase after the car that just took off with most of our band equipment. *And*—I know that car. A dark blue Buick. The license plate and the old Chippendales sticker and the *"Trucker's Wife"* window decal.

My thieving former sister. Sara's her given name, but she *earned* the name Satan.

She lost her name when she physically attacked me for standing up for *my* mother and then took my niece, Zoe, away from me—my mini-me. But I couldn't let her keep stealing from Mom and not call her out on it.

Not only do I know that car and the person driving, but we also saw that hooded figure—the corner creeper—jump into the passenger's seat after tossing Mike's Marshall amp head into the backseat. His hood fell off while running, long, red straggly hair clear as a slap in the face.

What the hell is she doing chumming around with my abusive ex from high school?

Who freaking knows? He's probably buying his coke from her and her husband now.

I run as fast as my boots and the electric shocks of nerve pain shooting up my legs allow me. But none of us can outrun a cokehead behind the wheel of a car filled with hot goods ripped off from the little sister whose life reminds that driver how much of a lowlife she is.

I really wish we were driving instead of running right now.

Just as the thieves run a red light, a huge Peterbilt pulls in front of their car, slowing them down as both vehicles merge onto the highway's onramp. Ronnie, with his long legs and spastic energy, jumps onto the trunk.

I pause, reach down to slip out my throwing knife. But I hesitate.

What if I hit Ronnie instead of a tire?

But I gotta do *something*. What other options do I have? I can't run fast enough. And they have my band's gear!

Oh, shit. Nausea gurgles in my gut as I wobble in my platforms. Dizziness hits hard. My fingers fumble trying to unsnap the sheath.

What the hell am I thinking? This isn't a damn movie! No matter how good I think I can throw, I'll never hit that freaking tire. I'll probably stab Ronnie instead.

I straighten up, rub my stomach, try regaining my balance. Doesn't work.

Bending forward, I hurl undigested home fries and ketchup and a whole metal show's worth of alcohol onto the sidewalk.

Maybe I shouldn't've had that fourth margherita.

I wipe my mouth on my forearm and stand back upright.

Satan swerves back and forth, making the Buick shimmy. Ronnie slides side-to-side a couple times before one arm loses its grip, dangles.

"Fuuuuuuuck!" I start running again.

Ronnie slips off the back of the trunk.

His legs hit the pavement, but he grabs onto the bumper. As the car drags him further up the on-ramp, his feet scrabble for purchase as though he could run along with the car. The Peterbilt swerves onto the highway. Satan punches the gas and follows suit, and Ronnie loses his grip. He hits the pavement hard and rolls off the side of the on-ramp into the ditch.

All we're left watching are the red taillights of the Buick as the thieves speed off down the highway through the foggy full moon night.

And I'm left in awe at…well…everything. Ronnie really put in some extra effort. Maybe I've finally found *the one*.

Or maybe he just really wants that gear back.

♬ ∎ ♪

At work the next day, my supervisor's face twists with shock when I tell him about filing police reports at the Portland PD until four in the morning.

"After the night you had, I would've understood if you called out. Remember, I'm not just your boss. We're friends, Dahl. And we don't have any burials today." Jack rests his liver-spotted hand on my shoulder. "Wanna go home? Get some rest?"

I shake my head. "Nah. I'd much rather be here. Work is a welcome distraction from last night's bullshit. But thanks." I straighten up a bit, rigid, scoot to the edge of my seat. "Dude, we just scored recurring gigs at Geno's after our set, then that thieving psycho stole half our gear. You'd think I'd be used to this sort of thing by now since that's how my oh-so-great life tends to roll—take a step forward only to get kicked backwards three more steps." I shake my head, sink back into the desk chair.

Jack's eyes widen. "Recurring gigs at Geno's? Dahl, that's kickass! Are you sure you don't want to go home, try to find your gear somehow? Maybe check with some local pawn shops?" He pauses, runs his hand down his long beard. "Or you *could* always borrow my amp. That will at least cover you until you hopefully get yours back."

I consider this a moment.

"Thanks for the offer, but your digital Line 6 has a completely different sound than my tubed Mesa, and it works so differently. It'll mess me all up. Pawn shops though? That's a great idea! Thanks! But nah, I really shouldn't leave work. I can't afford to lose the hours. Plus, Ronnie's tending to his road rash, and seein' that bloody mess gives me the ick-shivers."

A new look sprouts on Jack's face. Not just shock, but confusion. So, I'll bite my tongue about Ronnie's newfound jealousy rearing its ugly head when we got back to my place this morning. I don't even want to think about it, let alone tell someone who I already know doesn't like him. I haven't even had time to think about it. Everything happened so fast. And my exhaustion makes my thoughts all rattled.

"Ronnie's at your place right now? Without you there? Did he stay the night?" He steps back and leans against the office counter beside me.

I look up at him, serious as all hell. "Yesterday, he just showed up at my place with all his shit packed up in his car, ready to move in. Made me literally speechless. He has his own house, so it makes no sense.

Though his house does need a shit-ton of work." Groggy, I shake my head, try knocking the confusion against my skull to make it make sense without me needing to think too hard right now. "But still...I was shocked mute. And with our gig last night, I just haven't had time to address it yet. Plus, I have no idea what the fuck to say."

"You tell him no—*that's* what you say. Shit, Dahl. What the hell is Jordan gonna think when he finds out?"

Dammit. Leave it to Jack to sound like a dad. Maybe I should've waited to tell him that too, at least until I figure all this shit out myself. "If only it were that easy." I stuff a handful of almonds and raisins into my mouth and turn away.

"Um, yeah, I'm pretty sure it is." An irritated huff comes out of him.

"Yeah, but Jack, he was so sweet about it, saying how he just wants to wake up next to me every day, and knowing I live where I live to help Mom, he saw this as the only way."

Jack rolls his eyes.

"Yeah, I know. It's way too soon. But I don't know how to break it to him. You didn't see the excitement on his face."

Silence. Uncomfortable, like neither of us knows what to say.

"Oh, yeah, forgot to tell you the rest of my good news." The sarcasm filling my voice causes Jack to cock his head and stand at attention. "The divorce papers were delivered to me yesterday too."

"What? Divorce papers? I could've sworn you two would end up back together, that this was all just a hiccup. Man..." Jack shakes his head and rubs his sweaty forehead with the back of his dirt-caked hand. "You two are made for each other."

"Huh...Yeah, that's what I thought too, once upon a time, but all fairy tales—real fairy tales—end in tragedy." I turn away. "Huh...Tragedy...Story of my fucking life."

As I pick at my raisins, knowing I should eat more but not really feeling it, I think back to my last argument with Jordan. Heat rushes to my cheeks.

When I had left the last marriage counseling session with Jordan, I could barely breath. The things he'd said...

"I've never wanted kids."

I asked, "Then why did you act all excited and start planning to have a baby with me? You even went as far as picking out names with me and deciding we'd start trying after my graduation? We even joked about how we'll probably embarrass our kid when he's a teenager. We've talked about teaching him how to play music, how we want to play music together as a family, buying a camper van and going on family vacations. Why did you make all these plans with me when you knew none of it was going to happen?"

"It made you happy. I've always loved your smile—it's intoxicating."

"Do I look happy *now*?" I'd been crying through most of the session, and my face felt flushed, my eyes stung.

"Well, not now, but you were then."

"So, how long did you think you could keep me happy telling me fantasy stories? Making false promises? Did you think I'd never find out?"

"I guess I never thought about that."

"You never *thought about it*?" Rage bubbled up inside of me, and I yelled, "A five-year fucking lie and you never thought about it?" I didn't mean to raise my voice, but something came over me as he sat there staring at me, unblinking, like a deer caught in the headlights.

He shrugged, and silence fell over the small, white and sea green room. The counselor had remained quiet.

How could Jordan sit there and not shed a tear? How could he suddenly seem so cold and nonchalant? It was a side of him I'd never seen before.

After a few moments of my sniffling, sobbing, and stuttered breathing, the counselor said, "Dahlia, tell Jordan how that makes you feel."

It took me a moment to control my breath enough to form words. I grabbed a tissue, wiped my nose, and said, "I thought we were going to grow old together, play music together with our kid, hold hands until our dying breaths. You're my home. Every picture of my future…you're in it. But now…" My sobbing kicked back into overdrive, and I just shook my head and wiped my nose, unable to finish my sentence.

He yelled, "I'll be a terrible father! Is that what you want?" He paused, lowered his voice, and shrugged. "I guess I'm just selfish. I like my time."

I told him how I felt, and he yelled at me?

The weight of his words pressed down on me, suffocated me. I couldn't speak. Only cried.

The session ended when the counselor said, "I think the only option for you two is divorce. I don't see either of you coming out of this."

That was it in a nutshell. Jordan said nothing, though I saw him nod slightly. My sobs increased so much I thought I might hyperventilate.

When we got out to the parking lot, he grasped my hand gently before I walked off to my vehicle and said, "I'm sorry, Dahl. I didn't mean to hurt you like this. I didn't mean to make you hate me."

The look in his eyes felt like pity. It hurt so much, I couldn't hold eye contact. Sobs overcame me. I turned away, got in my Jimmy, and left.

It felt like he'd pulled my whole life right out from under me.

I've been free falling ever since, into an abyss of loneliness and uncertainty, with no place to call home, no one to cry to, every battle I now have to fight alone.

And I've been fuming ever since that last encounter. I did *not* need him to feel sorry for me. He took the pain he caused me and turned it on himself, trying to make me feel bad for his hurt feelings over me hating him for this. Really? "*Selfish*" was certainly the right word to describe him. Add "self-absorbed" to that too.

"Maybe you should try talkin' to him again?" Jack cocks an eyebrow.

"Yeah, well, maybe he shouldn't've lied to me for the past five years and gone through all the motions of wanting to start a family after my grad school graduation in three months. He completely fucked me over. Not only did he leave me high and dry financially, but my biological clock is *tic-tic-ticking* its final countdown." Tears welling in my eyes, I remain turned away. I hate looking weak. "And based on our argument at our last counseling session, all these months apart haven't changed his mind. Guess he'd rather be without me than take on another adult responsibility." A *ping, ping* sounds near my feet as a few almonds hit the floor from the baggy I'm crushing inside my clenched fist. "He's nothing but a selfish little man-boy, too scared to grow the hell up. Just kick back in his recliner, pound another beer, watch TV, go to the bar or a concert whenever he pleases. Fucker!"

Tension squeezes every muscle in my body as a lump forms in my throat. Eyes sting. I can't handle this conversation right now. It hurts too much.

Anger is much easier to deal with.

"Sorry. That really sucks. I just don't get him." Papers crinkle as Jack shuffles around through the upcoming burial records, obviously feeling uncomfortable and trying not to look at sad and pathetic little me.

Releasing the death grip on my lunch, I shake the baggy of almonds and raisins and consider reaching in for another handful, but my stomach has other plans. I lurch, cover my mouth. With eyes wide and holding back what I know is coming, I hold up a finger to Jack as I jump from the office chair and run to the bathroom.

Bent over the toilet and hurling everything out of my stomach, I hear Jack knock on the door. "I'll be out back having a smoke. Feel better. Meet me outside when you're done."

After swirling my gut chunks down the drain, I wash my hands and splash cold water on my face. The mirror hangs above the sink, taunting me, trying to lure my eyes to my reflection. I refuse to look. Not wanting to see the mess I've turned into, I turn away, grab a paper towel, and head back out into the office.

I grab my work gloves and head toward the front door. My old, black GMC Jimmy sits parked out front in the gravel patch between the road and the office. Just as I step down the front steps, a dark blue car speeds past. Something flies out of the driver's side window.

A loud, metallic *bang* and a shattering *crash* sound as the back window of my truck implodes. It stops me in my tracks. Shards of glass fly and scatter everywhere.

"What the fuck?" I run down the side of the road, chasing after the car. "You motherfucker, I know who you are, you crazy cunt!"

An arm pops out the driver's open window, middle finger held high, as the car—a dark blue Buick—speeds around the corner out of sight.

By the time I stop running and turn to head back to the office, I see Jack, cigarette in hand, running out from behind the office.

"What the hell was that?" Red paints Jack's angry face as he stubs out his cigarette on the bottom of his steel-toe boot.

Fuming and ready to rage, I shake my head. "Just another visit from oh-so-loving Satan."

"What the hell is your sister's problem?"

"My existence, apparently." I grith my teeth. "And *never* call her my sister again. It's Satan."

He nods, smirks. "Well, now she's fucking with my workplace. This shit needs to stop."

The window of my truck now lies in pieces across the ground. It's mixed with what look like ceramic shards.

"What in the world did she throw? A rock?" Jack leans in close to inspect the shattered window. Broken glass peppers the inside of the truck.

Bent over, I search the ground. "I'm not sure, but I don't think it was a rock." I kick around some pebbles, looking for any sign. "Motherfucker! I don't have money to fix this…and I sure as shit don't have time for her fucking bullshit."

Something shimmers differently from the bulk of the mess near the rear tire. I slip on a work glove, reach down, and grasp a shard of what looks like ceramic. Red and white and green paint. The words *Ho, ho* and the tip of a candy cane image decorate the surface.

"Found it!" I stand upright and turn toward Jack.

He pulls his arm out of the back of the truck with something held in his gloved hand.

The red ceramic handle of a coffee mug.

We hold our finds out on our palms, hands side-by-side as we inspect.

Jack looks into my sunglass-covered eyes. "A Christmas mug?"

A loud, sardonic laugh shoots out from deep down in my core.

"What's so funny?" With quotation marks etched into the skin between his eyes, Jack looks confused, and a bit concerned. Or am I reading that wrong?

"Her idiocy, *that's* what's so funny." My hand curls into a fist around the sharp shard of ceramic. "Don't you remember what she wrote in the comments of my Facebook post a couple weeks ago? Calling me a hypocrite for celebrating Christmas with our family and a Satanist for my Wiccan beliefs? Come on, Jack, don't you see the connection? And last night, my band's stolen gear and her car speeding away? Shit." I turn away, lean against the Gator loaded with landscaping tools parked beside my truck.

With the toe of his work boot, Jack's kicking around debris at the side of the road, searching for more evidence.

I shoot my free hand out. "Stop! Don't mess with the crime scene."

His foot freezes. Eyes wide, he looks back to me and nods. "Shit. Yeah, my bad." He tosses the mug handle back into the truck and pulls his cell out of the leg pocket of his cargo pants.

"I'm so exhausted and there's all this shit going on, I forgot to tell you who else was at the show last night. Her partner in crime."

"What are you talking about?"

"Aiden."

Jack's eyes widen.

"What? *Aiden* came to your show?" He steps closer to me. "And he *helped* her steal your band's gear? What the fuck is going on?"

Words don't come to mind. I just shake my head and shrug my shoulders, feeling frustrated and angry and cornered and ready to explode…or just un-exist. *Poof.* Gone. No more stress. No more crazy. Death, a welcome escape.

I shake my head, try tamping down the darkness like tamping down a freshly filled grave.

Man, I really could use a toke and a drink right now. Maybe I *should* leave early, go home and call Beth, party at her place like the old days, blow off some steam with a buddy and forget my shitty life.

Jack holds up his cell and heads toward the office. "Let's go call the cops. I'm your witness. I saw her too."

Unsure how I'm supposed to keep my shit together, I look up at Jack, no idea what to say.

He winks. "Yes. Sure as shit…I saw that bitch. I saw her throw that mug too. That crazy cunt isn't getting away with this."

I dread the idea of calling the cops again. Spending the morning before work at the Portland police station sucked, and I'm exhausted! I didn't get any sleep. Can you have a hangover if you never slept?

And the number of times I've had to call the cops on the same person—a sibling, no less—is getting old, time-consuming, and extremely tiresome and embarrassing. It doesn't help that the cops look at me, the little woman that I am, and think I'm bringing them my petty family drama, which is so far from the truth I could spit nails. And all the times I had to deal with cops in my teens because of bullies at school and because of Aiden, whom they never busted for all the abuse and stalking and terrorizing he dished out on me and my family. When your calls to the police station become so frequent they've memorized your phone number, address, and your name, it doesn't reflect well on you as a person no matter what the issue is that you're calling them about. They simply get tired of dealing with you, and they brush your problems aside as quickly as they can. My history of dealing with the PD in this town has left a bitter taste in my mouth. Plus, I'm not too keen on dealing with authority figures with my "Fuck you *and* your rules" attitude. I despise their smug, power-hungry stares.

But I sure would love to finally get Satan busted. With Jack backing my story, maybe they'll believe me this time.

I don't know. Going to Beth's sounds a lot more enticing.

As we step through the office door to make the call, I try to smile, but my eyes sting and my face refuses to comply with my effort. Dealing with this crap is the last thing I want to have to do. My life is a mess right now, and psycho Satan has nothing better to do than go and compound it with her hatred and jealousy. Man, I wish she would disappear.

I really need a drink right now. Smoke a bowl. Something to escape all this bullshit.

I feel a warm touch on my shoulder.

"Maybe sit and take a minute…Decide what you're gonna say." Jack's concern is palpable.

Two minutes pass. I remain standing. Steel-toe boot *tap-tap-tapping*.

Relaxation isn't in my wheelhouse of skills.

And dealing with cops right now…

Rage threatens to bubble to the surface as I reach for the office phone. I close my eyes, take a deep breath, and form a fist around the receiver. My mind flashes back to freshman year of high school.

I was on the payphone between classes talking to my then-boyfriend Aiden, when a group of seven senior girls surrounded me. My quarter's worth of a call was not yet up. But that didn't matter to them. They started taunting me with "Hurry up, slut!" and "End the call, whore" and "Cunt, it's our turn." I tried ignoring them so I could just finish my conversation before the bell rang for my next class. If I didn't check in with Aiden throughout the school day, he immediately accused me of cheating on him or hiding shit from him. This phone call check-in protected me from a potential argument and assault after school. But what happened next changed the course of my entire freshman year, as well as the rest of my high school years.

Cara stepped out of the group of harassment surrounding me, walked right up to the payphone, and slammed her hand down on the hangup lever. "Enough of this shit already," she said. With her face merely six inches from mine, she smugly stared down at me.

I stood there in shock. Disbelief. All I could think was, *this bitch I don't even know has the nerve to hang up my phone call? Now she's right in my face. What the hell does she plan on doing next?*

My hand squeezed the black phone receiver tighter, worried about whatever else she might do. Without thinking, I punched her in the face—with the hand still holding the phone receiver.

Cara instantly covered her face with her hands. Blood oozed through her fingers and gushed down her chin. She blinked away a tear. Then she grabbed my hair, yanked my head back, and we fell to the floor.

After a quick blur of wrestling to get her out from behind me and remove my hair from her grasp, I kicked my legs up and over my head, backward somersaulting myself over her. Then, I wrapped my arm around her throat from behind and squeezed as tight as I could.

I wanted to fucking end her, or at least scare her enough to get her and her bully buddies to never mess with me again.

I squeezed tighter and tighter. She tried telling her friends she couldn't breathe.

With my mouth right beside her ear, I shouted, "How the fuck do you like me now, bitch?"

A gasp later, all six senior girls pounced on the five-foot-two, 100-pound freshman me and started punching repeatedly. I covered my head and face with my arms, blocking their blows as rage ignited within me. Finally, the assistant principle, Mr. B., and the school's police officer, Deputy Brown, broke it up.

As Deputy Brown led me to the principal's office, my besties Beth and Allie came scurrying around the corner, eyes bugging out, worried, asking what happened. I couldn't even shrug as the officer man-handled me away from them and shoved me through the office door out of sight. Like I was the aggressor. Like I was the bully. Like I had started all of this.

Mr. B suspended me. No one else received so much as a detention. I suppose since Cara came away bloody with a broken nose and a fractured cheekbone, and I came away unscathed—at least physically—I must've been the one who started it. Right? Even after I was acquitted in court after Cara's parents tried to charge me with aggravated assault, not one of the girls who bullied me were ever disciplined.

I dropped out of school.

Returning to school my sophomore year, I paid that unfair school administration back by making the honor roll every semester of the three years it took me to earn my high school diploma.

People should never underestimate my resolve.

Sitting in the cemetery office with the old-school phone receiver held to my ear, I await the inevitable.

The 911 dispatcher answers, and I report the vandalism to my truck, making sure I don't leave out the detail of Jack and me seeing who did it.

An hour after the call ends, an officer arrives at my work. The police station is less a mile away. Officer Delany, a husky man with pale skin and a freckled face, asks us a handful of questions.

"What time did the incident occur?"

"Where were you two when it happened?"

"What did the car look like?"

"Did you touch any pieces of the broken mug?"

"How did you two respond?"

How did we respond?

What type of question is that?

Does he not see and hear us standing here reporting the crime to him? Does he not realize the time of the incident and the time of my 911 call were within minutes of each other?

Officer Delaney—or should I say Deputy Brown—stares at me, unblinking, as though waiting for me to slip up with my "story." As though analyzing every one of my words. As though I'm the one who broke my own truck window with a fucking Christmas mug.

Hey, but I did the right thing. Didn't I?

Man, I should've just left work, called Beth, and got drunk to forget all this bullshit.

Well, looks like Satan's going to get away with all the torment she's been dishing out on me.

It's a week after the Christmas mug incident, and the cops still haven't pressed any charges against her. They say they can't prove she did it. I called bullshit on that and told them to get prints off the mug since our witness statements obviously mean nothing. They told me they only got partials, not enough for a conclusive ID. If I had caught it on camera, they told me that would've helped. I could only laugh at that.

How was I supposed to know someone was going to vandalize my vehicle? Should I just walk around with my phone at the ready 24/7? Plus, I'm a gravedigger and groundskeeper; if I carried my phone around at work, it would get damaged. And this small-town cemetery certainly can't afford CCTV.

Idiots!

They also couldn't bust her lapdog husband last month when I caught him on my CCTV outside my house stealing one of my medical marijuana plants.

They told me the hood he wore masked too much of his face, and they didn't get a close enough shot of his license plate. The fact that I had just served Satan the day before with a restraining order for physically attacking me *on my property* and for leaving numerous death threats against me on Mom's answering machine didn't seem to have any sway in their ability to at least get a search warrant.

I don't understand what those small-town cops even do around here. Not their jobs, obviously.

And that little hooded weasel stole my medication! I can't afford to buy it, which is why I grow it. Dammit! If it wasn't for Mom and Jack loaning me money to fix my truck window, I wouldn't have a vehicle to drive right now because of that psycho.

What good are the cops in this town if they can't bust career criminals the police department is always receiving complaints about, and not just complaints from me? Satan's neighbors have filed numerous complaints, her sister-in-law has filed complaints, parents from her youngest daughter's sporting events have also complained. These so-called cops need to stop that menace before she causes even more harm.

And the theft of my band's gear—the Portland PD hasn't busted anyone for that little crime either. Our gear has probably already been sold to the highest bidder or traded for pain pills and cocaine.

We just landed a recurring monthly gig at Geno's, the best rock club in Portland—possibly in all of Maine—and now we need to somehow find a way to replace our gear before that first gig gets here. And the studio session next week…Dammit!

Just when something good finally happens, Satan swoops in and crushes it. Story of my life. If it wasn't her, I'm certain it would've been something else getting in the way. I have no idea how I'm supposed to replace my Mesa Boogie the company no longer makes. Even if I bought a different amp, the pay at my cemetery job isn't enough for me to buy new gear, especially not a Mesa. I scored that kickass amp on a wicked used gear sale at Buckdancer's Choice seven years ago.

At least they didn't nab my guitar. I always carry that with me, and Ronnie and I took my Jimmy to that gig.

Ronnie. There's another fucked-up situation I've landed myself in.

When he jumped on Satan's trunk, as crazy as that was, my drunk ass took it as a sign that he was the one—the one to stick by me no matter what, the one to do anything in his power to try to fix a terrible situation. But oh, how quickly that changed. A change I didn't want to mention to Jack because he would just get on my case even more about Ronnie. I already know how fucked up this is. I don't need the reminder. I just need more time to figure this shit out.

After Ronnie noticed the wink Mike gave me at the diner that night, Ronnie keeps accusing me of having a three-way with Mike and his wife. A fucking three-way?! I'm not even into that shit, and I certainly wouldn't do that with Mike behind Ronnie's back. We're in a goddamn band together! And our band is hot right now. I don't want to screw that up. But his accusatory bullshit is starting to make me wonder about that since it's triggered him to have delusions of *"proof"* he says confirms I'm lying. He's apparently gone a bit nutty on me. Plus, once I give him the boot from my apartment—since I never invited him to move in in the first place—he'll probably get the guys to boot *me* from the band anyway.

I need to time this out just right.

My grad school project includes my band going into the studio to record three songs about sympathetic villains to include with my essay, my PowerPoint presentation, and my novel manuscript for my thesis. As soon as I get that CD in hand, I can give Ronnie the boot, preferably with my steel-toe boot. If I do it sooner, my project is screwed. No, my project is *not* why I started dating him—that didn't happen until after I joined the band and after Jordan kicked me in the head with his five-year lie.

Dammit, why did I add the musical part to my project? Why do I have to reach so high, always trying to go above and beyond? Just so I can fall flat on my face? But if Jordan didn't abandon me, this never would've happened. Well, I guess he didn't make the decision for me to start dating Ronnie. But still…

Man, desperation is a fucking bitch! Pushed me right into the arms of a paranoid and jealous shadow, who knew exactly what to say and when to say it.

My life sucks!

Vulnerability and desperation, man.

If Jordan hadn't flaked out on me and lied to me all those years, this never would've happened.

Sure as shit—I blame it all on him.

Yeah, maybe I don't always make the smartest choices, but…

My biological clock is ticking louder than machinegun fire and speeding up as fast as a crazy train with Casey Jones driving that bitch. With the shitty family I've got, I need to make my own, choose my own, get the hell away from the ones trying to drag me down and ruin my life.

To hell with my family! Mom is my only family. Shit, she's my best friend.

Living in the apartment above Mom's unattached garage has been a gift. Makes it easier to help her out with her big, old house and large property she can no longer take care of by herself. Paying her rent rather than some slum lord also helps her pay her bills since waitressing and bartending most of her life didn't leave her with a retirement plan. Plus, I get to see her almost every day. Yeah, sometimes she gets a bit annoying with the multiple calls a day when I'm trying to get my writing done or work on school assignments or practice music. But I can deal with that. I don't know how much time she has left, and I want to remain as close to her as I can until that dreaded day arrives.

Thank goodness Ronnie works third shift. Maybe now I can smoke enough ganga to sleep like I'm in a coma and forget about all the crap swirling around me. Looking around my apartment and seeing all his belongings now where Jordan's once were feels unnatural, unsettling. What did I ever see in him to begin with? Yeah, he said all the right things at the right time, and we do seem to have a lot in common: we love the same music, we both love horror, we've both been in a number of bands and gigged out a lot over the years, we both love to go hiking and spend time in nature. But he tries so hard to be like Jordan, it makes me wonder if he knows who he really is himself. He even plays the same instrument and loves the same metal bands. It's strange. But their personalities are miles-apart different.

Pulling open the desk drawer below my laptop, I see the corner of my favorite picture sticking out from under the packages of Sticky Notes. I slide aside the notepads to get a better look. The photo shows Jordan, our nieces Zoe and Nat, and me at a Christmas celebration at my mom's. We're all wearing ugly matching Christmas sweaters and performing "I

Wish It Was Christmas Today" from the old Saturday Night Live skit with Jimmy Fallon, Tracy Morgan, Horatio Sanz, and Chris Kattan. Jordan's holding a keyboard while Zoe plays the melody I'd taught her. I'm singing and playing acoustic guitar, and Nat stands stone-faced, though trying so hard to keep a straight face, while swaying along in Tracy Morgan's role. We barely made it through the whole song without laughing our asses off. So much fun! I miss those days.

I tuck the picture back under the Sticky Notes and close the drawer.

Jordan always tries to make people laugh. Always has a funny joke or story to tell. Always tries to help my mom any way he can. Always dependable. Nothing like Ronnie's serious and paranoid ways. Always trying to be better than others. Always wondering what others think of him, what they think of our band. Always remaking himself. Always on edge, ready to pop like an overinflated balloon. Why didn't I notice all this about him sooner? Just because we have some of the same interests doesn't mean we should be a couple. And him jumping on Satan's car was probably only for the sake of getting the band's gear back, not to do something to help me. Why was I so blind? Did all his promises of making my dreams of having a family come true and his promises of how devoted of a family man he'd be create rose-colored glasses for me?

All bullshit. Phony people stick to me like those spikey seed pods from the pricker bushes I accidentally ran through when I was a kid. Those things tore the flesh on my legs to a bloody, painful mess. I miss being a kid. Just playing and having fun. No worries. No phonies and liars.

Phony people hover around me like junkies pining for a fix.

This isn't how my life was supposed to turn out. Growing old together with Jordan, finally having that son I thought we were *both* dreaming about, watching that son grow up and take on the world, and Jordan and I making music together until our dying breaths—*that* was the plan.

But my plans always seem to go haywire.

After clicking save on the story I've been writing for the past five hours, I shut down my laptop. Good thing I took that stroll through the trails out back in the woods earlier. Spending time out there always fills me with inspiration. My story's almost submission-ready. That'll make my third story submission this month. Hopefully one of the publishers bites. It's been over six months since I subbed my first novel—to five different indie publishers—and I *still* haven't heard a peep! Feels like rejections to me.

And it sure does amp up my Imposter Syndrome. Big time. They probably never read my book. Why would they? I'm a nobody.

If I chose the wrong direction with grad school, I'm completely screwed.

I grab a drink from my practically empty fridge, pick up a packed-full bowl from the coffee table, and head to my bedroom. Ronnie's two bass guitars hang on the wall next to Jordan's side of the bed, right where Jordan's Jamaican wood-carved masks once hung. Masks we bought in Negril when we got married ten years ago. The TV remote taunts me from my nightstand. I grab it, click to the Chiller channel, and settle back against my pillow.

Underworld is playing for the umpteenth time this month. Great movie, but I can recite it almost line-by-line. With a couple more clicks, a *Supernatural* rerun appears on the screen. Yeah, I can recite every episode of this show line-by-line too, but the characters comfort me. Feels like chosen family, or best friends I've had forever.

After a few tokes and half a mimosa, I crash, fast asleep, and find myself entrenched in a nightmare-memory—part memory, *all* nightmare—unable to escape.

Down in Aiden's underground hideaway-escape-hatch under his grandmother's trailer, the trapdoor creaks open overhead. Aiden's sinister grin peers over the edge. The beer stench reeks on his breath as he laughs.

Instant monster—just add beer.

With a guitar string wrapped around one of his hands—the low e— he jumps down into the tunnel-hole beside me. Stroking my long, tangled hair, he leans close and whispers into my ear. His beer breath sets my nerves on fire.

"My perfect little angel. So pure. So innocent. You think you know best? You think you're better than me?" His voice changes to a growl and increases in volume when he says, "Think you can flush my kilo and get away with it? Think again, wench!"

Grabbing a clump of my hair, he yanks my head back and tries to make out with me. I force my lips into a tight, flat line, refusing to let him in. I try to wiggle free, try to pull away, though I have nowhere to go to get away. In the dream, there's no secret tunnel leading out to the backyard like in real life.

He's so much bigger and stronger than me, fighting him is futile. I've tried many times before, only to have it end in more pain for me. I've tried numerous times to leave him, but all attempts ended with him causing harm to my friends and family. With his cunning ways, he has evaded arrest so many times I've lost count. All these real-life-thoughts swirl round my nightmare-mind.

When he stops slobbering all over my face, he releases my hair and wraps the guitar string around my neck.

"How do you like that? Strangled to death by the string from the thing that takes all your time away from me."

His lurid laughter makes my ears bleed.

He yanks the string so hard, so tight, dizziness consumes me.

"This is called poetic justice, my perfect little angel."

The phone rings, saving me from nightmare-murder. Drenched in sweat, heart racing so fast and so hard it pounds in my head, I open my eyes and look at the clock.

Three A.M.

I hope Mom's okay!

As soon as I grab the cordless phone, I see Ronnie's cell number displayed on the caller ID.

What's so important he needs to call me from work this early in the morning? Doesn't he have some cinnamon rolls to bake?

Dammit! I just want to get some rest for a change.

"Hey, Ronnie. Everything okay?" I cough, take a sip of my drink.

"Hi. What do you mean? Why wouldn't everything be okay?"

"Uh…I don't know. Maybe because you're calling me from work at three in the morning."

"So. You're usually up at this time writing or doing schoolwork. Do you have company or something? Who's there?"

"What? It's three in the morning. No one's here except Sam and Dean Winchester."

"What the fuck!? You've got *two* guys over there?! I fucking knew…"

"Whoa…Slow down. I'm watching TV. *Supernatural.* They're characters on the show. No one's here. *Jesus.* Enough with the accusations. What do you need? Why are you calling me from work?"

Jordan would've laughed at my Sam and Dean reference. He knows who they are. This is our show.

"Some guy just threw a trash can through the front door of the bakery and smashed out the glass. Cops just left. I had to fill out a statement and everything."

My glass bowl tumbles onto the floor, spilling ganga everywhere, as I sit up bolt straight. "Holy shit! No way? Seriously? Are you okay?"

Wait. Another broken window? What the hell is going on? Could it be Satan again? But he said it was a guy.

Aiden?

"Did you see what he looks like? Did he come in? What did he want? Did the cops get him?"

"Yeah, it's all good now. They're gone. I called my boss, told her. But that's not why I'm calling."

Why does he sound so calm? Some freak just smashed out the front door of the bakery where he works alone all night. Something like that would normally freak *anyone* out.

"Oh…Okay. Happy to hear you're alright. What's up? Is your car acting up again? Do you need me to pick you up in the morning?"

"No. Car's fine. I just…One of the cops…One of those fucking pigs is related to your ex-husband. Did *you* send him here? Are you trying to fuck with me?"

I fling the covers off and jump out of bed, heat rising, face flush. "What the hell are you talking about?" Groggy and confused as a motherfucker, I start pacing my small apartment. Bedroom to living room to kitchen and back. "Jordan doesn't have any cops in his family. What the fuck?!"

"Yeah, well this guy looked just like him but without long hair. And his name was Officer Jordan. He's your fucking brother-in-law. Just admit it. Jordan sent him here to fuck with me. Why the fuck won't he just go away already?"

"Um…Hate to break it to ya, Ronnie, but my brother-in-law is a fucking math teacher not a cop. And *Jordan* is that cop's *last* name. They go by last names not first names. I wouldn't be Officer Dahlia. And why would Jordan's brother have the same name as him. His name is Corey. What the hell is *really* going on? Did some guy really smash out the front door? Why are you calling me? I need to get up for work soon."

"Yeah, well, I was listening to the radio before that guy showed up, and the DJ kept telling me Jordan was coming, Jordan was watching me, and I needed to call the cops before the glass shatters. Oh, and I ordered Rosetta Stone for you."

"Wait. What? The DJ was talking to you? They were talking to you about Jordan?" I shake my head, rub my forehead. What the hell is this nutjob talking about? It's too freaking early in the morning to deal with this shit. What kind of game is he playing with me? Is he trying to get me to slip up, thinking I'm cheating on him, got some guy over here while he's at work? Maybe he thinks Jordan is here. "And you bought me Rosetta Stone? Why?"

"Yeah. I ordered it from an infomercial. I had the little TV on before the radio. The commercial came on. They kept telling me I needed to buy it. It's for you. That will make you happy, right? You said you've always wanted to learn Italian. So, I ordered it for you. Aren't you excited?"

What the hell is going on? Am I still dreaming? Is this really happening right now?

Releasing an irritated sigh, I step over to the window and pull the tapestry aside, look out into the driveway. My truck, with all the bumper stickers on the back window, is parked in front of the garage. Mom's pickup truck is parked in front of the walkway to her front door. No one else is here. The towering trees surrounding the property sway in the moonlight. Their shadows dance, wave, and shiver.

"Well, thank you for thinking of me, but Ronnie, you know money is tight right now. You told me yesterday you're behind on your car payment. You shouldn't've bought that for me. You need to return it. Call them back, cancel your order." I plop down on the bench in front of the window. "And what about the door of your work? Is the whole front of the bakery open to the outside? Is your boss coming to seal it up?"

"It's all boarded up. She already sent her husband to cover it."

Scratching my head, I stand and walk back to my bedroom. This shit isn't adding up. What's really going on over there? At my bureau, I pull out some clothes.

"Well, I can't imagine they'll be opening with that busted front door. Why are you still working? Why haven't they sent you home yet?"

"Time to make the donuts." Ronnie's sing-song voice sounds flat. He laughs a tight, un-humored chuckle at the retro reference to the old

Dunkin' Donuts commercials. "Okay, I'll call and cancel my order. But I thought you wanted to learn Italian? Aren't you happy?"

Holy shit! What is he talking about? Why does he not sound concerned about what happened with that guy smashing out the window of the door? Something weird is going on.

"Happy? Honestly…I'm half asleep and trying to figure out what is going on over there. So, you still have to finish your shift? The bakery is still opening at six? Even though the front door is all smashed to shit? Or are you heading out soon?"

He laughs again but still doesn't sound amused. "You just said it yourself…I'm behind on my car payments. I can't leave work early. I need to get my hours." *Clinking* and *clanging* drift through the phone. "I've got three huge pans of cinnamon rolls to put in the oven. Of course I'm working. I'll cancel the Rosetta Stone. So, no one's over there with you?"

As I'm pulling on a pair of jeans, I balance the cordless phone on my shoulder. "*No*, Ronnie. I'm alone. The only one here with me is Sam and Dean *on the TV*. Mom's next door, sleeping, I assume. It *is* fucking three in the morning." Shifting the phone to my other shoulder, I pull open another drawer and grab a hoodie. "Ronnie, if you're alright, I really need to go to bed. Four o' clock comes real fucking early."

"Four? Why you gettin' up so early?"

"You already know why—I get up early to do more writing before work. I still need to polish up my manuscript before it's due at my last school residency in a few months." I stuff my feet into my Docs beside the front door. "Goodnight, Ronnie. Get back to work. I need to go to sleep. I'll see you later."

We hang up.

That studio session can't get here quick enough. I really can't take his shit anymore. This is fucking crazy!

I grab my truck keys off the hook beside the door, thunder down the stairs, and march out into the crisp October night.

My drive to the bakery flashes by in blur of confusion and exhaustion.

The twinkle of the red streetlight shimmers across the black hood of my SUV. All the parking lots of The Maine Mall and the shopping plazas around it sit empty. No customers. No employees. No one.

It's three-thirty in the morning.

I yawn. I guess no writing for me this morning. I'm immersed in Crazy Town instead.

The bakery where Ronnie works is only two more streetlights away. If that front door window isn't really broken, we're going to have a serious issue.

Rather than pulling into the front parking lot of the bakery, I shut off my headlights and turn left just before it and circle around the back.

Getting only a partial look at the front door, I don't see any plywood covering the window. But it's dark, and I didn't get a clear view. Only a couple dim interior security lights are on. I need to get closer.

I pull into the parking lot of the plaza behind Ronnie's work. His little red car sits parked beside the backdoor of the bakery.

Hiding under the hood of my black sweatshirt, I quietly open my door, step outside, and ease the door closed. Sticking close to the outside wall of his work, I circle around to the front of the building. I step up onto the sidewalk leading to the patio tables and chairs and the front door, and I now confirm that no plywood covers the door of the bakery. But a window *is* shattered.

Not the window of the front door.

The large window beside the door is gone, busted right out.

Shattered glass is everywhere out here. All over the tables and chairs and cement, reaching all the way to the tarmac of the lot.

What the hell is going on? Why is there so much glass outside if the guy threw the trashcan into the bakery?

Maybe that's possible. I don't know.

I need to move closer to get a better look. If I can find whatever he threw, find the trashcan—because obviously nothing was cleaned up after the incident for some reason—then I'll know for sure if he's lying. But with all these big windows out front, he'll probably see me sneaking around. The untrusting girlfriend.

Oh shit. A dining room light turned on.

I slip back away from the sidewalk, hide around the corner from the front patio. Ronnie must be coming out of the back kitchen. What if he's coming outside to finally clean up this mess? A mess he said was already cleaned up.

Isn't that what he said? Maybe he said his boss *was sending* her husband over, not that she *already sent* him over. I'm so freaking tired, maybe I heard him wrong? Or I'm remembering wrong? Whatever he said, it still doesn't make any sense.

Dammit!

I need to get out of here before he sees me.

♫ ▮ ♪

Four-thirty in the morning, my fingers *clickety clack* across the keyboard at a rapid speed. With no time or ability to sleep after checking on Ronnie's sketchy story and seeing the broken window, I threw myself into my writing when I got back home. I can't afford to call out of work, and I need to get ready at 6:00. That gives me an hour and a half to bleed across the page.

Better than bleeding across the floor from slicing my wrists or blowing my brains out. Razor blades and bullets: great song title!

But nope. I chose door number three.

Write.

Maybe I'll put that song title to use when I get home from work tonight.

Checking up on my multiple novel submissions could've waited. That ate up fifteen minutes of my limited time this morning. Don't know why I did that before diving into my writing. Always makes me anxious, sometimes defeated. Still no replies. Waiting for replies is agonizing! Don't publishers realize they're holding onto our children, our creations, while we're left worried if those children will ever have the chance to become part of the world?

The wait time's so long, I might die before ever hearing back.

Dramatic much, Dahl? Suck it up. You chose this path. This is how the game's played.

I at least need to stay alive long enough to get to the bottom of Ronnie's story. It's driving me mad with confusion! Yeah, I could've called the police, *again*, about the broken window, try to figure this out right now, but I don't have time for Ronnie's mindfuck games. He can deal with that. It's his workplace, and he's a grownup. I have to go to work and get my school work done.

Smashing my head against the wall repeatedly also crossed my mind after getting home from the bakery and realizing Ronnie isn't just paranoid, jealous, and confused about his identity.

He's playing mind games with me. Trying to catch me in a lie. His behavior reminds me so much of Aiden's from back in my teens it makes me sick to my stomach.

Did I unwittingly let another Aiden into my life?

All Ronnie's belongings surround me as I just keep writing.

The manipulative sonofabitch lives with me!

I'm in a band with him.

A band that's scheduled to record in the studio next week.

A band who's helping me finish my grad school thesis project.

A project that's due in six weeks.

What the hell have I gotten myself into this time?

"Well, look what the cat dragged in. You look like dogshit, Dahl. You alright?" Jack stands beside the Gator with the motor running and all the burial equipment loaded into the back. Smoke trails up from the end of the cancer stick hanging from the corner of his mouth.

I always wonder how he keeps that nail-for-his-coffin from torching his long beard and mustache.

"Didn't sleep. Ronnie's fucking with my head. I worked on my thesis early this morning. Don't ask any more questions. I don't have the energy to talk about it right now." I grab my travel coffee mug from the cup holder and my work gloves off the passenger's seat. After slamming my truck door, I jump behind the wheel of the Gator. "Let's go dig this fucking grave and bury someone already."

Thirty minutes later, shovel in hand, I smash the tip of the spade into the dirt wall of the open grave over and over, imaging all that dirt and rocks I heave over my shoulder is all the bullshit from my life that keeps dragging me down and holding me back and clogging my brain.

"Why the frig is your sister hanging out with Aiden? That's what I want to know." Jack jumps down from the seat of the backhoe-excavator combo and grabs another shovel from the back of the Gator.

I pause, swipe my arm across my sweaty forehead, then roll my eyes up to look at Jack standing on the edge of the open grave, smoke curling up into the cloudless azure sky from another cigarette hanging from his lips.

"*Stop* calling that psycho my sister. And yeah, great question. Probably a new coke customer for her and her loser husband. Anything for money with those shysters." I slam the shovel into a clump of rocks and dirt. Clanging metal rings out as sharp pain shoots up both of my arms. "Damn rocks!" I pause again and lean on the handle of the spade. "Leave it to her to buddy up with another psycho *and* the abusive dickhead from the worst time of my life. That psycho thought he could ruin me?" An irritated laugh shoots out of me as I start digging again. "Fuckface never should've underestimated me. Thought I was his 'little angel'? Ha! He never really knew me *at all*."

"Why the hell the cops can't get a search warrant to see if your gear is at her house or his blows my mind. Especially since everyone in your band saw her car *and* her license plate."

"Jack, we fucking *chased* them to her car. So, the guys also *saw* both of them, not just the car. Plain as fucking day. Yeah, Aiden thought his hood would hide him, but running made that thing fall right off. We all saw him. The guys may not know who he is, but they all gave the same description to the police: long, reddish-auburn hair, burly build, about five-foot-eleven. There shouldn't be *anything* holding up the fucking pigs from finding our gear before those assholes sell it. But…here we are." I stop digging, lean the shovel against my thigh, and hold my arms out to the side. "Don't forget who I am. Shit always goes wrong for me. Nothing ever happens as it should in my life. If there's a way for shit to go haywire, even the *slimmest* chance, it will."

With a fling of my arm, I toss the shovel up out of the hole. Grabbing the grassy edge of the open grave, I jab the steel toe of my work boot into the rocky wall and haul my ass up and out. After I grab my iced coffee from the cup holder of the Gator, I plop down on the grass next to the pile of gravel beside the grave. "Man, it's smoldering hot today for freaking October." I shake my head. "I guess Hell *has* finally risen." Sweat trickles down my temples. "Man, Maine and its bipolar seasons…Wanna know what the weather's gonna be for the day? Step outside and find out."

I tip my mug toward Jack, who pauses from digging and looks at me with concern creased across his forehead. "Speaking of psychos and Hell—Have you told Ronnie to get the fuck out of your apartment and go back to his own place yet?"

"Damn it, Jack! I want to. Believe me. I need to find our gear and get the band's studio session over with next week. I *need* those tunes to finish my presentation for my thesis." Leaning to the side, I reach over and clean out the leaves from around the headstone beside the grave we've been digging.

"Is it so important that you'll risk your own safety and wellbeing?" Jack heaves another shovel full of dirt out of the grave.

"What do you mean 'safety'?" I sit back upright, take a haul off my coffee, and stare at him.

What is he talking about? I never told him about what happened last night with the call from Ronnie and what I saw when I drove to his work. I don't want to even think about it, let alone talk about it. It's too maddening. And I have too much on my plate right now. My mind can't handle more. I texted my bestie, Allie, before I came in, but she's busy pulling a double with her job and doing an overnight caring for her disabled brother. Hopefully she'll have time to get back to me later. And Beth's out of town, going to a metal show down in Worcester. Now I'm just too tired to deal with any of this. I just want to forget about it. Give my mind a break.

Jack shakes his head and keeps digging, shaping the perimeter of the hole to fit the cement vault for the casket. "Dahl, I'm a guy. I know his type. You're not safe with him. I worry about you." He stops and looks up at me. "You *need* to get him out of your place as soon as possible."

"Shit. You sound just like my mother."

His eyebrows arch up over his safety sunglasses. "Oh, so your mom doesn't think you're safe either?"

I laugh, though I'm not amused. Looking down, I pick at the grass while I tell him, "A couple weeks ago when I told her Ronnie was taking me to Salem for my annual fall visit, she made me write down the make and model of his car and the license plate number." I glance at him over my sunglasses. "She was worried he wouldn't bring me back. I just laughed at her. But now…I don't know." I turn away, keep picking at the grass and fallen leaves.

"What? You think she was on to something, don't you?"

No words come out of me.

"What aren't you telling me, Dahl? Has he hurt you? If that motherfucker lays a hand on you, I'll…"

"Hell no, Jack! No one lays a freaking hand on me and gets away with it! I learned my lesson the hard way. Aiden trained me well; I'll give him that. I will *never* take abuse like that ever again." I look away, start cleaning more leaves out from around the headstone next to me. "It's just that…something really messed up happened last night, woke me right out of a recurring nightmare." I tell him what happened with Ronnie's phone call and me driving to his work to check up on his story.

"Holy shit, Dahl! He's fucking crazy! You really need to get him out of your place. *Now.*"

"Yeah, but Jack…that's never happened before. He's nothing like that normally. I think he was just so exhausted from working third shift and getting no sleep. I think it's really messing with him and…"

"Stop making excuses for him. He's a freaking psycho and you know…"

A little red car pulls up on the gravel road beside the family plot we're working in. It pulls closer and the window rolls down.

"Hey, Dahl." Ronnie holds up a big, freshly baked cinnamon roll. "Can you take a break? I brought your favorite." A warm smile spreads across his pale face.

I turn toward Jack and cock my head. "See?" Standing up, I brush dirt off my jeans and grab my coffee. "I'm going to take a fifteen. Cool?"

Jack nods, turns away, goes back to shaping the newly dug grave.

♫ █ ♪

Sitting in Ronnie's passenger seat in the back of the cemetery behind the old crypt where they used to keep the bodies stored before the burials, back before refrigeration and all the luxuries of the modern age, I pick and peel apart the huge, warm cinnamon roll while Ronnie talks band logistics. Though the sweet, gooey pastry smells and tastes delicious, it's hard to digest. After receiving Ronnie's phone call and discovering what I saw at his work, I've felt sick to my stomach.

I haven't even heard a word he's said. Well, I've *heard* him, but I haven't actually *listened*. Shock and confusion consume my mind as I wonder how he's able to act so casual, like nothing weird happened earlier this morning. Just another night at the bakery, making tasty treats to distract people from his mind games. To distract *me* is more like it. But I haven't forgotten. How can I? It's too messed up to drop it and forget.

"Ronnie, I gotta ask you something," I say in the middle of him still speaking about the upcoming studio session or gig or something. "What the hell really happened at your work last night? Did some guy really smash out the door window with a trashcan? Did you really have to call the cops and fill out a statement?"

"What? Did someone really bust out the door? Yeah, it happened just like I told you." He says this like whatever happened is a common occurrence I should have no reason to question, while his expression remains blank and difficult to read. His eyes look everywhere but at me. "Why would I lie about that?" He looks out the driver's side window, fusses with his long bangs.

"Well, you're acting all calm, like you're not concerned about it. Like it's not unusual or anything." Trying to will him to turn around and face me, I watch for any telltale signs of him lying.

He has already displayed common signs of someone who might be lying: answering a question with a question; not giving any details; refusing to look me in the eyes; shifty eye movements; turning away from me; fussing with his hair. But that's not proof. I need proof.

Screw this!

"Ronnie, *look* at me."

He turns toward me, still wearing a blank expression. But he looks past me out the passenger side window behind my head.

Shit. Should I tell him I drove to his work to see if he was making shit up last night? If I do, he'll think I don't trust him.

But I don't trust him!

No. It's best to bide my time before telling him. I need to do more digging, figure this shit out.

"What did the cops do when they showed up at your work? Did your boss come in too? Who cleaned up the mess? You said someone boarded up the door?"

"Wow. That's a lot of questions all at once." Ronnie turns away, looks down, appearing distraught. "I'm trying not to think too much about it." After a pause, he turns to me and looks me straight in the eyes. "I was really freaked out last night. *Not* something I want to remember." The sunlight shimmers in his eyes, making it look as though he might cry. He grasps my hand and gives it a gentle squeeze. "Getting to see you this morning really helps calm me down." Reaching his other hand over, he wipes icing off my cheek, licks his finger, then leans in and kisses the same spot. "Now you taste extra sweet." A timid, childlike smile emerges as he pulls away.

Maybe he is telling the truth. Maybe I took what I saw out of context and made unfair assumptions about the uncanny event. Plus, I was in a dead sleep when he called, so maybe I'm remembering the conversation wrong. Or maybe I heard him wrong. I was so confused and exhausted.

He reaches into his pants pocket and pulls out an envelope. "I forgot to tell you last night." After unsealing the envelope, he pulls out two tickets. "I got us tickets to go see *Sweeny Todd* on stage in Portsmouth this weekend." Waving them in the air, his smile widens and his eyes twinkle.

Quite the change in demeanor. Maybe a date night will be good for us. Give us a chance to forget about all the crazy bullshit surrounding us lately.

But what about his overdue car payment and his gear he might need to replace? Those tickets must've been expensive. But he looks so happy. I don't want to ruin his mood by bringing up bills and boring responsibilities.

I grab the tickets. "No way! That is freaking awesome! I had no idea that play was even going on. How did you know I'd love to see this?"

"You're a horror girl. Duh." He gets playful, laughing and shaking his head all willy-nilly. Then he sticks his tongue out, like he'd be crazy for not knowing I'd love to go see this play. "Plus, you love plays. It was a no-brainer."

Yes, both great points.

But wait.

How does he know I love plays? I've never told him that.

Oh well. He's in a good mood, not acting all jealous and accusey. And it's a relief he's not still accusing Jordan of having a cop-brother and sending him to his work to mess with him. I'll take it. Maybe in the chaos of the moment he really did think it was Jordan's brother? Afterall, he hasn't brought that part up again, even though he was so mad about it when he had called. He might realize how wrong he was and just wants to forget he made that mistake, and he might feel embarrassed about it. The poor guy never gets enough sleep working third shift; it's no wonder why he sometimes can't think straight. I don't want to make him feel bad by bringing it up again. And maybe I did mention I like plays and just forget about it. It's time to have some fun and forget about my problems. I lean over, hug him.

"Thank you for being so thoughtful. I'm wicked excited!"

Yes, the idea of seeing the play excites me, but going with Ronnie…The surprise *is* thoughtful, but something feels off.

Whatever. More craziness is not what I want to dig up. Maybe I need to lighten up and have some fun.

I lean back, peel another piece from the cinnamon roll, start eating again. My break is almost over, and it's close to the end of my short cemetery shift too. Wish I could get more hours. I've been begging Jack to schedule me for more, but the old sexist millionaire prick who heads the board of directors doesn't want "the girl" working fulltime. We're too delicate and weak to perform too much *man*-ual labor. Yeah, he's another motherfucker who can kiss my fed-up ass. But that's a whole other problem I don't have the energy to deal with right now.

I wish I hadn't lost my teaching job back in June. Working as a long-term sub and teaching creative writing was great, until I advocated for a student who was wronged by the principal, not allowed to win *Student of the Month* even though all the teachers had voted for him. I was hoping that gig was going to turn into a permanent teaching position, but I guess that's what I get for speaking up for what's right. This cemetery gig fell into my lap right when I was desperate for a job; with Jordan moved out, I didn't have the luxury of having time to go without a paycheck while searching for something better. And the cemetery is only five minutes from my house. I'd love to find a better gig, but that takes time, and time is in short supply at the moment. I just need to last a few more months until graduation, then I can get a better job. I just need to hang on a little longer. Hopefully I can land a good job before my damn student loan payments kick in six months after graduation. Damn you, Jordan, for putting me in this position! I never would've signed up for this if I'd known you were going to flake on me.

Ronnie mentions something about trying to find our gear, or looking for used gear, or something. I don't know. We'll figure something out. Maybe Jack's pawn shop idea. With everything going on, my thoughts keep swirling, making it hard to focus.

Why does drama surround me everywhere I turn? And I'm starting to see a common denominator in each situation—men. Well, except for Satan. But she *did* pull in a man from my past to help her torment me. So, yeah…men suck! At least the ones I've met.

A tightness forms in the pit of my stomach and the middle of my chest. Slight nausea gurgles in my gut. An ache radiates from the base of my neck down my back, shooting out tendrils of tension and needle-like pain through my limbs. My head feels like an echo chamber, muffled and tinny, ringing in my ears. A vision hits me, one looking down at us sitting in this car right now, like an out of body vision. The sudden need to escape fills me. A rapid pounding knocks against the inside of my skull. What the fuck is happening? Is this what an anxiety attack feels like?

I shake my head and roll the window down. "Whew, it's stuffy in here." I take in a deep breath of fresh air.

Man, going home and losing myself in my school project sounds like a great idea to help pull me out of this, make me forget all my troubles. More research and writing about sympathetic villains…Ha! Maybe that will help me figure out Ronnie, if in fact he is a villain. Or maybe I'm just paranoid from all my studies about this type of character, not to mention my past with lunatic-Aiden.

Hmm…No wonder why I have a fascination with the character type I'm writing about.

Well, I also need to practice for our studio session next week—that should certainly help me relieve some of this stress, shake off this weirdness, and release some pent-up rage. And now I've got that new song idea: Razor Blades and Bullets needs to come to life. Good thing Jordan bought that small practice amp for my last birthday.

Thankfully, Ronnie won't be at my place. His mom's working today, so he'll probably go to his parents' house to watch their dog.

"Well, don't forget, if you want to have a baby, we need to get all the date nights in that we can before that happens." With a beaming smile, he reaches over and squeezes my knee.

A sudden vise-grip sensation hits my whole body, making it hard to swallow the bite of pastry in my mouth. My stomach churns.

I *do* want a baby. And at 37, I'm running out of freaking time. But…

Jordan.

All my visions of my family, my future, even my music—Jordan appears in every one of them.

My excited mood to go to the play crashes. I stuff it down deep, smile, and say, "I've really gotta get back to work now. Break's over."

He leans over, kisses my cheek again. "Yeah, I gotta get to my folks' place and walk Toby. I'll be home for dinner before my shift tonight." His warm expression grows gushy and overly emotional as he says, "*Our* home." A manic smile spreads wide across his sunken-in cheeks, clashing with his watery puppy dog eyes.

In my mind, those eyes bulge and swirl in chaotic spirals as his head lolls around in a crazy, trippy manner *Clockwork Orange* style.

Holy shit, what have I gotten myself into? Is this really happening?

I turn away, blink a few times, brush away the image from my spiraling thoughts.

His puppy dog eyes remain riveted on me when I turn back to face him.

I need space.

I need to get away.

I don't want to be here anymore.

This cemetery shift can't get over with soon enough. I need to get back into a creative space, my shedding-shadows space. Write a new tune, crank my guitar, and release some tension. Escape all the crazy for a bit. But focusing on anything right now…I don't know.

A sick, suffocating feeling overwhelms me. An emptiness at my core, hollow. How can emptiness hurt like this?

Thoughts spin.

Before sunrise at Ronnie's work. Shattered glass, like thousands of shiny lies, strewn across the pavement.

My last fight with Jordan. Yelling. Crying. Pain in my chest. Dreams, like raging tidal waves, crashing down around me.

How could he do this to me? After 10 years married, 15 together. How could he?

Today. Tuesday. Jordan's day off.

That motherfucker's five-year lie pushed me right into this mess.

I can't focus.

Man, I really need a drink.

Once Jack and I finish prepping this grave, I'm beelining it to…

Under the strange heat of the October sun, I empty my mind and jump back into the open grave.

Jack turns around and looks at me, mouth parted, about to speak. I hold up my hand.

"Let's just forget about him and get back to work."

He clamps his lips shut and nods. "You got it."

As I slam the spade over and over again into the walls of this final resting place for bones, digging out rocks and hucking them over my shoulder, muscles aching and screaming, sweat drenches every inch of my body. It seeps out of my pores, and every swipe across my forehead feels like I'm wiping away my worries. I refuse to think about any of it right now.

Just move.

Mind blank.

Breath the fresh air.

Feel the sun on my skin.

And keep moving.

Two straight hours of intense physical labor later, I punch the clock and head on home.

After a quick shower to wash away the day, I take my landline phone off the hook, shut off my cell's notifications, do a few stretches, and go to my music room. Still no return call from Allie, which really sucks. I could definitely use someone to talk to. Mom's not home to lend an ear either. But at least I have music to help me escape, and...

No distractions.

The setting sun shimmers through the window above my practice amp. Orange and fuchsia paint the sky around wisps of gossamer clouds. Lengthening shadows of tree branch arms stretch and reach and wave across the ground. Standing in a beam of sunshine, breathing in the light, I try imaging that light filling me with positive energy.

I strap on my guitar, tune up, plug in, flip the switch and start noodling. "Razor Blades and Bullets" tumbles around my mind, chasing rhythms, searching for a melody to weave into song. As I ride a wave of a catchy riff, lyrics begin forming on the tip of my tongue, sailing on the notes spilling from the tips of my fingers.

Razor blades and bullets, weaponry of the mind
Tripping through life, always wanting to hide

Razor blades and bullets, weaponry of the mind
Battling shadows, always follow behind
Razor blades and bullets, no longer part of the hive
Razor blades and bullets…

Word after word,
Line after line,
Verse after verse,
Riff after riff,
Scene after scene,
I write.

I lose myself in the music of each line, the poetry, the actions, the story. The only things occupying my mind.

After recording a rough idea on my phone's voice memo, I jot down lyrics, chord changes, and a melody line in my songbook. My pen dances across the pages, filling each staff of music with my visions.

Songs: stories set to music.

My sore neck and wrists throb and ache by the time I finish and finally look up. The sky outside the window no longer shimmers with vibrant colors. The silvery sheen of the moon fills the forest around my home. Diamonds twinkle across the black canvas of the night sky. Tree shadows twirl and sway with the wind. Whip-o-wills sing their nighttime lullabies.

I yawn, click off my amp, set my guitar in its stand, and glance at my watch. It's long past dinner. Ronnie's work shift began over an hour ago. He must've eaten dinner at his parents' place. Probably left a ton of messages on my cell by now. But I refuse to check.

I shut off my phone and forbid myself from replacing the receiver of the landline back into its cradle.

The quiet embraces me.

I eat a small, healthy dinner, meditate, and go to bed, trying my hardest not to think about what horrors await me tomorrow. I close my eyes to darkness, hoping for a visit from the baby boy of my wanted future rather than nightmares from my haunted past and present.

Determination to find our music equipment kicks me into gear and drives me through the day. Our studio session needs to go off without a hitch. Once that's past me, the time to clean out my dumpster fire of a life sets into motion.

After the third pawn shop of the day and traipsing along one cobblestone street after another, we've discovered not only my Mesa amp, but also three quarters of the rest of our band's gear that was stolen. Now, out on the sidewalk at Longfellow Square, I pull out the lead detective's business card, along with my cell, and dial him up.

"Yes, that's right. Not only are there signature flaws—dings and scratches—that we have documented in pictures matching the gear in these three shops, but we also double checked the serial numbers. Everything matches."

Mike's at my shoulder, his long beard brushing against my shoulder as he listens in on what Detective Blake says. His gear's also irreplaceable, at least not available brand new. Eagerness to retrieve our belongings surges through him as much as it does me, I'm sure. Buckdancer's Choice still sells Ronnie's and Kyle's gear, though needing to rebuy everything would take a while to save money for. Mike hangs on every word coming through the phone. I do too.

And, yep, there it is—Ronnie's giving me the stink eye.

Friendship running through a band helps hold the band together, at least that's what I've always believed. But Ronnie obviously thinks my friendship with the guys—specifically with Mike for some reason—runs deeper than platonic camaraderie. I don't understand. We only hangout when it involves the whole band. We're a crew. A team. Well, that's what I've hoped to build with these guys.

No doubt Ronnie's jealous streak links directly to the fact that he swooped in when my marriage was at its weakest point, when I was at my most vulnerable and desperate, and tried to steal me away. But I don't have time to deal with his bullshit right now. I need to get my fucking gear back!

With a huge smile and shooter-marble-sized eyes, Mike pulls away and slaps Kyle on the shoulder. "He's coming to get our shit back, man. Can you believe it?"

"Hell yeah, dude!" Kyle raises his hands and looks up to the clear sky. "I can't fucking believe it!"

Mike and Kyle high-five, fist bump, shoulder bump. All their excitement comes out in playful jabs at one another. Ronnie still stands staring at me, loaded eyes and tight expression. Why can't this guy take the win and be happy, at least for a moment?

I slap high-fives and pound fist bumps with Mike and Kyle. When I turn to Ronnie for more of the same, he turns away and starts reading flyers on the sidewalk billboard nearby. Tension tingles through me. Mine or his, I'm not sure.

Whatever. He can wallow in his misery all he wants. As for me, I'm on a mission his assholery cannot thwart. We've got tunes to record soon.

By dinner time, my gear sits in the back of my Jimmy as I'm heading home. At least one thing has worked out for me. Maybe now my life will take a turn toward better days.

♫ ◼ ♪

"Mom, what's going on? I thought you'd be excited about the news. *I* sure as hell am."

After unloading my amp and hauling it upstairs to my apartment, I ran next door to tell Mom the good news and to bring her the groceries she had called and asked me to pick up for her on my way home. I found her and her friend Jody sitting at the kitchen table, with a deck of tarot cards and a quartz crystal sitting in the middle, a coffee in front of both of them, each looking like *their* valuables got stolen. And Mom keeps scratching her head incessantly.

Were their tarot readings that depressing and foreboding?

I sit down between them. "What the hell's going on?" I turn toward Mom. "What's wrong with your head? Why do you keep scratching?" I lean closer. "Holy shit! You're bleeding! And there's a bald spot there?" I reach over and gently pull her hand away from her head. There's blood under her fingernails and on her fingertips. "Ma, you've gotta stop that." I gently place her hand on the table.

Jody hands me a napkin.

"I can't even believe what she's puttin' me through," Mom says without elaborating. She stubs out her cigarette butt in the ashtray, puts her nasal cannula back on, and takes a deep breath of pure oxygen.

I hand her the napkin. "What? Who?" I turn to Jody. "What's she talking about?"

"Ya sista. She sto'med in heah earlier when Alex and Dan were heah to give ya motha the receipts for the materials they bought to fix ya motha's apa'tment building. We were all just shootin' the shit ova coffees, then Sarah threw open the front door, swearing up a sto'm, then came into the kitchen and punched Alex in the face. Told ya motha the guys a'e rippin' her off and buying shit for themselves with her Home Depot credit cahd."

Tears threaten to fall from my mother's eyes. She starts scratching her head again and says, "Doesn't that idiot realize I get all the credit card statements? I'd know if they were ripping me off. She's still pissed off I hired them to do the work instead of letting her husband do it to work off the money they still owe me from loaning them the downpayment for their house *and* for bailing her out of jail for that fight she started at the bar a couple years ago." A derisive laugh escapes her. "No wonder why The Devil landed in the past for my reading. I never should've let them borrow all that money."

No surprise. Even Mom sees my former sibling as evil.

As I pull her hand away from her head again, I'm furious. "I hope you called the cops this time?"

"No, she didn't. I told her to. But she won't. You should heah all the horrible messages ya sista's left on the machine already. I think it's up to at least five by now." Jody gets up and goes to double-check the doors, making sure they're locked. "I already told ya motha I'm lockin' these damn doors every time I come ova to visit. I'm not lettin' that shithead do this to my friend anymore. The'e's not much I can do to stop her, but I can at least do that." She grabs a dish towel from the oven door handle, runs the corner under warm water at the sink, and comes back to wipe the blood from my mother's scalp. "Look what she's doing to ya, Penny. There's no need of this."

"If you're not going to do it, I'll call the fucking cops *right now*." I get up and head to the phone in the dining room. Before I grab the receiver, it rings. The caller ID displays Satan's number. "It's her. Should I answer it?"

"No…Yeah, go ahead. Let's see what she has to say for herself."

Over my shoulder, I see Mom grab her coffee mug with a shaky hand. Coffee spills over the edge, and Jody hands her another napkin to dry off the tablecloth.

"Hello."

"Why the fuck are *you* answering the phone? Put Ma on." Her venom shoots through the receiver, poisoning my ear.

"Hello to you too, *sis*."

"Just put the gullible traitor on the fucking phone."

"Um, do you realize Mom's over here scratching bald spots in her head because of what you're doing to her. This really needs to stop. *You* need to stop. She's your freaking mother. Treat her with some respe…"

"Fuck you, you stupid cunt! How dare you talk to me like that? I'll put you ten feet under if you even think of speaking to me like…"

It takes all my willpower to remain calm and keep an angry tone out of my voice. She wants me to stoop to her level, so she can put some sort of *blame* on me. I refuse. "Are you listening to yourself? Do you hear the insanity coming out of you? Mom can't deal with all this stress. You know she's been sick. Her freaking oxygen delivery's coming today, and here you are…"

"I'll fucking beat you senseless, you spoiled little bitch! Put *my* mother on the phone. *Now*!"

As she continues screaming into my ear, I hold the cordless receiver away from my head. Jody and Mom look at me, mouths agape. They can hear the craziness all the way in the kitchen. I look at them and shrug. Then, I hang up the phone.

Ten seconds later, the phone rings again. I let the answering machine take it. And, yep, it's her again. More screaming. More swearing. More venom. More threats to kill me. Nothing new.

No one answers it.

The phone rings again and again. At the end of every string of rings, the psycho leaves another message full of threats and name-calling. By the end of my twenty-minute visit with my mother, she has received fifteen calls and fifteen more nasty answering machine messages from the person people expect me to call my sister.

If she acted like a sister, if she'd never assaulted me, if she didn't steal from me, if she didn't try to destroy my property, if she treated Mom and me with respect, and if she didn't feel joy every time something bad happens to me—like when she smiled at the news of my separation from Jordan—maybe I would still call her sister like I used to. Like when we were close many years ago.

But no. I no longer call her my sister. I no longer call her by her given name.

She's Satan.

As I pull Mom's hand away from her head again, Jody hands her a clean, wet dishtowel to wash up the fresh blood.

"If you insist on *not* calling the police, at *least* take the damn phone off the hook so you don't have to listen to all those hateful messages that are obviously stressing you the hell out."

"I can't take it off the hook. I need to be available for my tenants. Rent is due, and only one has paid yet. I need to be available so I can get paid. I need some money to order oil and pay my contractors."

I have no idea why she only takes cash for the rent. But I'm not a landlord, so what do I know? Maybe because it's her retirement money she needs to live on. Maybe it's so she doesn't have to go to the bank when she needs cash. She refuses to learn how to use online banking, and she refuses to use a debit card to make purchases. I don't know why she does what she does. She's a woman stuck in her ways.

At a loss of what to do to better this situation, and needing to put in time on my thesis, I tell Mom, "If things get any worse, call me. I'll be home all night doing schoolwork." Leaning down, I give her a hug and a kiss on the cheek. "And stop that damn scratching before you're *completely* bald." With a playful bump to her shoulder, I laugh, trying to lighten the mood.

She looks up at me with teary eyes and smiles. "At least then I won't need to color the gray anymore."

We all laugh.

Mom thanks me for picking up some groceries for her and asks me to help with her laundry. Going up and down stairs weakens her and makes her short of breath, which is why I help take care of her house and do some chores. A big part of why I live in her garage apartment. And it's cheaper than owning a home while I finish grad school. Not that I could afford one now anyway, but still…Sacrifices, man. Gotta do what I gotta do. Plus, Mom needs my help. That's important to me.

Once I finish her request, I set the basket of warm clothes beside her chair. "If *she* doesn't call me," I say to Jody, "will you please call me if things get worse?"

Jody nods and smirks. "You *know* I will, sweetie."

As I walk across the driveway back to my apartment, I pray no crazy phone calls ring into my house later tonight.

Late Saturday afternoon, I step out of the shower after a long and unusually sweltering day of working a burial ceremony at the cemetery and see my living room filled with rose petals strewn across the hardwood floor and lit candles all around. After quickly drying off in the bathroom and taking my hair out of the towel wrapped around my head, I slip on my silk bathrobe and step out into my flower-filled apartment.

A vase of pink lilies, one of my favorites, stands perky and bright on the mantle. A potted purple orchid, another of my favorites, sits atop the stereo cabinet. And on the island in the kitchen sits a huge vase of at least two dozen red roses. It smells sweet and magical. I smile so wide my cheeks hurt.

I search my small two-bedroom apartment to find Ronnie, but he's nowhere. And I don't see his car anywhere out in the driveway. The only vehicles parked out there are mine and Mom's truck.

What the hell?

Still smiling, I shrug and start getting ready to go see *Sweeny Todd*.

By the time I'm dressed and have finished applying my armor—eyeliner and mascara—Ronnie pulls into the driveway and comes clomping up the stairs to my door. He clammers around in the kitchen for a few minutes, which gives me time to finish getting ready.

I step out into the living room just as he turns on the stereo. "Like a Stone" starts playing, and Ronnie spins around to face me with his hand held out, smile emerging, beckoning me for a dance. He knows how much I love Chris Cornell. He knows how much this music makes me happy.

I take his hand. He gently pulls me close.

We dance.

After a few moments, smiles still plastered on both of our faces, he tells me, "That baby you want so much could be coming sooner than you know."

My stomach drops.

What the hell is he talking about?

I pull my head away from his chest, look up at him. His smile is so huge he looks maniacal. A Joker's smile. Eyes wide, he continues twirling me through the dance.

"What are you talking about?" I try not to sound negative, but I already don't like where this is going.

First, he showed up at my house with his car filled with most of his belongings, insisting he's moving in. Then, he starts getting all accusey and jealous. And the sketchy bakery story? Now he's trying to rush having a kid with me. We haven't even been dating that long. My divorce isn't even final. I'm not even sure I want a divorce.

"Turns out I can reverse my vasectomy. I scheduled an appointment with a doctor to discuss the procedure."

Whoa! Vasectomy? That's news to me.

Yeah, maybe I'm not so sure I *really* want to have a kid with him, but he promised to give me the child I've been dreaming about. I know that sounds odd, but it's a matter of principle.

I halt the dance, let go of him, and step back a few feet. "What are you talking about? You had a vasectomy? When did you plan on telling me this?"

His expression morphs from manic to faux surprise. "Yeah, five years ago. I told you that. When I was dating Tanya. She didn't want kids, and I didn't want to wear a rubber, so I got fixed." He laughs like it's no big deal.

Yeah, it is a big fucking deal. He lied to me! Doesn't he remember why my husband and me got separated in the first place? Lies. Lies. Fucking lies!

That bakery story he dished out to me now sounds like a whole ton of lies.

And who gets a vasectomy just because they don't want to wear a rubber? Seems quite drastic to me. He only dated Tanya for a year, unless that's a lie too. But why lie about that?

Who the hell am I dating?

Flames instantly light my rage, setting my head on fire, flushing my cheeks. My heart's pounding so hard, so fast, it just might pop right out of my chest.

"You knew the reason why Jordan and I separated, and you rushed right up, trying to sweep me off my feet with the promise of the future I've dreamed about—knowing all the time that it would never happen? Really?" I turn away and walk to the kitchen, feeling the need to put distance between us before I rip his goddamn lying face off. What a fucking phony! I open the fridge, grab the pitcher of premixed mimosa, and pour myself a drink.

As I drop the second ice cube into the tumbler, Ronnie's warm hands slide around my waist from behind. He presses his body against mine and leans down to whisper in my ear. "You never asked. But I'm reversing it. I'm doing this for you. For *us*."

"I never *asked*?!" I pull apart his interlocked fingers, remove them from my stomach, shove him away with my elbow. I spin to face him. "That is a piss poor fucking answer. You realize that, right? What else have you *not* told me about? What else have you *lied* to me about? Might as well get it all out on the table now."

I pause, think about the bakery's broken window.

"Like...who the hell really busted out the window at your work? Who was it, Ronnie? Was it some tweaked out homeless junkie, was it the bitch who busted out my truck window, was it her hooded accomplice, or was it..." Biting my tongue on implying he broke it himself, I allow breathing room for him to step forward and admit it himself—if my suspicion is in fact true.

Or...maybe it *was* Aiden, and all the crazy from my life is too much for Ronnie to handle. I don't even know how to deal with all of it myself. I mean, look what the hell it's doing to me. Nothing good, that's for sure.

Sometimes...I wish to not wake up in the morning.

Sometimes...I want to slit my wrists, let the pain and loneliness bleed out as I drift away into a forever peaceful sleep.

Sometimes...I want to drive right off a fucking bridge and pretend I'm flying, never to come down again. Just...fly away.

I need wings.

He steps back, leans against the counter opposite from me. "Why are you so hung up on that broken window? I've dealt with it. Now, let's move on."

Shock shakes my head. Trying to get a grasp on his nonchalant attitude about the crazy occurrence, I scramble for words to respond.

"Come on, Ronnie, that shit isn't normal. Stuff that that doesn't happen hardly ever, especially around here. This is Maine, one of the most mellow, peaceful states in the whole goddamned country, so, yeah, I'm hung up on the broken window. And why? Because *you* act like it's no big deal and keep avoiding talking about it. That is very fucking weird. What the hell? Stop spinning this to make it look like I'm making a big deal out of nothing. It isn't nothing! Who broke the window?"

Eyes wide, he stares me dead in the face. "Some sketched out junkie, I guess. I don't know. I only saw him running away. Portland's filled with 'em. Junkies everywhere. So, no, it's not unusual. And, yes, you are making a big deal out of a small problem, a problem I already took care of. I already told you..." Taking a long-legged step across the narrow kitchen, he comes up close to me again. He looks down and gently grasps my chin. "You have so much on your plate, so much stress to deal with about your sister and your schoolwork and taking care of your mother and, well, everything..." He pauses to kiss my overheated cheek. "I don't want to add to your stress with my problems. That's all." A smile spreads wide as he slips his arm around my waste.

Why does he sound so convincing? Is he really telling the truth? Am I so used to crazy that I see crazy everywhere, even when crazy isn't there? I don't know what to think anymore.

As he goes on and on about how deep his love for me goes and how he would do anything to make me happy, I remember his comment the day he showed me the *Sweeny Todd* tickets. *"I know how much you love plays."*

I know I never told him anything about my love of theatre. He doesn't seem like the type who would be into that at all. He's a poor punk rock boy who barely graduated high school and has played in punk and metal bands his whole adult life while working a variety of jobs to pay for his ramshackle house. Plus, I haven't even been to a play in over five years. It's not like the topic of theatre sits on the tip of my tongue to talk about.

My mind spins so fast I feel a bit dizzy. Where's an anchor when you need one? Rebuttals escape me as my tornado of thoughts swirls on.

Shit. I need a drink. Or a toke. Something to slow this storm down.

He keeps on talking, trying to convince me of his undying love, as I tip back my drink and think of all the other things I never told him but he somehow magically knows about: my love of old blues tunes, how I think saxophone is sexy, my secret desire to hang out in jazz clubs, the Arizona vacation Jordan and I took a few years ago, Jordan and me getting married in Jamaica.

How does he know about all of that?

A sneaking suspicion creeps into my muddled mind.

Has he been stalking me?

♫ 🚪 ♪

Loneliness envelops me like a shroud though I'm not alone. The desire for a warm hug and a comforting shoulder eats through my insides like maggots devouring me. A heaviness weighs down on my chest, pinning me to the bed. A demonic incubus feeding on my soul, piercing my heart with horns of malice. Tears of emptiness and frustration trail from the corners of my eyes, tickling my temples like tiny insects feeding on my sorrow. Fuseli's *The Nightmare* painting lives.

The pressure on my head pounds and aches, a vise crushing a grapefruit to pulp. How much did I drink to get me through the night? Maybe too much, but certainly not as much as Ronnie. He drank so much, I had to drive us back home.

His foot touches my leg again. I cringe and shift my body over to the edge of the mattress as far away from him as I can get without falling right off the damn bed. Sleep has evaded me for two hours already, subjecting me to the torture of hearing Ronnie breathe and smelling the scent of his nauseating cologne as it assaults my senses. It seems pointless to keep lying here trying to accomplish the impossible—having a peaceful night's sleep while lying next to my potential stalker.

Oh yeah, he did assure me earlier tonight during the drive to the *Sweeny Todd* play that he found out "all sorts of interesting things" about me by going through my Facebook posts and pictures when I mentioned I was interested in auditioning for his band. He also assured me that the doctor reversing his vasectomy told him he'll be able to have kids once the procedure is complete. But his assurance doesn't make me feel assured. I don't know shit about vasectomies—except they prevent the dude from having kids—or if what he's told me is true until I speak to a legit doctor. As for my love of plays and whatnot, he would've had to go way back to very old posts and pictures to find out some of the stuff he knows about me that I never told him about. I haven't been sharing much on social media in the past couple of years. And some of that stuff he mentioned I don't remember ever posting on social media.

Well, that's an easy tell. All I need do is check to see if some of the things he knows about me that I never told him can be found on my Facebook page. Easy-peasy.

The need to finally find the truth to *something* lifts some of the heaviness from my chest. With slow and steady movements, I ease myself out from under the covers and off the bed. I wipe my eyes on the sleeve of my T-shirt. My fuzzy socks allow me to slide my feet across the hardwood floor rather than make noisy footsteps out of the bedroom.

I snatch my phone from the kitchen counter, unplug the charger, and go hide in the bathroom.

And, yep, after thirty minutes of searching, I found one post from ten years ago with a couple pictures of my wedding with Jordan in Jamaica. Ronnie might be telling the truth about that one, though it's still a bit creepy seeing how far back he searched through my posts and pictures. Sure seems like a stalker move to me. But what about my love of plays?

After another thirty minutes of searching and finding no posts or pictures on my Facebook about my love of plays, or anything at all about me going to even one play, I revert to a general search through posts from around the time period when I remember attending the last play I had seen before tonight, *The Lion, the Witch, and the Wardrobe*. That was seven years ago. I thought it was only five years ago. My bad. But that's not the point. The point is—

In the only post on my Facebook with any mention of the play, I talk about taking my niece, Zoe, out for some "Me and Mini-Me Time". It says nothing in the post about taking her to see the play. A picture accompanies the post. It shows Zoe and me sitting at a patio table under a rainbow umbrella on a sunny day in front of The Cookie Jar, with each of us taking a messy bite from our huge raspberry bear claw. The detail about the play comes in the comments under the post.

My friend Beth had asked me in the comments about what brought us to The Cookie Jar, and my response told her we were in South Portland to see *The Lion, The Witch, and the Wardrobe* at The Portland Players Theater, which is close to the bakery. I also told her how happy I was that Zoe wanted to see the play because "*I absolutely love live theater performances*". Those two comments are buried amidst a sea of comments proclaiming how adorable my niece is and how much she looks like she could be my daughter.

How did Ronnie find that? He must've been searching every single post and picture and comment on my page to discover that detail about me. But why? What's the point? To try to play up the whole idea of *"Wow, I love plays too—we have so much in common."*

Classic. Just like Henry Rollins sings about in "Liar."

After all this searching and wondering and speculating, my rising frustration and irritation scream for a drink. Plus, hiding in the bathroom for so long has made me cold and uncomfortable, and there's no need to keep searching. I found the proverbial needle. Now, what can I poke with it?

I go to the kitchen, pour myself a mimosa, and plop down on the couch with the silky chenille blanket wrapped around me. The first couple of sips taste sweet and refreshing. The third sip helps me melt into the cushions, and I rest my head back on my velvety Edgar Allen Poe throw pillow.

Why did Ronnie scour my social media page to find things out about me instead of just asking me about myself like a normal person when they want to get to know someone better? I swear social media has created a communication breakdown, making people forget how to communicate in person. Body language—what's that? Vocal intonation—what does that even mean? Tone of voice—why does that matter? What tech giants promote as progress for society I see as regression for humans. But that's a topic I don't have the brain power to think about right now. I'm too pissed off at *one* person. I don't have the energy for anger against a *whole group* of billionaire techies.

Whoa! This drink's already getting to me, pushing my mind right down the rabbit hole of outrage. Ronnie better watch out. At this rate, I just might stab him to death in his sleep. No, but really…I'll save that type of rage for my songwriting. But if he wakes up now, he's in for one hell of a fight. I'm so fucking irate! Why did I let him make me second-guess myself?

All this anger's got my body tied in knots. I zipped straight from a deep hole of lonely depression to fire-in-my-eyes fury! I don't know which is worse.

Both suck equal bags of donkey dicks.

Why can't I just make it all stop, disappear myself from the ugliness of life, say "Goodbye, cruel world" and drift away?

Man, I could really use a professional massage to help calm my nerves. If it wasn't so late, I'd call Nine Stones and put that birthday gift card I still haven't cashed in to good use right now.

I sink deeper into my pillow and pull the blanket up to my shoulders, trying to relax. But my hurricane of thoughts refuses to slow down, kicking up even more rage.

I don't care if Ronnie swears his vasectomy can be reversed. Yes, all the research he showed me before we left for the play backs up his claim, but those research findings also say, "The more time that passes between the vasectomy and the reversal, the lower the chances for success". He fails to see the importance of that statement. But that shit doesn't even matter. I don't care about the research! I don't care if the vasectomy can be reversed! What I freaking care about is he kept it from me! He not only kept an important piece of information from me, but he also knows so much about me I no longer feel comfortable around him.

Now that I'm thinking about it, I don't know if I've ever really felt *comfortable* with him. His jealousy puts me on edge, questioning everything I do, wondering if my behavior or what I say will somehow make me look suspicious of something and then push him to make accusations. Just when chatting with the guys in the band I find that I censor my wording and my actions to make sure I don't say or do anything Ronnie might take the wrong way.

Shit. My glass is empty. I need a refill. Gotta be quiet getting in the fridge. The last thing I want is for Ronnie to wake up and try talking to me. If I even see him or hear his voice right now, this glass will meet his face, hard. But first, refill it and drink it.

Ah…That's better. Back to my warm spot on the couch.

No, don't touch your phone again. No more scrolling. I already know. I already found it.

This is fucking insane! What the hell am I doing with my life?

Everything I try to accomplish fails. I had to drop out of the first college I went to because their tuition is too expensive, and I'm poor. I wasted five years of my life applying to a graduate program that refused to accept me, even though I graduated college in the top 10% of my class. Then Jordan encouraged me to follow my dreams, encouraged me to take my writing more seriously, encouraged me to go for my MFA and start a new path. Then, he abandons me when I'm in the thick of it and only working part-time. Now, finishing my master's degree may never happen at the rate I'm going with all my life's setbacks getting in the way. Every person I've ever had a relationship with has either physically abused me, mentally and emotionally abused me, cheated on me, or lied to me. Most of them did more than one of those things. After a ten-year marriage, my husband refuses to create a family with me, refuses to even talk to me about the possibility. Then there's Psycho Satan—the arsenic icing on my mountain-high shit cake—who attacks me in some way pretty much every other week, and her actions are pushing my mother closer and closer to an early grave. And Aiden, the worst memory from my past—the blood-filled cherry on top of my dessert of despair—has come back to torment me for whatever insane reason.

Dammit! I hate my shitty life! What's the point in trying to make it better? Every time I get two steps ahead, something or someone kicks me three steps back. Two steps ahead. Three steps back. Two steps ahead. Three steps back. Over and over again. I just can't deal with it anymore!

I wish I had the money to move away from it all, start over somewhere else, a place where nobody knows me.

Yeah, that doesn't sound lonely at all. Not one bit.

This apartment feels like a fucking cage, claustrophobic. I need to get out of here. Go somewhere. Get some fresh air or something.

Or maybe if I just *do* something, *any*thing. I gotta get out of my head, get out of these thoughts that won't stop bombarding me, dragging me down.

But where am I supposed to go at two in the morning? What the hell can I do at this hour that won't wake up the sleeping pile of lies on the other side of that door? I can't go next door to Mom's. The "I told you so" look on her face that I'm *certain* will appear is not what I need right now. She's still not home yet anyway, probably playing cards at her friend's house down the street. Plus, I need space to think. I need to figure this shit out on my own—like a big girl.

I could always do some writing. That's therapeutic, right? Take out my anger on some fictional characters maybe? No, but really—Writing is nice and quiet, especially if I take a notebook and pen outside to the porch swing. There is a section of my thesis I've been struggling with. Maybe I can step away and work on that. Nature's hug and freehand writing always help tap into the creative pathways of the psyche.

Or maybe a warm bubble bath to drown my sorrows, slip under and fade away, escape. As long as Ronnie doesn't wake up and try to join me. I'd rather slit my throat with Ronnie's damn straight razor than share a

bath with him right now.   

Good thing I brought the blanket out with me. It's chilly outside. The cool night air's refreshing against my angry-hot skin. I don't think I'll doze during this impromptu writing session, that's for sure—as long as Ronnie doesn't wake up and come ruin my time alone because if that happens, I'll be sure to make myself fall asleep to not have to deal with him.

I should've brought a flashlight out with me so I could walk the trails in the woods and do some writing at the old tree fort. But no, maybe that wouldn't be a good idea. Just reminds me of when Jordan and I built the fort with our nieces, Nat and Zoe. Plus, I love this swing. Maybe I'll go walk the trails tomorrow, climb some trees, pretend I'm a kid again. That sounds pretty freaking awesome!

I love the woods, the trees.

I miss being a kid. Carefree. No stress. No worries.

Curled up in the corner of the bench swing, I affix the booklight to the top of my notebook, take a sip from my mimosa, and put pen to paper. With the waxing gibbous moon so bright overhead, the shadow of a tree branch sways and shimmies across the page, dancing around with my pen strokes. A barred owl calls out through the trees. Its hoots sound almost like it's saying, "Who cooks for you? Who cooks for you all?"

Not hungry at all, neighbor. Rage and despair have my stomach tied in knots.

Maybe I should journal a bit first, or write lyrics or poetry. Something to help me process everything going on. I don't know. Whatever flows, flows. I won't force it.

Mimosa, good friend that she is, pours all my thoughts out of my mind to splash across the pages, uninhibited. The fault lines of my internal earthquake split and crack, releasing demons from deep within. These creatures of darkness run amuck, moving my pen at their will, like a session of automatic writing.

But what is my question?

My subconsciousness already knows the question, I'm sure, even if it's not written down. I know of many questions I need answers for. But are any of those the correct question, *the* question?

Will I ever start making the right choices for my life? Am I on the right path? Will this hellscape I call "My Life" ever lead to peace and happiness besides that which comes with death? That baby boy who comes to me in dreams, will he ever come into this world as my son?

Will we ever build sandcastles together, climb trees and build forts together, read books and play music together, like in the visions that dance across the backs of my eyelids? Am I meant to have a child, a family? Will I ever finish grad school? Will I ever stop struggling financially? Will I ever be treated as an equal, not just in the world and in my work, but as a partner? Are there any men who don't lie, cheat, and abuse their partners? Is anyone really trustworthy? Or are most people scum? What will…

Before I read the words I wrote in my notebook, the bell chime hanging on my front door jingles and clatters against steal.

"What the fuck?" Ronnie's groggy voice carries to the backyard from the driveway. "Where the hell is she?"

I shift on the swing, trying to stay quiet, trying to stay hidden, but my foot kicks over my empty mimosa glass. It lands on a stepping stone in the flower garden and shatters.

My life is that glass.

"Yeah, no vocal isolation booth or laying down guitar solos after. We do strictly live recordings here at Rock Coast Studio." Ryan, the audio engineer, reiterates the recording procedure as he props open the door at the top of the loading ramp in the back parking lot of the studio.

"Cool. *We're* a live band, so we're all good." Mike hauls his Marshall cab out of the hearse and sets it down next to Kyle's two bass drums.

"Sounds good." I try to not make eye contact with Mike unless absolutely necessary. With Ronnie acting weird lately, I also make sure not to get too chummy with Kyle, even though he's never gotten all accusatory about Kyle and me. I wonder why. Maybe Ronnie and Mike had some sort of beef between them from before I joined the band. Whatever it is, I stick to an all-business-and-nothing-but-business vibe with the guys. I need this session to go smoothly. No drama. No setbacks. Finish it for my school project and move on. Professional is my middle name.

As I open the back door of my SUV and grab my backpack with my guitar pedals inside, I see Kyle pulling out pieces of his kit from the hearse. No way in hell is Ronnie's jealousy going to make me not offer to help Kyle carry in his kit. That's like an unspoken rule for all non-drummers of a band—at least in my book it is.

"Here, let me grab something for you." I step over and grab the high-hat stand and the double bass drum pedal.

As he turns away with a bass drum in his hands, Kyle says, "Thanks." He doesn't look at me at all and heads toward the loading ramp of the studio.

Huh…That's odd. Kyle normally shows a lot of appreciation every time I help him, and he always tells me I don't have to help.

Come to think of it, neither Mike or Kyle have spoken to me much since I arrived. Just simple acknowledgements of my arrival and one- or two-word responses to anything I've said. I wonder if Ronnie has gotten all accusatory with Kyle too and just hasn't laid into me about it yet? Or maybe they're just pissed off about all our gear getting stolen by people I know.

Hey, at least I was the one who hunted our gear down and got it all back in time for our studio session. Whatever. Either way, I foresee an uncomfortable recording session ahead.

Just remember—breathe, stay calm, stay professional.

This recording session can't get over with soon enough. I need this piece of my thesis done, so I can finish digging into how the hell Ronnie knows a bunch of stuff about me that I've never told him. Besides the fact that he stalked my Facebook page. I didn't have the energy to confront him about it after he came outside and found me writing on the swing the other night. I needed sleep, not more stress. Recurring arguments and tension, sandpaper scraping away my psyche, are wearing on me, muddling my mind.

But, man, I also want to find out what really happened at his work the other night with that broken window and the weird phone call from him. It was all so strange. Or is that just my obsessive find-out-who-dunnit mind speaking? Or is it my try-to-fix-them-and-make-them-happy people-pleaser side?

Why does all that matter anyway? Why does anything really matter? He's been driving me mad! Every time I see him now, I'm trying to find out if he's lied to me about something.

What if that's on me though? What if my history of dealing with liars and psychos is making me turn everyone into liars and psychos even when they're not like that?

Whatever. I don't care. I need the madness to end.

Once this session ends, kicking him out of my apartment won't affect my project, my thesis. And I have a sinking feeling *that* is the *only* ending that will fit this mysterious tale.

Yeah, kicking him out of my place will most likely lead to me getting kicked out of the band, but I can always find another band to join. Or better yet, I'll quit this band and start my own fucking band! But that entails starting from scratch *all over again*. This is the fifth band I've been in already.

Why is it so fucking difficult to keep a gigging band together?

Once our gear is loaded in and we get all set up, we sound check. Playing our longest song helps us get our levels set and gives us a warmup before hitting that record button. No one says anything to one another when the song ends.

"All right. Sounds great! I've got a good mix back here," Ryan says through our headphones. "If everyone's ready, and if no one needs to use the bathroom, you can go ahead and play all three songs. You can repeat any if you're not happy with the first go-through. We'll wait until the end to have a listen and see if we need any more takes."

"Sounds good," I say into my mic. No one else in the band says a word. I turn and look at each of them when I say, "Does anyone need to use the bathroom before that red light goes on?" No one looks at me except Ronnie. Mike and Kyle both say, "No," as they tinker with their instruments. Such obvious displays of avoidance, I feel like calling them out about it on the spot, but I don't want to rock the boat in the studio, setting an even more negative vibe than the one I've already been feeling. I need to get good takes for my school project.

Ronnie's eyes remain riveted on me.

"How about you? Need to go before…"

"Nope." Wearing a blank expression, he stares at me for a few uncomfortable seconds. Then he thumps a few notes on his bass and says, "Let's roll," as he turns away.

I nod and turn back to my mic. "Looks like we're ready whenever you are, Ryan."

We pound out our three tracks. Tracks one and two take three go-throughs, but we nail them both on the third go-round. Once the mistake-free second take of the third song ends, we've got plenty of time for a listen in the control room and a few audio tweaks to level everything out. And we'll still have about twenty minutes left on our time slot to break down, pack up, and load our vehicles.

Ryan continues working on the tracks while we clean out.

In the back parking lot, we pack our vehicles in silence. No one says anything. Nothing about how the session went. Nothing about practicing for our next Geno's gig. Nothing.

"Here you go, guys and gals." Ryan's walking down the loading ramp of the studio with four CDs in his hand and a USB drive. "I burned the tunes to a CD for each of you. I also sent them to you through Dropbox, but I thought you'd like to have something in-hand when you leave."

I rush over, anxious to get the tunes in my possession. "Hey, thanks a lot, dude. Much appreciated!" I pocket the USB drive.

We shake. He waves to the rest of the guys, who are still loading their gear. They all wave and shout, "Thanks." Then Ryan heads back into the studio and shuts the back door.

After passing out the CDs to the guys, I help Kyle load the last of his cymbal stands into the hearse. After he flings the back door shut, I turn toward my SUV and see Mike and Ronnie standing nearby. No one's talking.

I step over to the guys and hold up my CD. "I can't wait to crank this baby on the way home. Great job in there, guys!" Throwing a smile to each one of them, I wait to hear what they think about how our session went.

"Yeah, same." Standing beside me, Ronnie tucks his CD into the front pocket of his pullover hoodie.

Mike and Kyle share a look I can't read. Then Mike looks at me, then at Ronnie.

"Yeah, well, I hate to say this, but I'm done. The band is done."

His blunt words hit me like a punch in the gut.

Speechless, I glance at Kyle. Stone-faced, he just nods.

Then I turn toward Ronnie, who looks as shocked as I feel.

I turn back to Mike. "Okay. Well, I'm real sorry to hear that. I thought the session went pretty fucking awesome, but…"

"It's not that…" Mike stops short before elaborating, looking as though he's trying to figure out how to say what he wants to say.

Before Mike gets another word out, Ronnie hauls his arm back and punches him in the mouth. "I know you've been fucking my girl!"

I jump out of the way.

Kyle takes a step back and looks as though he's assessing the situation before reacting.

"What the fuck…Motherfucker…" Mike touches his jaw, wiggles it side-to-side. He turns toward Ronnie, eyes ablaze, and then wraps his arm around his neck. Mike gets him in a head lock, and a full-on brawl takes place right there in the parking lot of the studio.

Punches and kicks start swinging. Mike throws punch after punch against the side of Ronnie's head. A swift leg swipe from Ronnie takes Mike's feet out from under him, releases his headlock grip, and sends him to the pavement. Ronnie dives on top of his friend and bandmate and throws a couple jabs at his face. Blood and spittle fly everywhere.

But the beatdown doesn't last long.

Kyle, the biggest guy out of all three, at six-three three hundred pounds, steps in and pulls each one of them off each other like they're grade school kids in a playground tussle. "Whoa now. Let's all calm down and get a grip on ourselves. The band's just breaking up. No need for overreactions."

The brawlers each step away from each other, wiping their faces, straightening out their hair and clothes.

"I never fucked '*your girl*,' you insecure fucking prick! We've only been bandmates."

Ouch! I thought we were friends too. Guess not. Business only.

"This…" Mike points back and forth at Ronnie and me. "Your obsession over her is why this band is fucking done. You stalked her online for years until you saw just the right time to invite her into our band. Then you swooped in when her marriage went south, promising all sorts of bullshit you have no intentions of delivering on just so you can get into her pants. Now this? Fuck this is bullshit! We're out." He waves at Kyle to follow him to the hearse.

Kyle looks at us and shrugs, then follows Mike.

So, it's true? And they both knew all this time? And no one told me? What the fuck? I guess we were never really friends.

Dumfounded, I stare at Ronnie. He's wiping blood from the corner of his lip, looking like a wounded puppy dog, all apologetic eyes, obviously wanting sympathy.

In the final words of Mike…

Fuck this bullshit! I'm out.

My suspicions were just confirmed.

I turn away, open the door of my SUV, hop in, and drive away.

Without a damn clue how to calm my boiling rage, I gun-it down Forest Avenue. Weaving in and out of traffic, I head straight toward I-295, punching the steering wheel and screaming obscenities the whole way. Flames of fury engulf my head. Pounding pain throbs at my temples, and my cheeks feel scorching hot. Not to mention the bolts of lightning shooting painful jolts down both my forearms and ricocheting around my wrists like a billion tiny needles. Please, don't tell me I'm going to need carpal tunnel surgery on top of everything else I'm dealing with.

Son of a bitch! I can't deal with any of this right now. It all needs to go away, vanish.

Why do I have to exist at all?

Sometimes I wish I were never born.

Disappear me, oh great magic from beyond the stars. Reach down from the cosmos and wipe me out of existence, please. Toss me into a black hole, or whatever it takes to wipe it all away and strip me of the torment of all the heaviness.

Maybe going for a drive and blasting some tunes will calm me down. Or maybe I can find a very large, old Mr. Oak to clear my slate, eliminate the madness for me.

Man, I could really use one of Jordan's amazing massages.

No! To hell with Jordan, the scared, little lying man-boy that he is. I do still have that Nine Stones gift card he gave me for my birthday though. But I need to get my gear home. I don't want to get ripped off again. For all I know, some psycho could be following me.

What if Ronnie goes right back to my place? His face is the last thing I want to see.

Nope, I don't want to go home right now.

I need to get away, to escape.

"I know this is last minute, so anyone who has an opening is fine by me." I take the next exit off I-295 and head back in town toward The Old Port. "Shanelle in twenty minutes sounds great! Thank you!"

Wow! I can't believe someone's available. Navigating through downtown traffic and finding a parking space will eat up most of the twenty-minute wait. As anxious, stressed, and depressed as I feel, the prospect of a massage fills me with excitement. I've only had a professional massage once before, and that, too, came as a birthday gift quite a few years ago. Spa treatments fit like a square peg in the small circle of my tight budget. Plus, I've never really been a spa-type girl. Poor artists like me have better things to spend our pennies on, like books and guitar effects pedals and weed medibles.

The CD from today's studio session screams at me from the passenger seat. Our songs run about four to five minutes in length, so I'll be able to listen to a couple songs on my drive to Nine Stones. I stop at the next red light and pop the CD into the stereo.

"Medicated Zombification" is the first track. As the light turns green and I step on the gas, I anticipate hearing Kyle's kickass drum opening, but instead, I'm greeted with Kyle counting us in and hitting his sticks together with each beat of his four-count.

What the hell? Why didn't this part get cut? We're not supposed to hear the drummer counting the band into the song on a studio mix. What the fuck kind of hack engineering job is this?

I need to present this to a whole audience-filled room in a couple months, not to mention my thesis advisor, my writing mentor, and the director of the graduate program.

Okay, just try to calm down and listen to how the rest of the recording came out. Afterall, I'm in a creative writing program, not a music program, so maybe this won't matter.

But it matters to me! This is my music! I wrote it! A lot of people are going to hear this. I want it to sound good. Plus, this session cost money, money I could've certainly used for fuel this winter instead of a shitty recording.

I hit the back arrow to start the song over. An uncomfortable cringe surges through me when I hear Kyle counting us in again, but I push through it and focus on the rest of the song as I turn left onto Congress Street.

The rest of the song sounds pretty freaking killer!

Oops. Maybe not.

Between the second chorus and the solo comes a click sound, like the engineer punched-in the solo section. Did he take the solo from one recording and paste it into another? If so, why? And why do I hear the punch-in?

Another click-sound-punch-in comes after the chorus too, dammit!

Man, I might've wasted my limited funds on a hack of a studio with a shitty engineer. But don't get ahead of yourself. Maybe it's just this song.

During Ronnie's short bass line interlude before the last chorus, an image of his manic smile and swirling crazy-eyes flash across my mind. I push it away as best I can as I make the last turn onto India Street to find a parking space near the spa.

Shit! Now I'm going to be late for my damn appointment. Bumper-to-bumper parked cars line both sides of India. Parking in Portland sucks! If I didn't just make the appointment, I might be able to call and reschedule. But I need this *now.* If I cancel without a 24-hour notice, I still have to pay, and if I'm too late and waste my gift card, I can't afford to make another appointment. My Jimmy moves at a turtle's pace as I scour the street for some place to park. That's when I hear it.

Between track one and track two, Kyle says, "Which song next?" Then my voice comes through the speakers. "How about 'Dead Inside', and then we go right into 'Bury Yourself'. Cool?"

And again, I clearly hear Kyle counting us in with his voice and his drumstick hits.

What the fuck type of shit-ass recording did I just blow my fucking money on? I'm embarrassed to have to share this when I present my thesis at my senior residency in a couple months. I don't know how to fix this myself, and I have no more money to put toward another recording session at a different studio.

Plus, I don't have a band anymore.

Dammit! If I were tech savvy at all and had a DAW program on my computer, maybe I could fix this myself. But if I had tech skills and recording gear, I wouldn't've had to pay for a studio session—I would've done it all myself like all the younger musicians are doing these days. Fuuuuuuuuck!

I hit the back arrow to listen to all the mistakes again. Probably a bad idea at the moment, but I do it anyway. It's a waste of time, though, because I'm more focused on finding a parking space than listening to this suck-ass recording.

"Dead Inside" plays as I circle around the block to find parking. My revved-up heart rate pounds in my head, pain throbbing in my temples, when I realize I have to circle the block *again*. Shit! The *tic-tic-ticking* of the clock in my head knocks against my skull. I *am* going to be late. Can I get anything right? I can't even get to a fucking appointment on time, an appointment I just made ten minutes away from the place! Heat rises from under my shirt collar as stress sweat breaks out around my neck. When I find an empty space on the opposite corner of the block from the spa, I realize I didn't pay attention to "Dead Inside" at all. When I cut the engine, I'm already ten minutes late. Man, just trying to get to this freaking appointment has made me more stressed than when I called to book it—if that's even possible.

What a fucking pathetic freak I am if I can't even handle looking for parking space and running a few minutes late for an appointment.

Holy crap I need this massage!

I grab the blanket off my back seat and the towel from the floor and spread them over my gear in the way-way back to hide it all as best I can. I don't want to take any chances of getting ripped off again. With shaky hands, I clip my keys to my purse and book it down the sidewalk to my appointment.

After arriving and giving my gift card to the teenage girl working the front counter, a twenty-something woman, wearing a warm smile, strolls around the corner, greets me, and leads me down the sea green hallway toward a tea station.

Twenty minutes late and counting.

Great. And when I leave here, I have the joy of listening to a shitty studio mix of my former band's demo while I drive home to face Ronnie, the guy who's been stalking me for who the hell knows how long and is living in my apartment.

Lovely.

It doesn't matter how long this massage lasts. It could go on for two hours or more, but it won't make a difference. Nothing will.

Rage, anxiety, and depression fill my entire being, clinging to me like a fungus, eating me from the inside out.

♬ 🎙 ♪

So much for a relaxing and refreshing massage. I'm more wound the hell up now than I was before. My body should feel better, and yeah, it did during the massage, but my screwed-up life still has me all tied in knots. I can't get out of my head! At least the wind blowing through the open car window feels good. I take in a deep breath of fresh air, hoping it will help clear my head.

Maybe I should've driven home in silence instead of listening to the shitty mix of our tunes. That, of course, made me think about how embarrassed I'm going to be when I present this with my thesis in a couple months. Even the levels are all wonky, the reverb's way overdone, and the vocals are buried in the mix. It sounds worse than when we all listened to it together before packing up. Maybe my professors, the director, and my writing mentor won't care about that part. But *I* care. There'll be an audience listening to that crappy mix. This recording was also supposed to be our demo—the first of our tunes to be recorded. Tunes we could share online and with venues we haven't performed at yet. Not that *that* part matters now that the band split up. But still…Maybe I'm being too much of a perfectionist. But I paid for a good recording, for Christ's sake, and that's what I should've walked away with.

Maybe that's not it. Maybe it's…I don't know…Just hearing the tunes I wrote with that band puts Ronnie's crazed face into my headspace. Not a pleasant sight.

And now, there's my mailbox up ahead. I hope Ronnie's not already at my place.

No, it will never be "his place." He'll be gone soon. Very soon.

As I pull down my long driveway, the urge to spark a joint and pour myself a drink intensifies.

But wait.

What the hell?

Son of a bitch, what the fuck am I arriving home to?

Looks like that toke and drink won't happen soon enough.

Jesus Christ! Can I ever catch a fucking break from the insanity?

The front door to my apartment is ajar. No vehicles in the driveway. Not even Mom's truck.

Guess my gear will have to stay in the Jimmy for now. No idea what the hell I'm about to walk into. I hope no one's still inside my place!

After shifting to park, I slip out my boot knife from inside my tall Doc Marten before easing myself out of my vehicle. The surveillance camera above my front door dangles from the cord, smashed. I hold my cell phone up to record that and whatever else I find, then shoulder the front door open further. That's when I notice the open door at the top of the hallway stairs. Looks like someone kicked it open. A partial tread from a shoe marks the center of the bottom half.

Walking up the stairs quietly proves difficult in my heavy-clomping boots, but I try. Knife at my side, phone held out in front and facing forward, I step inside and turn the corner to see…

A total fucking mess. Graffiti everywhere.

Graffiti I recognize.

The signature pointy knife-like lettering, red paint dripping like blood. Wings. Roses. Skulls.

My heart sinks.

He knows where I live. Knows when I'm not home.

But I was supposed to be home. The massage was a last-minute decision.

Has he been stalking me again?

I search my apartment. As I move through the living room, I navigate around bits and pieces of the smashed-up DVR I use for my surveillance system. I check closets and under the bed but find no one, just a mess and more graffiti. Skulls. Demons. Daggers. More red dripping paint. Bureau drawers all emptied, clothes thrown around. Mattress stripped and flipped. Then I see the huge black wings spread wide across the wall at the head of my bed, red paint dripping as though the wings were severed and now bleeding. Pointy, knife-like lettering with drips of red paint arches over the top: *Angel Baby*.

Motherfucker. It *was* him!

After a complete go-round with my cell, capturing all the damage on video, a memory from my teens hits me. When Aiden snuck in through my second-floor bedroom window after he'd been watching the house from the woods to see if I'd brought home a guy friend from school, whom I had previously mentioned wanted to start a band with me. My uninvited company proceeded to smack me around and raped me just for making him worry I'd brought a guy home from school. That was the day he first started threatening to harm my friends and family if I ever reported his abuse or attempted to leave him.

Attempting to shake off the memory with a shake of my head, I set down my boot knife and grab the buck knife—bigger and deadlier—from beside my small Marshall practice amp and unsheathe it. Good thing I keep a knife hidden in every room. With a life like mine—gotta stay armed. After a peek out the music room window and no sight of anyone lurking around outside, I scurry to check out all the other windows.

When I make it to the second set of windows in the living room, I turn left toward the kitchen and realize how visible I am from the outside. To my right—the tall, double windows beside the couch that I just looked out of. To my left—the sliding glass door leading out to the back deck, back yard, and the woods. The last window for me to check.

I hesitate.

Tightening my grip on the hilt of the knife, I drop to the floor and crawl toward the door, making myself a smaller target. Aiden never owned guns back when I dated him, but who knows how he's changed since then. Everyone and their fucking Grandmother owns at least one gun, if not more, these days. Maybe he does too.

Or maybe I'm just paranoid as all hell.

Rightfully so after finding my apartment vandalized.

I wish I owned a gun right now.

Lying flat on my stomach with my head near the bottom edge of the doorframe, I peer out into the back yard and the woods beyond. Vibrations from my blast beat heart rate pounds against the tile floor. Sweat tickles at my temples. Breath holds tight and shallow, tensing every muscle.

No one on the deck or in the back yard.

My eyes move further out toward the tree line.

The bottom branch of a hemlock sways slightly.

Maybe a bird?

A shallow breath later, the patch of ferns between that tree and the oak beside it, leaves rustling.

A squirrel…maybe?

Higher branches on the hemlock bounce and sway. Then I see it.

A foot. Then another. Read and black. Maybe sneakers? Higher branches bounce as the feet move out of sight. Shit! Why am I still watching? Someone's in the fucking tree outside my back door!

Someone?

No. There's only one person that can be. And after the graffiti…

Call the fucking cops already, you amateur sleuth!

I backward shimmy away from the door and across the kitchen floor. Once I make it to the living room, I jump to my feet, grab the landline, and call 911. While telling them why I need them to send help, I scurry back through the kitchen to lock the front doors. First, the one at the bottom of the stairs. Going down the stairs sets my heart rate soaring. Then, back up the stairs to lock the apartment door behind me.

Oh, shit. Can't lock this one. The psycho kicked it in, dammit!

I crouch down in the far corner of the living room near the big closet door where I'm hidden from every window in the place.

Shaking.

Sweating.

Knife and cell in hand, landline sitting beside me.

I wait.

And wait.

And wait.

Thirty minutes later, a cruiser finally arrives. I hear it pull in, see its flashing blue lights reflect through the front windows and shine across the wall. The police department is five minutes from my house, and my small town employs ten officers. Not sure what takes them so long, but Officer Palisano finally shows up, alone.

I guess they don't think I'm in danger.

That means they have no idea who did this or who's out in that tree. Well, after those lights flashing down my driveway, *whoever* I saw in that tree is probably hightailing it right out of here.

"Came home and found it like this. Didn't touch anything except closet doorknobs when I searched. Looks like nothing was stolen, though I couldn't do a thorough search without touching stuff. So, I waited for you. But I saw someone out back in that tree right there. See? That big hemlock." I point out the sliding glass door. "Red and black shoes. I think maybe sneakers." I lean closer to the glass. "I don't see anyone now, but that tree's bushy, and now with your lights…I don't know. Maybe they're gone now, but still…Can you please check there first? It's freaking me out.

"Sure thing." Officer Palisano leans close to the window and peers out into the trees as he unlocks the slider. Grabbing his flashlight from his belt, he aims it toward the tree's thick branches as he steps outside and then conducts a search around the hemlock and the whole back yard.

I stand by the slider, white-knuckling my buck knife, and wait.

Five minutes later, he climbs the back steps and comes back inside.

"No one's out there. Saw a bunch of footprints around the base of that hemlock, along with a few cigarette butts." On the palm of his gloved hand, he shows me five stubbed-out cancer sticks. "American Spirits. Know anyone who smokes those?"

"Huh, yeah, at least one, but that was years ago. But that's exactly who I suspect did this," I say, sweeping my hand through the air, motioning to the graffiti, "and that's who I suspect I saw in that tree."

Nodding, he pulls out a baggy, inserts the cigarette butts, seals it, and repockets it.

He takes a step closer to the kitchen cabinets to inspect the free artwork I received while away from home.

"Hmm…Yeah, I recognize this handiwork. The signature tag. Officers have seen this around town. Spotted around Portland and Westbrook too." He points to a little squiggly, psychedelic image near the lower left corner of a cabinet door covered in skulls. Not an actual signature of a name, but a graffiti tag. Aiden used to practice creating his own tag back in our teens. He covered his bedroom walls in graffiti art, as well as a ton of street signs and business signs around town.

I tell Palisano the time I got home and how long I've been gone, though I can't speak for my mom next door.

The whole visit is short and quite uneventful.

After strolling through the apartment and snapping some pictures and dusting for prints, Palisano stands beside the door at the top of the hallway stairs. "Well, I, too, have my suspicions who may have done this." He's no stranger to Aiden's criminal history. Afterall, Aiden grew up in this town where Palisano has been an officer for twenty-five years.

"I'd say, 'Check my surveillance,' but they smashed my equipment, my DVR." I point to the living room floor.

"It's not sent to your phone?" He looks confused.

I shake my head. "Haven't had the money to update it since my husband left earlier this year."

He nods. "Aha," is all he says. He holds up the little briefcase-like box in his hand. "If I can make a match to these prints, hopefully I can find him and make an arrest. Maybe forensics can get something off the cigarettes. Maybe not. We'll see. You can touch stuff now, and make sure to contact me if you find anything's been stolen or if you suspect someone's trespassing again." Palisano talks like he's already convinced who did this. "In the meantime, see if a friend can stay with you, or better yet, see if you can stay with someone else until you get that surveillance updated."

"Will do. Thanks."

Officer Palisano's heavy footsteps clomp down my stairs as I turn toward the mess I need to clean.

Trying to unwind and calm down with a fat bowl of ganga, smoke wafting out from between my lips, I make sure the Dr. is on hand—McGillicuddy's that is. The frosty bottle and shot glass sit on the coffee table in front of me. Cleaning that mess was a bitch! Then hauling my gear up here after…I am fucking beat! Unfortunately, I'm stuck with the graffiti until I can repaint. Need to see if I can borrow money from Mom to add a few deadbolts to my doors. I pour a shot.

Thankfully Ronnie didn't show up here before I pulled in. I dread his reaction to the graffiti, the break-in, but fuck him. Him and his shit will be out of here by tomorrow, or the next day at the latest. If I had it in me to act as vindictive as some girlfriends do, then I'd throw all his shit out the window and change my locks now. But it's late, I have no energy left to move his stuff and no money to buy new locks. And honestly, I don't want to stoop to his level. Knowing me, I'd feel bad about it after.

Guilt is a heaviness I refuse to carry.

But, man oh man, it feels damn fucking good fantasizing about it. Getting him the hell out of my life can't happen soon enough. I've been fuming about his bullshit since peeling out of the studio parking lot. Our demo sucks *and* Mike confirmed my suspicions.

On top of everything I've been dealing with, Ronnie, that jealous freak, *has* been stalking me. And here I had actually considered I was paranoid thinking that.

Nope.

Ronnie planned this whole thing. Right down to swooping in when I was vulnerable and separated from my husband. Promised to treat me like a queen, make the metal band I've dreamed of, make the family I've dreamed of, be the father I always imagined Jordan to be, or what I had thought Jordan *wanted* to be. And then I find out Ronnie's had a vasectomy and never told me. *Everything* was a fucking lie!

All his lies are exactly why he tries to buy my happiness. Like our *Sweeny Todd* night. No fun, though the actors put on one hell of a performance. I can't even believe I still went out with him that night. But I really wanted to see that fucking play! It's not like I can afford that shit with my part-time cemetery job.

And now this break-in?

I wonder if Mike and Kyle ever really wanted me in the band or if Ronnie just convinced them, in his manipulative way, to agree. He does have a way of talking big and putting stars in people's eyes, the ego-stroker that he is. He probably promised them I'd be the next Maria Brink or Lzzy Hale or Alissa White-Gluz. Probably promised them we'd be the next Arch Enemy or some bullshit star-studded lie.

I don't play music for recognition and fame. I play music because it courses through my veins. It's in my blood. It makes my soul sing. Music equals life.

Yeah, that last one…Not so sure now.

My life is a total fucking mess. The only good thing going for me right now—grad school. But now I'm stuck with a shitty recording to go with my project. Why can't I stop stressing about that? Yeah, maybe embarrassment will wash over me when I play that for the audience at my presentation, but it probably won't affect my grade. But it still sucks! My whole goal of going above and beyond to combine both of my passions to create a unique thesis project flew right out the fucking window. Going to grad school never seemed achievable for me, coming from a low-income, single-mom family with more than one kid. And now that I made it this far, I wanted to go big and finish with a bang. Now, that goal's been squashed. *And* I wasted my time and my money! That's how it typically goes for me, one disappointment after the other.

Just look at the shit-storm flying through my life, making it harder and harder to concentrate on polishing my thesis. Up until now, working on my project has helped me hide away from all my problems, bury my head in my work and forget about my crumbling life.

Now I find out that not only was my marriage based on lies, but so is this new relationship, the band, the studio engineer's recording abilities, my family. Everything is a fucking lie! I don't even know what's real anymore.

Psycho Satan's running around all buddy-buddy-criminal-co-conspirator with Aiden, the maniac who left nightmare scars on my brain, causing night terrors and me waking with the sweat-drenched shakes almost daily. Now he's crashed through my door again, literally. And who knows how often he's hidden in the trees, spying on me, stalking me. Yeah, maybe today was the first time, but knowing him, I highly doubt it.

How will I ever get a good night's sleep again?

My mother and best friend is knocking on heaven's door, barely holding on with her oxygen tank and her cigarettes and scratching bald spots on her head from all the stress caused by Satan.

And friends? I'd love to call on a friend right now. I wish I could talk to Allie, my bestie, but she's an "in-the-moment" chick who doesn't keep her cell on her all the time. I always have a hard time getting a hold of her. She works her fingers to the bone, then spends her off time caring for her aging parents and disabled brother. She's a fucking angel. Most of my other friends have turned into drunks or drug addicts, always looking for the next party. There's Beth, but she's probably at a concert or a party. She's always on the go, always hanging with a group of people I don't care to hang out with. My other two friends who haven't turned into drunks or drug addicts are always so busy with their careers and their families I have a hard time getting them to return my texts. I don't blame them though. Good for them for having their shit together. I'm happy for them.

As for me…

No matter how hard I work to make my life what I've dreamed it could be, everything falls apart. Everyone leaves or abuses or lies or steals or berates or sabotages all I've worked so hard to build and create.

And family, that's what I tried to have with Jordan. Been planning together for the past five years. We even thought of names for the little boy I see when I close my eyes. Then Jordan smacked me in the face with, *"Oh, sorry, I really don't want kids. I just didn't know how to tell you."*

A five-year-fucking-lie! Motherfucker!

And then there's Ronnie, not just a liar and jealous freak, but a stalker too.

Why do I have such a bad habit of allowing the worst people into my life, people who tear me down and stomp on me, people who hold me back, pull me down, and crush all my hopes and dreams? Why do I…

Oh, shit.

Here he comes.

The thud of Ronnie's footsteps stomping up the front hall stairs makes my muscles tense and my stomach turn.

I really need to get him out of my place and change my fucking locks. But dammit…What if Aiden comes back tonight? And I'm home alone? Even if Mom's home and that happens, there's not much she can do but call the cops. And by the time they get here, who knows what Aiden could do to me by then? To Mom? Maybe I should wait until tomorrow to kick Ronnie out…just in case.

This suuuuucks!

Not sure if I'm ready for this, but here goes.

"Where's my metal Goddess? Got great news!" Ronnie sing-songs his words as he saunters into the kitchen with a huge bouquet of lilies and sunflowers, two of my favorites. Again.

The ick-shivers run through me. I don't even try to force a smile. Even if I try, I know it will look fake.

Why didn't I see through his manipulative crap sooner? I need to burn those rose-colored glasses and tell him to fuck off.

Bide your time, Dahl, just make it through tonight. You can get rid of his ass tomorrow. One. More. Night. I shudder at the thought.

His squeaking sneaker announces the sudden halt in his steps when he notices the graffiti across the cupboards. "What the fuck is that?"

As a fresh hit wafts out from between my lips, I turn toward him and say, "I'm doing some redecorating. I call it 'Punk Rock Life'. Like it?" A sigh-laugh tumbles out of me, though I'm not amused.

He sits the large vase of flowers next to my Dr. on the coffee table in front of me. "Seriously?" He glances around. "Never knew you were into graffiti art, but that's cool."

What? Does he really believe my story? Damn. Maybe it's my turn to lie, at least to avoid more accusations I know he'll throw at me if I tell him the truth.

The thought of turning into a liar makes me cringe. I despise liars. But…

Fuck it! The truth can wait. For now.

I shrug. "The mood just hit me. What do you think?" I roll with it.

He smiles. "Maybe you can do our album cover art."

"We no longer have a band. Remember?"

"No worries. I already talked to some buddies. Got a new lead guitarist and drummer swinging by here tomorrow to talk about forming a new one." He sits down beside me on the couch, big smile, doe-eyes.

What the fuck is *this* all about? Does he not remember what happened about three hours ago?

Speechless, I stare at him.

I set down the bowl and lighter and replace them with another shot of Dr. McGillicuddy's. Weed mellows me too much, might make me lose my nerve to address the mammoth in the room. And I do *not* plan on remaining mellow. Not now. Not with him.

He leans toward me, aiming for a kiss.

I turn away, look straight ahead. Then I tip my shot back, enjoy the flavor, the invigoration.

Do you think he takes the hint?

Nope.

Out of my peripheral, I see him leaning closer and reaching toward me, as though to brush my hair aside, whisper sweet bullshit into my ear.

"Mmm, you smell so good. The smell of your patchouli always gets me going."

I can't take it anymore. I refuse!

Abrupt, I stand and push the coffee table out of my way, walk away from the couch.

He laughs. "Whoa! What's got your panties in a bunch?" He stands, steps toward me.

"Really? Am I the only one here who remembers what went down after our studio session?"

Stepping right up beside me, he loops his arm around my waist and pulls me so close our bodies press together. I pull my head away. He starts kissing my neck and breathing heavy in my ear.

"Come on. It's been too long." He squeezes my ass.

I shove him away. "What the fuck, Dude? You accuse me of fucking Mike, which I'm sure is what broke up the band, then you punch him in the face over your delusion? Now you think I want to fuck you? Man, you need to get a grip."

He reaches for my waist again, but I back further away, go over to the coffee table, pour myself another shot, tip it back, slam the glass on the table. Man, sure wish I could handle the hard stuff, so it would hit me quicker.

"And what about at your work, the crazy guy who broke the window? Did that even happen, or was that just an excuse to call me in the middle of the night to check up on me?"

Ronnie's face goes blank. Then a smile forms that I can't quite read. "What guy? What broken window?" He steps up beside me and rests his hand on my shoulder. "What is this all about? Are you drunk?"

My arm flies up, knocks his hand away. "Another fucking liar!" As I stomp away, I growl and grab my hair in frustration. Heat rises to my face so quickly it feels like flames engulfing me.

Do they *all* lie?

After taking a deep breath, I say, "Dude, I saw the broken window. I drove to your work right after you called. Glass all over the sidewalk and parking lot, broken window, no cops. What is *up* with you? What the hell is going on?"

"Hey, I have another surprise." He smiles wide. "I went to Buckdancer's Choice before I came here." Turning away, he heads toward the front door. "I'll be right back."

Thundering footfalls speed down the stairs.

What the hell?

So shocked I can feel my eyes bugging out, I stand alone in the middle of the living room. Wanting to go to the roof and scream at the world, I go back to the coffee table instead, reach for my bowl and lighter. I want to calm down. But if I calm down, I might not do what needs to be done. I set it all back down, reach for the bottle, tip it back, take a gulp. Fuck the glass!

Ronnie walks back in carrying a coffin-shaped hardshell guitar case. He lies it across the kitchen island, unclips the locks, opens the lid. As his head tips down toward what hides inside, Ronnie's eyes roll up to look at me. A manic smile appears. "My metal Goddess deserves nothing but the best."

He spins the case so I can see what's inside.

The Paul Allender, lead guitarist for Cradle of Filth, signature purple maple-top Paul Reed Smith with the bat inlays up the fretboard shimmers under the ceiling fan light. The guitar I've dreamt about but can never play with my tiny hands and that wide fretboard.

"What? How the hell did you pay for this? And why? You're behind on your car payments *and* your mortgage." Refusing to indulge his mania, I remain in the living room.

Ronnie stays silent. He pulls the axe out of its velvet-lined coffin and brings it to me. A Jimi Hendrix guitar strap dangles from the purple body. He lifts the strap and tries to loop it over my head for me to try it.

I step back, put my hands out, reject the offer. "No. You need to return that. This shit going on between us, a bouquet of flowers and my dream guitar will not fix or make me forget. What the hell is going on?"

His elated expression falls away, face pales, and his eyes widen. "Jimi's 'Purple Haze' came on the radio. *He* told me to get this for you, told me you needed it for the new band. Are you saying I should ignore Jimi's advice? Isn't he your hero?"

My mouth drops open and my eyes practically pop out of my skull. He actually thinks Jimi Hendrix talked to him through the radio? This is way more serious than I ever suspected. He's far beyond whatever I can do to help him.

Shit. What am I supposed to do?

With the guitar held out to his side, Ronnie sidles up beside me and wraps his arm around my waist again. I pull away, but he holds on tight and pulls me closer. Though I lean my head back, trying not to get too close, he leans in and whispers in my ear. "You'll look so hot with this sexy beast strapped across your body. Come on. You know you want to hold her. I want to see you hold her." He sticks his tongue in my ear.

I shove him away as hard as I can. "*Ronnie*, back the fuck off! This is serious. You're spending money you don't have to make me happy. You said *Jimi Hendrix* talked to you through the radio? Then there's the broken window at your work, the story about the guy who broke it, the cop you thought was Jordan's brother, and then the fight with Mike over your accusations of us sleeping together. I think you need to…"

"Facts! *Not* accusations." Rage paints his face; rage I've never seen from him since we met ten months ago. Worse than his fight with Mike. He tosses the PRS onto the couch. "Come on. You think I haven't seen the signs. You live in the woods. Then a month after you join the band, Mike says his family is shopping for houses out of the city with lots of woods for his boys to ride their dirt bikes. Then suddenly his wife hates you. The way he stares at your ass on stage. The way he has his nephew take all those pictures at practice. The way he changes his songwriting to please you. Come on. It's freaking obvious. You've been fucking! Stop lying about it!"

Me, a liar? This motherfucker just called me a liar? Oh man, it's on.

Fury bubbles up inside. The shakes surge through me. More heat rises to my face.

"Dude, if I wanted to fuck Mike, why the hell would I date you?"

"Great question. You tell me."

"First of all, I've only met his wife twice. And last time you accused me of fucking him, you said I was having a three-way with him *and his wife*. Now you tell me she hates me. Why does your story keep changing. And how can she hate me when she doesn't even know me?"

"Duh. She hates you because you're fucking her husband."

"No. I. Am. Not! Mike's not my type *at all*. He's a redneck, who loves to hunt. I'm a fucking vegetarian!"

"So what. That don't prove shit."

"The only time I've ever hung out with Mike has been with the band. He doesn't even know where I live! He knows what town, but that's it. And if you think I've been sneaking him over here, all you had to do was ask to see my surveillance footage."

A derisive laugh shoots out of him. "Yeah, you erased all *that* footage. I'm not an idiot, Dahl." As he shakes his head, a smartass smile appears on his psycho face.

A fucking smile!

I want to smack that smug look right off him! But I refuse to resort to violence. That will only work against me here.

I go on and on with more reasons why me fucking Mike is a batshit insane idea, but Ronnie has a rebuttal, albeit delusional rebuttals, for everything I say. Unable to contain my anger, I stomp off into the bedroom to get some space.

He follows me, yelling on and on about me hiding the affair.

As calmly as I can, I say, "Please, stop. Just give me some space."

He doesn't.

He moves toward me, uncomfortably close, spewing more insane reasons why he knows I'm lying. "You're a pothead, and now Mike smokes more weed than before you joined the band. He jumps on all your song ideas like you…"

The hanging shoe rack I've only half put together rests against the wall. I grab it, raise it over my head, then smash it against the floor with each word I shout. "I. Don't. Lie!" I drop the remaining broken pieces. "I'm not fucking Mike! This shit's fucking crazy. *You're* fucking crazy! Do you *hear* yourself? You. Sound. Crazy!"

Ronnie jumps back. Fear washes over his face. He scurries out of the bedroom, goes into the music room.

I'm relieved he walked away, leaving me alone to calm myself down. But then I wonder what he's doing near my music gear.

I go to the music room door and peer inside. Ronnie's crouched down in the back corner, shaking and looking like a scared little puppy. The closer I get to him, I notice he's crying.

Shit. Now I feel bad for flipping out with that shoe rack. But damn it, he wouldn't back off. I didn't know what to do. He's obviously having some sort of psychotic break or some shit. I don't know. What if he tried to hurt me? Wouldn't be the first time some dude cornered me and smacked me around, had their way with me. Nope. Not letting that happen again.

But now look at him.

I step over to him, reach my hand out to console him. He flinches. Fear fills his eyes.

"Ronnie, I'm not going to hurt you. You wouldn't listen or give me space. I just wanted you to stop." I reach toward him again. He doesn't pull away.

As I rub his shoulder to help him feel safe, he starts sobbing.

"What's going on? *Please*, tell me." I gently squeeze his shoulder, lift his chin so he'll look at me.

"I'm not crazy." His words come out stuttered. "I'm *not*." He buries his head in his knees.

I lean in, give him a hug.

Why am I like this? Why can't I stop myself from trying to help someone who treats me like shit?

"Your heart's too big, always gets you into trouble." Jordan's words bounce around my brain.

"Ronnie, I really think you need to go speak with someone, someone who can help you."

"I'm not crazy." The words come out choppy as he shakes his head, refusing to look at me.

"Let's call the crisis center, get you in to speak with someone. I'll drive you there. I'll be right there with you the whole time. Come on." I squeeze his shoulder and give it a slight pull to nudge him up off the floor to come with me.

He shoves me away, jumps to his feet. "No fucking way! Don't try to turn this all on me! I don't need some head doc telling me I'm crazy just to make *you* look right," he screams in my face, spittle flying.

It's like I flicked a switch.

He grasps my upper arms, picks me up off the ground, and carries me to the bedroom. A twisted creeper-grin emerges on his sweaty face.

A memory flashes across my mind—an image of Aiden straddling me, my shirt torn open, knife to my throat.

"Never again!" I kick and scream, trying to squirm free, but Ronnie is much taller, stronger, and filled with psychotic rage.

Another flashback flickers across my mind: Aiden, picking me up, carrying me to his bedroom, shoving me through the trapdoor in the floor into his hideaway-hole/escape-hatch under his trailer. The memory flies from my mind as Ronnie throws me onto the bed. He unzips his pants, hauls his stiff dick out.

Why the hell is he aroused right now?

He jumps up onto the mattress and tries to straddle me.

At least this psycho doesn't have a knife to my throat.

Wish I had my knife right now.

Maybe this time I can get away.

My knee flies up and nails him in the balls. As he grunts and falls to the side, cradling his crotch, I start scooting off the bed.

But I don't get far before he grabs a handful of my long hair and shoves my face between his legs.

"Time to soothe the pain with those soft lips of yours." Rubbing his shaft, he shoves his dick in my face. "Wrap your lips around this, baby. You know you want to."

I start screaming, "No! Stop! Please, stop! Someone help!"

"No one can hear you out here in the woods, sweety." He wraps his hand tighter in my hair, getting closer to the scalp. It feels like my flesh is tearing open.

Struggling to get away, I kick and scream, knock everything off the nightstand. The lamp crashes to the floor. The alarm clock falls off the edge, hanging by its cord. Notebooks and loose papers scatter everywhere. A couple more kicks and the clock radio blares to life. Sting's "Every Breath You Take" blasts through static. I grab for my cell teetering on the edge of the table. Though I can't see what I'm doing, I squeeze the side buttons, signaling an emergency, fumble with the SOS slide, try contacting 911. *Hope* it's contacting 911. I've never done this before.

Ronnie yanks my hair. My cell slips from my hand. The more I wrestle to get away, the tighter he latches on.

How's this skinny asshole so fucking strong?

"Get your fucking hands off me, *psycho*!"

He keeps grabbing at me, yanking my head closer, trying to get me to suck his dick, but I keep fighting back.

He doesn't give up.

As much as it disgusts me to even be this close to him, I finally open my mouth, insert his cock, and bite down as hard as I can.

"Arrrrrrrgh!" His scream pierces my eardrums. He immediately releases my hair and backhands me upside the head. I fall to the floor.

I shake it off, reach under the mattress, retrieve my knife.

"You stupid whore!" Cradling his dick in his palm, he drops his legs over the side of the bed to get up. As soon as his feet touch the floor, I drive the blade into his left leg just above the knee.

"Motherfucker!"

He winces, backhands me across the face, and shoves me to the ground. My ass hits the floor. He wraps his hands around the hilt of the blade, grunts as he yanks it out, then throws it across the room. A crimson river runs down his calf, dripping onto the hardwood floor. He still stands up.

Towering over me, he steps closer, appears barely phased by the injury.

Just like psycho Aiden, who still fought off my protectors after they beat him in the head with nun-chucks.

I bury the memory—*again*.

Ronnie glares down at me with his red-rage face, sweat-drenched hair, and bugged-out eyes.

Crab-crawling away, I grab my cell, yell down at the screen, "Help! Someone, help me! Please, someone…"

"You're not as smart as you think you are, cunt! No one can hear you!" Leaning down, he grasps my ankle, pulls me under him. "But *I'll* help you." That last line comes out creepy-calm, almost soothing. But I know better, know where it's coming from. Grabbing my other ankle, he twists my legs, flips me onto my stomach.

I reach out, grasp at the floor, trying to pull myself away. Making it only as far as the doorway, I feel Ronnie lower himself on top of me. His knees tighten around my hips, freeze me in place. Warm moisture soaks through my jeans on my left hip. The copper scent fills my nostrils, making me gag. Though I keep reaching and pulling at the doorframe, I can't pull free from his leghold. His stiff cock presses against my ass.

Leaning down against my back, he flattens me to the floor and slowly lowers his face beside my ear. His beer breath makes me want to retch as he whispers, "Now I know you like it rough. No more teasing. Take it like the whore you are."

He reaches underneath me, fumbles for the zipper of my jeans.

Sirens blare outside my windows.

Wow! That was fast. Thank God!

A few more fumbles with my zipper and more kicks from me. The sirens grow louder and the blue lights swirl and flash across the walls beside the living room windows.

"Help! Up here! Please, help me!"

Ronnie's knee-grip on my hips loosens, and I pull away, hair all disheveled and sticking to my sweaty face and neck. I scrabble across the living room floor toward the kitchen.

Multiple footfalls thunder up the hallway stairs. The front door flies open, smashes against the wall.

Just as I make it to the kitchen and start lifting myself to my feet, crying and sniffling, two police officers rush in, guns raised.

I turn in the direction of their aimed guns and see Ronnie, stiff dick in his hands, blood river running down his leg, staining my authentic, handwoven Navajo rug from Arizona.

"Freeze!"

"Stop right there!"

Ronnie's hands fly up into the air, face flush, shaggy hair sticking to his drenched forehead. His erection hangs out of his unzipped jeans, and for some bizarre reason, it looks like it's stiffening even more.

What the hell is wrong with this freak?

The taller, female cop rushes toward Ronnie, gun aimed. "Put your dick in your pants, then turn around with your hands behind your back!" She ignores the knife wound, not bothering to ask if he's okay.

Ha! I like this chick!

Ronnie complies, slowly.

The older, male officer, the one who's worked for the town's PD since I was a teen, steps over to me, gun still aimed at Ronnie. His salt-and-pepper hair sticks out a little from under his hat. "Dahlia, are you okay? Do you need medical services?"

Shaking my head, I look down at my rumpled clothes, run my hand down my front to straighten myself out. I don't want to look back up. I don't want to look him in the face. I don't want to make eye contact.

I'm fucking mortified.

This isn't the first time Officer Frank Palisano has saved me from a psycho boyfriend.

How the hell do I get myself into situations like this?

As I try to control my sobbing, I wipe the tears and snot from my face, attempt to neaten my hair. That's when I notice Ronnie's reddened handprints on both of my upper arms, one already starting to bruise. And the blood stain on my favorite jeans. A couple stuttered attempts at deep breaths later, and now I'm fucking pissed. My shoulders hike up to my ears as I breath in one more time and look up at the female cop cuffing Ronnie. My words come out as calm as I can manage. "Get that fucking psycho out of my house, please."

Officer Palisano steps over to them and nods at his partner. She steps back and lets Palisano take it from here. And he doesn't take it easy.

Palisano glances down at the leg wound. "Looks like she needs to practice her aim." His eyes roll up and glare at Ronnie.

He yanks Ronnie's arms back, makes him wince, shoves him toward the door. As they pass by me, Palisano looks down at me, attempts a smile, though it's more of a smirk. "I'll take care of this creep for you." He side-eyes the graffiti on the cupboards. "You *really* should have someone stay with you tonight."

It's hard to talk. It's hard to look him in the eyes, but I do. And all I can bring myself to say is, "I really know how to pick 'em, huh?"

Palisano's smirk remains as he slowly nods and then looks back toward Ronnie. Just before he shoves him toward the stairs, Palisano says, "There ain't no smacking me around like you did to this young woman. You're done, asshole."

♫ ∎ ♪

Alone at home in the woods at midnight, with no one to stay with me and no place else to stay, my head pounds, my entire body aches, and the deluge of tears hasn't let up. I texted Beth. I texted Allie. I received the *"Notifications silenced"* message both times. Still no return texts. Still no calls. I sent those texts an hour ago. But it's late, so I guess I understand. Still sucks. I could go sleep at Mom's. But she isn't even home yet. Her blackened windows look ominous. I'd still be alone inside there. And I have no idea where she is. She refuses to own a cell phone, so I can't call or text her.

So, I sit on the bench in front of the living room window and gaze out at the night sky, stars twinkling, full moon shining bright, whip-o-wills filling the air with their songs, bats swooping over the yard as they feast and soar. My Jimmy sits parked in the driveway in front of the garage. Mom's parking space is still empty. Jordan's parking space is empty. My bottle of Dr. McGillicuddy's is now empty. And I feel empty.

How could I be such a fool? How did I let another psycho rapist and abuser into my life? How am I thirty-seven years old, on the verge of divorce, no kids, no house, no career, still going to college, still an amateur writer, still no publications, still living in my mother's garage apartment, still dealing with psycho Satan, still driving an unreliable vehicle, still broke as shit, and still struggling to keep a gigging band together? This is not how I'd imagined my life would turn out. This is not where I want to be. This is not the life I chose. This is not the life I dreamed about as a child, but still, somehow, I'm here. Alone. Broken, beaten and scarred. No one to confide in. No one to cry to. No one to hold. No one to tell me everything is going to be all right. Because everything is *not* going to be all right. The sun may rise tomorrow, but *I* don't want to. I don't want this life. I don't want this fucked up bullshit. I can't deal with it anymore. I'm tired and fed up with every*thing* and every*one*.

It's not like I have time to meet someone new, get to know them, cultivate a relationship, grow to love and trust them, and then conceive the child I've dreamed about, start the family I've been planning—alone—for years. I'm fucking thirty-seven! I'm running out of time.

The moment Ronnie showed up in my driveway with his car packed and ready to move into my place without even asking, I should've immediately said, "No way in hell," and got rid of his psycho ass then.

Woulda, shoulda, coulda. Always living with regret of my stupid-ass decisions.

What is wrong with me? How do I get myself into messed up shit like this? As much as I try to make the right decisions, I keep fucking up over and over again. Why can't I get my shit together? Why do all these horrible people flock to me like I'm fire and they're moths? I can't make it stop. It's maddening!

Little, white crumpled clouds of cotton cover the floor around me. Like I'm in the sky. But no. I'm out of tissues again. I don't have the energy to move to go get more. It's like a weight is on me, pressing me down, making me feel...heavy.

Like that old painting: *The Nightmare.* The incubus on the sleeping woman. A perfect depiction of my life, how I feel. Depression. Like a monster holding me down. Preying upon my life force, my essence, my soul.

How is it that I feel so low, so alone, so lost, when I've worked so hard my whole life, worked so hard for the things I want, worked so hard to make my dreams come true, only to end up living a fucking nightmare?

All I want to do is escape, get away from all this bullshit, get away from all that keeps dragging me down. All I want to do is sleep. Close my eyes...forever.

My bowl sits on top of the stereo speaker beside the bench. No matter how much I smoke, it does nothing to make me relaxed or happy or calm. If only I did heroin instead. Then I could just nod off, wrapped in a velvety soft opiate blanket, and drift away.

My head pounds like a hammer to the skull, thundering through my whole achy body. My upper arms throb, heart in a crushing vise-grip, teeth grind, jaw tense.

The bench creaks under my weight as I stand up. Joints protest as I hesitantly put one foot in front of the other. Dizzying anxiety makes my movements slow and choppy. Once I get to the bathroom, I refuse to look in the mirror. I can't stand to see the mess I've become. When I open the drawer next to the sink, Ronnie's straight razor shimmers under the overhead light. I reach for it, pull it out, flip it open, and sob.

It won't take much effort to make it all stop. Right here. Right now.

The cold steel feels refreshing against the clammy skin of my palm.

My shoulders bounce along with my sobs. My head feels like it might burst from the pressure. My tears fall, crashing around me. The salty rivers flow down my cheeks nonstop. I don't know what the fuck to do with myself anymore. I'm a fucking wreck!

I could call Jordan, confide in him, see if he'll reconsider coming back, reconsider creating a family with me, the family we've *talked about* creating for the past five years. But I don't want to sound desperate, and I don't want to make him think I'm only calling because Ronnie went psycho on me. Plus, Jordan made it clear during our last fight he no longer wants to talk to me about this subject.

If I call one of my other friends, they probably won't answer this late. Plus, I don't want to be the Debbie Downer, bringing them down with all my life's boo-hooing woes. Squashing other people's happiness and contentment is the last thing I want to do. It's bad enough for me to deal with. I don't want to dump my shit on anyone else, especially not my loved ones.

But I really need someone right now. I could use a shoulder. An ear. A hug would be fucking wonderful. Where the hell is Mom? She gives the best hugs! Why isn't she home yet? This is so weird. I don't remember the last time she stayed the night somewhere else. And of all the nights she doesn't come home…Why tonight? When I need her the most?

I feel selfish even thinking that. She deserves to have a social life. At least someone around here does.

I grab my cell. Make sure the volume's turned up. Check my texts.

Still nothing.

I toss it aside, sink deep into the couch.

I'm alone. Empty. Hanging onto the frayed ends of sanity by my fingertips. And slipping.

Maybe if I pack Ronnie's shit and move it to the garage, a wave of closure will wash over me, lift my spirits.

Or maybe I just need to go outside, get some fresh air, listen to the leaves sing in the wind.

I don't know.

What I do know—there's no way in hell I'll be able to rest and fall asleep right now.

I have no idea what the hell to do with myself, how to get out of my head full of spiraling out of control thoughts. Why can't I find a way to make them all stop, or at least mellow out?

I wish so desperately to talk to someone.

I wish Mom was home. But her house sits dark and empty. Like me. And though she'd talk my ear off most nights, if I brought these feelings to her, she'd urge me to get help, call Opportunity Alliance, the crisis center. Call the suicide prevention hotline. Call the professionals.

But a stranger? Why would I want to dump my shit on a stranger? Though that is their job. They get paid to listen to people like me boo-hoo and piss and moan.

Man, I feel so pathetic. What a fucking weak loser I am. I just want to feel better. Please, just make it all stop! How can I make it all go away?

Cordless phone in my shaky hand, cell on the coffee table with the lit-up screen displaying the Maine Crisis Hotline, I dial 1-888-568…

Tears blur my vision. I wipe them away, see the rest of the phone number. My trembling finger hovers over the next number to press on the receiver. Chest heaves and shoulders bounce from my pathetic sobbing.

I can't do this.

I hang up.

Shit.

What a fucking mess I am.

Squeezing the receiver with a white-knuckle grip, a desperate scream erupts out of me. Tears waterfall down my steaming-hot cheeks.

Why can't I do this?

I *need* to do this.

I need to talk to *some*one.

If I don't let this out, it's sure as shit going to drown me, suffocate me, close my eyes forever, snuff me out of existence. That's a surefire way to never reach my goals, to never earn my graduate degree, to never have the family I dream about, to never meet the little boy who visits me while I sleep, to never see my work published, to not be around to help Mom, to never write and perform music again.

I.

Need.

To.

Do.

This.

Now!

Fuck it.

1-888-568-1112. Maine's Crisis Hotline rings into my ear.

"Maine Crisis…this…Holly. How…help…"

Out of breath and unable to stop crying, I catch only part of what the person on the other end is saying. I try to talk, but the double-breathing effect from my cries keeps words out of reach. I need to say something. What if they hang up?

"Hello?"

"Yes, sorry, someone's here. I'm here please don't hang up…I-I-I…" Sobs swallow my words. What am I supposed to say?

"It's okay. Take your time. Making this call isn't easy. But I'm here. I'm here as long as it takes you. I'm here to listen. And I look forward to hearing your story." The soft, calm voice rolls through the line, wrapping around me like a gentle hug, a warm blanket, a soft pillow to rest my head on.

My sobs intensify with the anticipation of dumping all my dirt into this stranger's ear. I grab a tissue from the roll of toilet paper sitting on the coffee table beside my cell, cover my mouth, and attempt to calm myself enough to talk.

As soon as I grow quieter, the voice on the phone says, "Are you calling for yourself or are you concerned about someone else?"

"Me. It's me," I manage to say.

"Alright. That's a good start. I am very concerned that you are so upset, and I want to help. I just need to ask you a few questions. Can you please give me your name and number just in case our call gets cut off, so I can call you back?"

My name and number?

I hesitate.

What the fuck is this all about? Is my name going to go into some database? A list of crazies to keep track of? A list of nutjobs to never hire for jobs or rent an apartment to or allow near children or…

"I want to assure you—our agency *never* traces *any* calls that come in to us, and we never share or sell your information to anyone or to any companies. This is a safe space. Sometimes cell calls get dropped or phones run out of battery, and I just want to make sure you are able to talk to me for as long as you need to."

"I'm on a landline, so I don't have to worry about that." My words come out choppy as I try to simmer down my crying. Giving her my name and number doesn't sit right with me, though her reasoning makes sense. But still…

"Are you calling from your home or someone else's? And is someone there with you or are you alone?"

"I'm at my home, alone." Though I hesitate, I give her my first name and phone number. Then I blurt out, "I don't *want* to be alone." My crying intensifies. Big time. I grab more tissues, try to calm down.

Why do I feel so out of control?

Before I realize what I'm doing, my dirty laundry spills from my mouth into the phone, starting with what happened tonight, Ronnie and the blade, the cops arresting him and hauling his ass out of here.

"Dahlia, you did the right thing calling the cops and reporting what Ronnie did to you. I am so sorry you had to go through that. And I imagine you must be hurting a lot right now, and it may seem like there is no way out, but I believe that I can help you, *if* you let me."

"That's not even everything. That's only what happened *t-t-tonight*. My life is a never-ending h-h-horror story." My breath hitches. I cover my mouth with a tissue, wanting to save her from listening to me cry more.

"Has Ronnie done this to you before?"

"No, n-n-nothing like that but…" An image of Jordan crosses my mind, which intensifies my crying, again.

"Dahlia, it's okay. Take your time." She waits while I quiet my sobs. Then she says, "Dahlia, I need you to tell me—have you put the straight razor away? And are there any other weapons you have that could harm you?"

"No, no more…weapons n-n-near me."

"Good. That's very good. Now, you said Ronnie's never done this to you before. What else have you been dealing with that makes you want to harm yourself?"

I jump back to the fight with Jordan, our separation, Satan's attacks, and work my way to pull all the story threads together to meet somewhere in the middle.

By the time I make it to the part about the studio session and the band breaking up, my one-way tale has turned into a mutual back-and-forth conversation, unfolding with much more ease than I had anticipated. A feeling of nostalgia surges through me, similar to déjà vu but stronger. The counselor's name is Holly, and for some odd reason, if feels like we've known each other longer than we've been on this call. After the first few minutes of talking with her, even the timbre and cadence of her voice started to sound familiar as though we've talked before. I'm not sure what to make of that. All I know is, the longer I talk, the easier it is to talk to someone about everything—even this stranger, who doesn't feel so much like a stranger anymore.

Our conversation lasts about twenty-five minutes or so. Depression and loneliness and feelings of betrayal still weigh heavy on my shoulders when I hang up the phone, but…

Now I have a plan.

And now I think sleep won't be as much of a problem as I'd thought before that much needed call.

I get up off the couch to return the phone receiver to the charger cradle and notice I'm no longer dizzy and off balance, no longer light-headed and brain-fogged. But when I glance into the bedroom and see Ronnie's two basses hanging on the wall and his clothes on the shelves and his blood on the floor, a knot forms in my stomach and nausea kicks in.

I take a deep breath and turn away.

The couch seems like a much better option for tonight.

Hey, did you really think one phone call would fix *every*thing?

Hell no!

All I can hope for is progress, improvement. One foot in front of the other, as the saying goes.

Oh, and not wanting to make myself bleed out of this life at a premature date—that's a pretty fucking big thing to hope for too.

The silky, chenille blanket on the couch calls to me. I plop my exhausted ass onto the sofa and see step one of my plan staring at me from beside my packed bowl and lighter. An appointment time with a counselor, scheduled for tomorrow, written on a purple Sticky Note. A few deep breaths help me melt back into the pillow. As I reach for my bowl and lighter to assist with falling asleep, my cell phone chimes. Is it Beth or Allie texting me back?

Nope.

The lit-up screen displays an email notification.

At this hour?

Probably some automated promotional bullshit.

But the odd timing piques my interest, and I can't stop myself from checking to see who it's from.

Philip Franco appears on the *Sender* line.

The name sounds familiar, but I can't place it. I click it open.

Is this real?

Did I just get spammed?

I open the "Submissions" folder in my Gmail account. Scanning past the recent submissions I've sent out that have not reached their submission deadline yet, I finally find the five novel submissions I sent out over six months ago.

There it is!

Philip Franco, Editor-in-Chief of the indie UK publisher Hallowed Ground Press.

No fucking way!

This does *not* feel real At. All.

They want to publish my novel!

Shit!

It's going to be really tough to fall asleep now.

But I'd much rather lose sleep from excitement than despair.

Maybe I *can* handle this thing called life after all.

Maybe.

Setting my phone aside, I grab the bowl of Indica and take a couple tokes. I hope this new counselor doesn't instantly want to put me on sleeping pills or antianxiety meds. Weed is much safer than those chemical concoctions.

My body feels relaxed now, but thinking about my novel acceptance sets my thoughts alight and sends them spinning. I need to tell someone the good news. But it's so late, no one will answer a text or a call at this hour.

Oh well, I can still send one.

Without thinking it through, I send a quick text to Jordan. I'm not sure why because I know he won't respond. I'm the last person he wants to hear from. As soon as the *Delivered* notification appears under my message, I lie down and close my eyes.

A text message chimes on my phone.

Why would Jordan be awake this late?

Probably a promotional text.

I reach out to shut off my phone, so I can sleep without interruptions. The screen lights up with the second text chime before I squeeze the buttons.

"Congratulations! I always knew you could do it babe I'm your biggest fan"

Jordan's text ends with a purple heart emoji.

The End

Author's Note

All profit and 5% of all proceeds from the sale of this book over the next ten years are being donated to The Opportunity Alliance, the organization that runs the Maine Crisis Line, to support their suicide prevention program. *TOA is a Community Action Agency providing integrated community-based and clinical programs serving thousands of people annually throughout the state of Maine.*
Every day, and in times of crisis, help starts here.
www.opportunityalliance.org/crisis

If you or someone you know is having a behavioral health crisis or having thoughts of suicide or self-harm, there is help out there. Help can be reached nationwide by dialing 988 to be connected to a crisis support specialist in your area. For people in Maine, you can call the Maine Crisis Line (MCL) by calling or texting 988 or calling 1-888-568-1112. For chat, go to their website at www.opportunityalliance.org/crisis. This is Maine's crisis response service answered by trained professionals, who provide free and confidential support via call, text, or chat 24/7, 365 days a year, day or night. **They serve <u>everyone</u>.**

Another great resource is the National Alliance on Mental Illness (NAMI). From their website: ***When someone experiences a mental health crisis and doesn't receive the care they need, they can end up in emergency rooms, on the streets, involved in the criminal justice system, or in the worst case, they could lose their life. A 24/7 crisis hotline can be the first line of defense in preventing these tragedies and an essential part of any continuum of care for mental health crises.***

https://www.nami.org/Advocacy/Policy-Priorities/Responding-to-Crises/National-Hotline-for-Mental-Health-Crises-and-Suicide-Prevention/

You are not alone. I see you. I feel you. I relate to you. Help is out there.

To contribute to the organization please scan this code:

Acknowledgments

First and foremost, I want to give a shout-out and a huge thank you to Mark Tullius, owner of Vincere Press, for inviting me to write this book for the *Try Not to Die* series. I am forever grateful for the opportunity to share this story with the world, with the hope that it helps others dealing with mental health distress and suicide ideation.

Mark's commitment to mental health awareness is refreshing and inspiring. He and I have both lost loved ones to suicide—three for me, to be exact—which is part of the reason why we both feel very deeply about this subject matter. Thank you to Andrew Najberg for all his valuable editorial feedback that helped make this book better. Thank you to artist Jun Ares for the amazing book cover artwork. And another thank you to Mark for his ongoing support and editorial feedback during the entire process of writing and developing this book. It was certainly a rough road for various reasons.

Anyone who has read any of the other books in the *TNTD* series will see that this book is very different than all the others; this is not horror for fun entertainment. This is dark fiction about a serious topic, one without demons or supernatural monsters; this story deals with human monsters and the gigantic monsters of suicide ideation and depression. Though this book follows the interactive theme of choosing your own path, many of those paths veer into dark and depressing territory rather than fun and exciting horror mishaps. Honestly, I struggled with that aspect of writing this story for various reasons, and I worried that fans of the *TNTD* series, as well as diehard horror fans, might come away disappointed that this is not what they might've expected; it's not your typical horror. Also, writing seven different endings for the same story—for someone like me who always says, "Endings are hard"—was definitely a challenge. But I love to challenge myself, especially creatively.

Thank you to The Opportunity Alliance and their Maine's Mobile Crisis Line for all the vital work they do to support people in communities across the great state of Maine, and thank you specifically to Lily Lynch, VP of Development and Communications, and Carrie Swarthout, Director of Crisis Services of TOA for their enthusiasm for this book and their interest in partnering with Mark and myself. Thank you to Bethany Cianciolo for introducing me to Carrie, so we could make this important partnership happen. A personal thank you goes to my husband, Jesse, for holding me up and lending an ear and a shoulder and a hand while I worked through the emotional toll of writing this story. I fought many inner demons, faced many traumatic memories, and unburied a plethora of personal truths along the bumpy road in order to arrive at the final product of this book you now hold in your hand. No, this is not an autobiography, but it is inspired by true events.

About that bumpy road . . .

I apologize if any of the content of this book triggered any of my readers. The act of writing this book set off my own personal triggers, but this story screamed and begged me to share it with the world. So, I pushed through to create an authentic story about the extreme difficulties of dealing with suicide ideation and depression because these are important topics to address. There are not enough discussions about these unsettling and debilitating mental illnesses. Too many people suffer with suicide ideation and depression every day. Many of these people have no resources to help them, no support system, no one to talk to, no family, no friends, and they have no knowledge of coping mechanisms to help alleviate their negative internal dialogue, depression, and suicidal thoughts. Some people feel ashamed to admit they are having mental health trouble and need help. Others might feel weak because of it. But I am here to tell you, everyone needs help sometimes, and there is no shame in admitting that—ever. Asking for help shows strength, determination, and it shows your commitment to your own personal wellbeing.

At a certain point in my life, I suffered from severe depression, debilitating social anxiety, and disturbing suicidal thoughts. I was an angry teenager, wishing I had never been born. Eventually, my untreated mental health troubles snowballed to the point of a suicide attempt. During that attempt, I had my first out-of-body experience. Hovering above myself, looking down at the mess I had become, I saw flashes of potential futures that suicide would have stolen from me. At that specific point in my life, I had lost so much that I thought my whole life was ruined, that nothing could possibly get better, that the pain would never go away, and that my struggles would keep growing. I felt like a complete loser who couldn't do anything right, and I felt like I would never figure out how to keep harmful people away from me. But seeing those potential futures made me realize that no one truly knows what tomorrow will bring. Where I initially saw more pain and loss and struggle, I began seeing and realizing that change is inevitable. I had the power to change, not just myself, but my situation; that power lies in the decisions I make.

From that point on, I vowed to never allow myself to feel that lost and helpless ever again. And I am thankful to say, suicidal thoughts have never entered my mind since. Not since that fateful day. Now don't get me wrong—it has *not* been easy. Not. At. All. The road I've traveled since then has been long, bumpy, and full of detours, but I say with the utmost sincerity—it was all worth it. All those struggles, all those hardships made me the person I am today, and I wear *all* my scars with pride. I've earned every last one of them with strength, determination, a shit-ton of tenacity, and a fierce fighting spirit. I still get depressed sometimes, and I still deal with anxiety in varying degrees, but I've learned how to better manage my mental health.

But—and this is a big but—I didn't do it all on my own. I've been to counseling a few different times throughout the course of my life, which helped me tremendously. I also earned my degree in psychology and worked in the mental health field for many years, so I could both learn more about myself and go on to help others struggling with their mental health. And the message I want to send with this book: You can make it. You can survive. You can make yourself happier and make your life better. You have the power of discovery and the power of change on your side. Help is out there. Help to guide you. Help to inform you of resources to help improve your situation. Help that will listen and be there for you and hold your hand along the way to a stronger and happier you and to a happier and more fulfilling life.

We are all in this together. Life gets tough, so let's be there for one another. If you know someone who is struggling with their mental health, reach out to them and let them know you're there for them. Let them know you'll listen. Sometimes that's all any of us need—someone to listen. And if you're the one who needs someone to listen, don't be afraid or ashamed to reach out to someone and ask for help. It can literally save your life.

One final note:

When Mark Tullius invited me to write this book for the *Try Not to Die* series, I jumped at the opportunity. Mark specifically asked me because based on my other works—*The Bone Cutters* and *Chisel the Bone*—he knew I could write about such a tough subject matter and make it raw, unflinching, and authentic; Dory, the protagonist of *The Bone Cutter* series, suffers from suicide ideation, depression, PTSD, and severe anxiety. You may wonder why I wanted to keep writing about suicidal characters when my book series already takes on that subject matter. Or maybe not, but I want to tell you anyway—One of the biggest reasons why I agreed to take on this project was because Mark's invitation landed in my *Inbox* about two months or so after I had lost a dear close friend to suicide. I hadn't been in touch with that friend in a few years because we had a falling out over his "dangerous" lifestyle. The last time we had talked, I reached out to him to let him know my husband and I were worried about him, we wanted to make sure he was doing okay, and we missed him.

However, his mental illness had sunken its claws in so deep he couldn't accept the love and friendship I offered to him. Though I'd told him how much we cared about him, he kept repeating that all his friends had abandoned him; he could not understand or internalize the words I'd said to him.

That's how depression works; it creates negative internal dialogue, making the sufferer think every*thing* and every*one* is only out to hurt them. The last thing I had said to him was, "We're worried that the next thing we hear about you is that you're dead." And that's exactly what happened. I beat myself up about this all the time, wishing I had reached out again after that last conversation, wishing we had tried harder to get through to him to let him know we cared, wishing we could've helped him stop with his dangerous lifestyle . . . wishing, wishing, wishing. So, when Mark came to me with the invitation to write this book, I knew I had to say yes. I *needed* to say yes. I knew I needed to write this book, not just for myself, but for Joey, and for everyone else out there suffering alone. I wasn't there for my friend Joey in the end, but this book lives on for him forever.

We love you and miss you always, Joey! We miss your smile that lit up every room you walked into. We miss your endless jokes and sense of humor. We miss your infectious laughter. We miss your music and your songwriting. We miss your artwork, all those amazing drawings. We miss you so much it hurts. I hope you're playing guitar in the stars, singing through the cosmos, and making your artistic mark everywhere your soul travels. Rest in peace, Joey.

We *will* meet again.

Sincerely,

Renee S. DeCamillis
July 31, 2025

About the Author

Renee S. DeCamillis is a horror author and freelance editor, and the author of the psychological thriller/supernatural horror novella *The Bone Cutters*, Book 1 in *The Bone Cutters* series, and *Chisel the Bone*, Book 2 in the series. Renee's short fiction appears in various anthologies, such as: *Dethfest Confessions: The Devil's Playlist*; *Horrors of the Deep: Startling Sea Stories*; *After the Burn: A Post-apocalyptic Anthology*; *Wicked Women: An Anthology of New England Horror Writers*; and more. Her poetry appears in the *Horror Writers Association Poetry Showcase Vol. IV*. She is a member of the Horror Writers Association, the New England Horror Writers, and the Horror Writers of Maine. Renee is also the lead singer/songwriter and rhythm guitarist for the punk-metal band Scars Aligned, and she's a tree-hugging hippie with a sharp metal edge.

Renee earned a BA in psychology, an MFA in Popular Fiction Writing, and attended Berklee College of Music as a music business major with guitar as her principal instrument. Renee is a former model, school rock band teacher, creative writing teacher, private guitar instructor, A&R rep for an indie record label, therapeutic mentor, psychological technician, and preschool teacher. She is also a former gravedigger; she can get rid of a body fast without leaving a trace, and she is not afraid to get her hands dirty. Renee lives in the woods of southern Maine with her husband, their son, and a house full of ghosts.

You can find Renee on BlueSky, Substack, Instagram, Facebook and her website https://reneesdecamillis.com/

Download Your Free Copy

Includes the first two chapters and one or two death scenes from each of the first 14 books in the Try Not to Die series.

Download for free.

For More Fun-Filled Deaths

please check out the rest of the

Try Not to Die series.

[Try Not to Die on Amazon](#)

Out Now:

At Grandma's House
In Brightside
In the Pandemic
In the Wizard's Tower
In the Wild West
At Ghostland
At Dethfest

Back at Grandma's House
On Slashtag
In a Dark Fairy Tale
At the Meadow Spire Mall
The Shadowlands
In This Damned House
In Arcranium
Escaping the Cult
Super High
In Brownsville
In the UK
By Your Own Hand

In the Works:

In Roswell and Beyond
With Satan Inside
In the Tournament of Mortem
At Desperation House
In Hollow 2
In a Prison Riot
In a Video Game
Between the Worlds
With No Way Out
On Werewolf Island
In the Asylum
With many more soon to be announced.

Try Not to Die Merchandise

Brightside

Thought Thieves

Telepathy is illegal and Thought Thieves are imprisoned in a beautiful secluded town. It's Joe's 100th day and he has to escape.

The First Time

A naughty short story about Joe's first intimate encounter.

Out of the Fire

The grass always seems greener, but living beyond Brightside will be Joe's greatest challenge.

Horror

90 Short Stories

Nonfiction

MMA

Exploring the
Motivations of Fighters
100 gyms
23 states
400 interviews

Brain Health

Facing fears of
dementia from
repetitive blows to
the head.

Jiu Jitsu

Current Project
A coffee table book
featuring Mark and
his family training
around the world.

Listen to the Books

You can listen to several books in the Try Not to Die series, short horror stories , suspense novels, or nonfiction. Find your next listen at your favorite retailer or www.MarkTullius.com

www.ingramcontent.com/pod-product-compliance
Lightning Source LLC
Chambersburg PA
CBHW070459300726
48975CB00007B/2241